I0727682

Hunting Camp 2

The Rise of Big Red

Gin Matters

Cover Design: Shawn Rohe
Designer: Jeanna Wiggins

Paperback ISBN: 978-1-7370936-2-6
E-book ISBN: 978-1-7370936-3-3

LCCN: 2025911423

Hot Tub Writing
Irving, NY

First Edition

Printed in the United States of America

CONTENTS

______

CHAPTER ONE

THAT'S NOT THE WIND

George looked out into the woods, then back at Phil and said, "That's just the wind."

Phil nodded and they both started walking back to the truck. Suddenly, they heard a gunshot. They both stopped and turned back toward the woods.

"Get the fuck off me!" A distant voice came from the woods.

Phil looked at his partner and said, "That's not the wind."

The two ENCON officers started running toward the voice; Phil leading the way. He knew the terrain. They were running along a path that had been established by hunters a long time ago.

"Die you fuckers! I hate you!" It was that voice again, except it sounded closer.

To Phil, it sounded familiar. A few seconds later they came upon a small opening and saw John. He was swinging his rifle like a baseball bat. The only thing he was connecting with was the air. Phil and George stopped about thirty feet away.

"Johnnie, relax." Phil said.

John turned the rifle around properly and pointed it at them. He pulled the trigger. A loud *pow* noise filled their ears. George couldn't see the bullet, but he heard it whiz by his left ear. He hit the ground and reached for his sidearm.

"I'll kill you. Come on!" John pulled the trigger again, but this time the rifle made a clicking sound. Phil noticed the terrified look on John's face. He was looking at something past Phil.

Phil didn't wait, he rushed John. John tried to turn the rifle around again like a bat but before he could, Phil tackled him to the ground. This didn't stop John from screaming. "Get off me! They're coming."

"Johnnie, stop. It's me, Phil."

John then screamed, "We have to go, now! They'll take us!"

Johnnie continued to struggle. He started screaming and thrashing. Phil was trying to pin his arms, but the kid was strong. He looked over at his partner, who was laying on his belly and pointing his handgun at John and said, "Put your gun down and get over here and help me."

George continued pointing his gun at John and screamed, "He tried to shoot me."

"George, put your gun down. Help me restrain him."

George lowered and holstered his weapon.

"Hold down his legs," Phil told him.

It took several more minutes for John to stop thrashing. The two officers zip tied John's wrists behind his back. They got him to his feet. He calmed down, like he wasn't a threat anymore. Phil said, "Johnnie, where's your brother?"

Without warning John drove his shoulder into Phil and started running back toward the camp, he screamed, "They're coming!"

Phil stepped back a few steps and briefly lost his balance. George started to reach for his gun. Phil shouted, "Stop! Put that away."

Phil's gaze was enough to make his partner holster his weapon.

The two men gave chase and eventually caught up to John behind the camp. George tackled him. John started screaming and crying, "Dead! They're all dead!"

Phil came up behind them and they got John to his feet again. This time they both had a good grip on him.

Phil asked, "Johnnie, what do you mean?"

John kept repeating, "They're all dead!"

Phil made eye contact with his partner. He could tell George was still shaken from almost being shot.

"I couldn't save them!" John wailed.

Phil looked back at John and asked, "Save them from what?"

John didn't answer Phil. He kept repeating that he couldn't save them. That they were all dead. It was pointless to continue with questioning. John was in shock, or at least that's what Phil was thinking.

George looked at his partner and said, "He's lost it!"

Phil gave George a stern look but said nothing.

"This kid is a killer. He tried to end me." stated George.

Phil shook his head and said, "I don't think he was shooting at you."

——

CHAPTER TWO

THREE DAYS EARLIER

Craig was surprised to wake up in an empty bed. He reached over to touch Cheryl before he opened his eyes, but she wasn't there. He looked over on the bed stand and found his phone. It read *6:24 am*. Before he could fully process the situation, a loud banging on the door broke the silence.

"Craig, open up!"

He knew the voice; it was Cheryl's father. He slipped his bathrobe on and walked out of his bedroom. The front door continued to resist the beating. Craig started to think of the reasons why Cheryl didn't come home last night. As he walked by the bathroom, he noticed the door was open and the light was off. Craig stopped and peaked in, but she wasn't there.

"Open the fucking door!"

Craig turned his gaze to where Mr. Peterson was trying to gain entrance. He continued walking towards the door. The room opened up, it was a combination kitchen and small living room area with the front door at the other end of the room. Mr. Peterson continued banging on the door, screaming for Craig to open. The two of them did not like each other. Craig wasn't good enough for Dave Peterson's daughter and had been told that by the man on more than one occasion over the past year. What really sent Dave over the edge was when Cheryl decided to move in, and her father wouldn't speak to her for three months.

"Coming!" Craig shouted back.

As he opened the door, Mr. Peterson walked in with authority like he owned the place.

Craig rolled his eyes and said, "Come on in."

"Where's my daughter?" Mr. Peterson walked by Craig and started shouting, "Cheryl, it's Daddy!"

Craig watched as Mr. Peterson walked into the bedroom, shouting his daughter's name, fully expecting her to respond. He checked the bathroom and then the kitchen.

"Cheryl, where are you honey?"

Craig closed the door. Mr. Peterson looked long and hard at him. Finally, he said, "Where's my daughter!"

"I don't know. I guess she didn't come home."

It was clear that these two didn't like each other. They were glaring at each other until Craig suddenly thought of Cheryl, turned away and walked towards their room. The thought of Cheryl in some kind of trouble started to overtake his soul.

"Where are you going? Where's my daughter?"

"I need to check my cell phone; she probably left me a message."

Craig found his cell phone and checked. There were no text or voice messages left by Cheryl. He walked back out of the bedroom and looked at Mr. Peterson and said, "Nothing, she didn't call or text. Let me try calling her."

Craig dialed her number. It rang until voicemail picked up the call.

"Hello, this is Cheryl. Sorry I missed your call. You know what to do at the beep."

Craig waited for his cue and then left a message. "Hey babe, where are you? Call me back, please."

"I tried calling too, but she didn't pick up."

Craig looked at Cheryl's father and said, "I wouldn't expect her to pick up your call! Are you guys even on speaking terms?"

Mr. Peterson responded, "That's none of your business!"

Craig shook his head and smirked back at Mr. Peterson; he really didn't like this man.

"Look, she probably stayed in town at Emily's. I'm sure she's fine. As soon as she calls me, I will call you and –"

"No! She's in trouble!" With conviction, like he was betting his soul, Mr. Peterson shouted, "I know it!"

Suddenly their tense moment was interrupted by a knock on the door. Craig and Cheryl's father looked at each other with bewilderment. Craig walked over and opened it. Two state troopers were standing outside.

"Are you Craig Bronson?

"Yes." Craig responded. "I am."

"I am Trooper Gonyea and this is my partner Trooper LaMay. We found your truck abandoned on

Forest Home Road about three miles from here, going toward town."

Craig asked, "What do you mean abandoned?"

"Can we come in?" Trooper Gonyea asked.

Craig stopped blocking the entrance and motioned with his right hand for the troopers to come in. They walked in and Craig closed the door. He noticed it was cold outside. Had to be in the teens.

Cheryl's father didn't wait for the troopers to get comfortable, he shouted, "Where's my daughter?"

The troopers shared a suspicious glance and then focused their attention on Cheryl's father.

"Who are you?" Trooper Gonyea asked.

"I'm Dave Peterson. My daughter was driving that truck last night."

Craig quickly filled in the details. "His daughter was driving my truck last night; she lives with me."

Trooper LaMay looked at Craig and asked, "Did she call you or text you at all last night?"

Craig shook his head. "No, I just checked."

He then pointed at Mr. Peterson and said, "He just banged on my door about five minutes before you guys showed up and started asking me where Cheryl was. That's when I noticed she wasn't home."

The troopers focused their attention back to Mr. Peterson.

Trooper Gonyea asked, "Did you have any contact with your daughter last night?"

Dave looked at the trooper and said, "No."

Trooper LaMay gave Mr. Peterson a piercing look and asked, "How did you know she was missing?"

"A father knows when there is something wrong with their own child. I can't explain why or how, but something made me wake up in the middle of the night and I just knew that Cheryl was in some kind of trouble."

Dave Peterson focused his attention on Craig and pointed back at him and said, "If my daughter is missing, that scumbag has something to do with it!"

"Hey, fuck you old man! Those two haven't talked to each other in months! Cheryl hates him!"

Dave Peterson snapped. He stepped forward and threw a right jab from his ear that connected with Craig's face. The old man immediately jumped back like a boxer while Craig crashed to the floor. He hit hard. The back of his head hit the floor last and ricocheted off the floor like a basketball. There would be no ten count. No need, Craig was out cold!

CHAPTER THREE

WHERE IS CHERYL

Mr. Peterson was arrested and booked out at Troop B headquarters in Ray Brook. The troopers brought Craig to the emergency room where he was treated for a possible grade two concussion. During his visit to the ER, the troopers asked Craig several questions and this just seemed to increase the intensity of his headache. He kept telling the troopers that the lights were too bright and he even asked them to stop talking so loudly. That didn't stop them from inquiring about where Cheryl was. Their questions seemed to target Craig, like he had something to do with her disappearance. He told the same story over and over. How he went to bed around 11:00 pm. Cheryl was working late. He hadn't noticed she didn't come home until Mr. Peterson banged at the door and that was at around 6:30am.

He had no truck, it was impounded. The troopers told Craig it was evidence. Craig reluctantly accepted a ride home from the troopers. His head was pounding. The old man had sucker punched him really good. They had given him headache medicine at the emergency room and that had helped. A frightening thought crept into his brain and he screamed out loud, "Cheryl! Where are you!"

Craig suddenly realized that he hadn't focused on the source of all the drama. Cheryl was missing. A weird upset feeling started to spread in his abdominal area. What if she had been abducted? What if she was in trouble?

Craig couldn't lay down. He had to go find Cheryl. He got up from the couch and made a few calls. There was no car he could use, everyone working. He couldn't wait. That feeling in his stomach was getting worse. They told him he might experience nausea, that it was a side effect from the concussion. He got dressed. The temperature outside was around freezing, high twenties and the sun was out. It had warmed up earlier that morning. He could do this. He grabbed his backpack and snowshoes. He would walk out to where they said the truck had been abandoned. He had to look around. Maybe she was still out there in the woods.

CHAPTER FOUR

NOR'EASTER

Phil, George and John shared a volatile ride to the state police headquarters in Ray Brook. John kept repeating that they were all gone; he couldn't save them. Occasionally, John would scream and thrash around in the back seat. He kicked at the door, smashing the side window. Phil pulled over and restrained his legs. The scene escalated when John kicked George in the chest. George punched John in the face and this seemed to pacify John long enough for Phil to zip tie his ankles. The three of them started heading down the road a moment later. Phil looked in the rearview mirror and made eye contact with John and said, "Sorry about that Johnnie."

George looked at his partner and asked, "Why are you apologizing to that felon? He tried to kill us! He shot at us!"

"I wasn't shooting at you."

Phil and George looked at each other in disbelief. Phil then asked, "Who were you shooting at John?"

"I hit it. It was going to attack George."

George raised his voice over John and screamed, "You tried to kill me, but you missed. You're lucky I didn't shoot back. You wouldn't be telling lies in the back seat right now!"

"I saved your life! It would have dragged you back into the woods and tore you to shreds. Like they tore apart Billy and Karl–"

"John." Phil interrupted. "You're not making any sense. Was it the cougar? Was there more than one?"

John started to raise his voice. "Like they tore apart Darrel!"

Phil and George again looked at each other, but this time they shared a look of concern. John started to thrash again in the back seat. He was becoming agitated.

"They're gone. I couldn't save them!"

They were almost at Troop B. Phil radioed in that they were going to need help with their passenger. A few miles later they arrived, and John was escorted into the barracks by two state troopers. Phil and George were met at the door by Major Viera, Troop B's commander.

"What's going on?"

Phil started shaking his head and said, "Looks like we have some more missing hunters."

The color of Major Viera seemed to bleed off his face. He motioned for the two ENCON officers to follow him. They conveniently walked in the back door, where the perpetrators entered the building. Phil could hear a commotion happening further up the hallway. A man was arguing with some other troopers, he shouted, "I need to find my daughter!"

They walked by the man and his hands were cuffed behind his back. The troopers were processing him at the front desk. Phil made eye contact with the man and knew him instantly.

"Phil, a little help, please." pleaded the man.

Phil looked at his partner and the major and said, "I will catch up in a minute."

The Major and George and the two troopers escorted John down the hall towards the lockup cells. Phil walked over to the front desk and asked, "Why is this man being arrested?"

"Hey Phil." responded Trooper Borden sitting behind the front desk. "Seems Mr. Dave Peterson sent a man to the emergency room."

"Overhand right. Knocked him right off his feet." said Trooper LaMay who was standing to Dave's right side.

Phil looked at his childhood friend but Dave Peterson kept staring at the floor.

Phil looked up at Trooper Borden and asked, "How long are you going to hold him?"

"We have to process him, you know the drill."

Phil looked at Dave and said, "Dave if you cooperate, you will probably be out of here in a few hours."

Dave Peterson raised his head and shot a piercing gaze through his friend's eyes and screamed, "I got to find Cheryl! I don't have time for this bullshit! I know that good-for-nothing boyfriend of hers has something to do with it!"

"Yeah." Trooper Gonyea said on Peterson's left side. "Mr. Peterson sucker punched Mr. Craig Bronson. The man is recovering with a decent concussion in the emergency room as we speak."

"Gentlemen, we all understand the duress Mr. Peterson must be going through." Phil gave all three troopers a nod and turned around and started to walk towards the major's office.

"Phil, I'm begging you, please!" shouted Dave Peterson.

Without turning around Phil said, "Cooperate Dave."

Phil walked up the hallway and found the major's office, he walked in. Major Vierra was sitting behind his desk and George was sitting in a chair to the far right.

"Close the door Phil. Your partner was just filling me in. How there were a total of six in his hunting party and according to John's admission, five of them are dead."

During the discussion the major asked if they thought John had lost it, if he was crazy. From his office, they could hear John screaming from his cell. George was adamant that John had tried to kill him and probably killed the rest of his hunting party. Phil told the major about how John said he had shot at something behind George, possibly a cougar. Major Viera decided to send in two BCI investigators to interview John.

"Phil, I need you to go out there with my search party. If the kid did hit something behind George, there must be a blood trail. As it sounds, I think your partner is probably right. I fear the worst for the rest of his hunting party."

Phil nodded at Major Viera. He had his doubts too. Things weren't looking good for Johnnie. "I've known this kid, his brother Darrel, and his father for over twenty years. I consider them friends of mine."

Major Viera said, "Phil, I'm sorry, but we got a job to do. I need you to go find those missing hunters. Get some kind of evidence. We have some bad weather on the horizon. A Nor'easter is about to hit in the next twenty-four hours. They're saying we could get two feet of snow dumped on us. Those hunters could still be alive, even just one."

Phil understood the implications of a bad snowstorm covering up a crime scene. More importantly, if one of those hunters were still alive, time was not on their side. The three men wrapped up their meeting. Phil and George were to meet up with a search party back out at Butch Fuller's hunting camp.

CHAPTER FIVE

BUTCH FULLER HUNTING CAMP

Phil and George arrived back out at Butch Fuller's hunting camp about an hour later. They were joined by the two BCI (Bureau of Criminal Investigation) investigators who had interviewed John. Another ENCON officer, Dean Hayes, was also part of their group. Phil had taken part in several missing person investigations over the years. In every case, the BCI officers always took the lead. When it came to the cabin, or hunting camp, the two BCI officers didn't want anyone else from the search party to enter. So, the rest of the party waited outside. After about thirty minutes, Phil knocked on the cabin door.

"Don't come inside!" a voice from within the cabin yelled.

Phil responded, "We're losing daylight. You guys can continue this when the sun goes down."

Several seconds passed by before Phil got a response from inside the cabin. "Okay, we'll be right out."

Ten minutes later the two BCI officers exited the cabin and the search party walked back to where the trail began. Phil and George directed the party to where they had encountered John. Over the next thirty minutes they collected footprints and took photographs. George was busy acting out his part. Describing how the bullet fired from John's rifle nearly missed him. The two BCI investigators walked over behind where George was standing, stopped, and both looked down. Phil walked over and noticed what they were looking at, it was blood. There was a light covering of snow on top of a layer of leaves. John's bullet hit something, and it bled out. One of the BCI investigators, named Morrow, was kneeling down looking at the blood. He then raised his head and looked off into the direction of where a blood trail led into the woods.

"Everyone stays here." Investigator Morrow stood up and started slowly following the blood trail. He disappeared into the woods. After a moment, he appeared to change his mind and shouted back, "Phil, can you come here please."

Phil followed his footprints into the woods. He came upon Investigator Morrow staring at what looked to be drag marks. Morrow looked at Phil and asked, "What kind of an animal would do this?"

Phil said, "Nothing human!"

Phil noticed where the blood trail stopped and pooled. "Whatever got shot by John, walked into the woods and fell at this spot. Then something else dragged it off that way." Phil pointed off to where the drag marks went.

"What kind of tracks are these?" Morrow was pointing to the snow.

Phil bent down and took a careful look at the impressions in the snow and said, "We found what looks to be the same tracks out on Forest Home Road."

"Do you think it could be a cougar?" asked Morrow.

Phil studied the tracks and then responded, "If that's a cougar then there has to be four or five of them hunting together."

Investigator Morrow looked confused and asked, "What's the big deal if they were?"

Phil looked at Morrow and said, "They are solitary hunters. They don't hunt in packs. I'm positive this isn't a cougar!"

The snow started to fall. The temperature was also falling by the minute.

"Found it!" A voice from back towards the search party said.

Phil and Investigator Morrow looked at each other and walked back towards the search party. When they came out of the woods, they saw the other BCI officer standing next to a tree.

"That's a gunshot." said Investigator Allen.

Everyone was looking at the mark on the tree. Morrow walked over and looked. He produced a pocket knife and started digging at the mark. It took him a few minutes, but he eventually extracted the bullet.

Investigator Morrow looked at George and asked, "Show me where you were standing."

George stood where he thought John had fired his rifle at him. The tree lined up in the bullet's path about fifteen feet behind him. Phil and Investigator Morrow nodded at each other.

"Whatever John Fuller shot, the bullet passed right through and embedded itself in the tree," said Phil.

Over the next two hours, the search party took more pictures of tracks. They also walked a couple miles into the woods, following tracks and footprints. The whole time the snow started falling more heavily. They came upon another clearing where several blood pools and drag marks were found, but no bodies. They did find two rifles, a Savage model 110 and a .30-30 lever-action Winchester. Phil had recognized the Winchester as Butch Fuller's hunting rifle. He explained that he used to hunt with Butch and that Butch probably passed the rifle down to his son Darrel. Soon the snow was falling hard and visibility was becoming a factor. The sun was dropping over the horizon. The search party had to leave. They had gathered all the evidence which included tracks, blood, rifles, pictures and a bullet. But they found no bodies. They made their way back to Butch Fuller's hunting camp and declared it a crime scene.

——

CHAPTER SIX

THE INTERVIEW

John was being interrogated by two BCI officers out at Troop B in Ray Brook. Investigator Morrow was about six-foot tall and he probably weighed around one hundred and ninety pounds. Both investigators wore high and tight haircuts and were clean shaven. They didn't wear the regular New York State trooper uniform, they both sported a white button-up dress shirt and gray slacks. Morrow had black hair and brown eyes. John thought he looked Hispanic. The other guy was just under six-foot and weighed around one hundred and seventy pounds. His name tag said Allen. He was a white guy with blondish hair.

John still had his ankles bound and he was hand-cuffed to the table. The room had bright fluorescent lights, a rectangular table and four chairs, that was it. The three of them sat there for the longest time, nobody said anything. This was perfectly fine for John. His mind kept slipping back to what had happened. How he hadn't been able to save his friends, his brother. Tears started flowing down his face again. His memory was interrupted by a voice in the room. "Did you and your brother fight a lot John?" asked Investigator Allen.

John shook his head no but said nothing.

"You've had a lot of anger since your father died. You blamed your brother for that, didn't you, John." Investigator Morrow followed up.

Investigator Allen didn't miss a beat with the next question, "Your father, he liked Darrel better. Is that true John."

"Why did you do it John?" screamed Investigator Morrow.

John looked up and made eye contact with him. He didn't understand the question.

"Where are the bodies John?" asked investigator Allen.

John turned his head toward the other investigator, but no words came out of his mouth. He drifted back to the clearing. He could see Darrel surrounded by maneaters. Then he watched as the monster lifted up its hoof and produced a claw and started ripping Darrel to pieces. John stood up and screamed, "Darrel! No!"

Investigator Allen stood up and pushed John back into his chair.

"Where's Darrel? What did you do with his body?"

"They ate him!" screamed John.

"Who ate him?" asked Investigator Allen.

John looked down at the floor. Their voices started to drift away. He could see Billy. He was pulling on his arms, trying to get him away from them. If he hadn't tripped backwards over that stump.

"Cut the crap! You shot them. You killed your friends and your brother!" Investigator Allen was pointing his finger at John.

"Why did you do it John? Did you get into an argument?" asked Investigator Morrow.

"Maybe they tried to kill you and you were protecting yourself."

Both men looked at each other like they had just discovered a truth, and then they looked back at John.

"Ya, self-defense. That makes sense. Just tell us where the bodies are." said Investigator Morrow.

John drifted away again. This time they were racing up I-87. The investigator's voices started to fade away. Darrel was telling him to pass Danny. Bill was laughing in the backseat. John liked this memory. He decided to stay here for a while.

CHAPTER SEVEN

EVIDENCE

Major Viera was in a meeting with Morrow and Allen. They told the major about the evidence they collected. The major looked at his two officers and asked, "So, what do you think happened?"

Trooper Morrow responded, "I don't think the kid did it."

His partner, Trooper Allen looked at him in disbelief. "What are you talking about? Of course, he did it. He even tried to kill Phil and George. We just don't know where the bodies are."

The major looked at Trooper Allen for a long time, and then brought his attention back to Trooper Morrow and asked, "Why would he turn his weapon on George and Phil and shoot at them?"

Trooper Morrow sat up in his chair; he didn't look comfortable answering the major's question. He paused for a few seconds and then said, "The kid definitely shot in their direction, but I don't think he was shooting at them. I dug this bullet out of the tree about twenty-five feet behind George and Phil."

Trooper Morrow handed the major the bullet in a small evidence bag.

The major looked at it closely. He then looked at

Morrow and said, "This just proves the kids shot at George and Phil."

Trooper Morrow gave the major a confident look and said, "No sir, there was blood at the base of the tree. I think the kid hit something."

The major looked over at Trooper Allen and asked, "What do you think?"

Trooper Alan looked at his partner and then back at the major. He seemed a little uncomfortable sitting across from Major Vierra, he hesitated in his rebuttal and then finally said, "We are making this more com-plicated than it really is. The kid is a mass murderer. He killed his whole hunting party. We're talking about his brother and lifelong friends."

Trooper Morrow raised his voice over his partner to ask, "Where are the bodies?"

Trooper Allen looked at his partner and said, "I don't know where the bodies are, maybe the kid hid them. Maybe a bear dragged them away."

The major looked annoyed. He raised his voice over both of them and said, "Let's get the blood sample tested. Let's also get the bullet tested, first for traces of blood. Then we'll send it over to ballistics."

The major looked long and hard at his officers, he could tell they were uncomfortable and asked, "Any-thing else?"

Trooper Morrow looked at his partner and then back to the major and said, "There has been talk amongst the locals that there are strange deer in the woods."

"Oh, come on. You're not going to start regurgitating that crap now?" said Trooper Allen.

The major lifted up his hand toward Allen, signaling him to be quiet and then asked, "Explain strange deer."

Trooper Morrow again looked over at his partner, who was shaking his head in disbelief. He then turned his gaze back to the major and said, "Deer with claws and sharp teeth. Maneaters."

The major looked long and hard at Trooper Morrow. The kind of look that intimidated a person, and then asked him, "Has anyone ever captured or shot one of these so-called strange deer in the park before?"

"To the best of my knowledge, no sir." responded Trooper Morrow.

The major continued to stare down Trooper Morrow. He then said, "Let's stop adding gasoline to a small spark. A spark that has been spread by ignorant locals that don't know the difference between a deer and a cow. Do I make myself clear trooper!" demanded the major.

"Yes sir." a very nervous Trooper Morrow said back to the major.

The major seemed to relax back in his chair. He scanned both troopers up and down and then asked, "How did the interrogation go?"

Trooper Allen spoke next. "The kid has lost it, sir. He keeps drifting back and forth. One minute he's lucid, the next minute he's screaming at his brother."

Trooper Morrow shook his head and confirmed what his partner had said about John. The major leaned back in his chair and brought his hands up to his brow and said, "Now I have to go out and face the press."

CHAPTER EIGHT

PRESS CONFERENCE

Major Viera waited out in the hallway for a moment before entering the ongoing press conference. He listened intently as a back-and-forth exchange of questions and updates transpired between reporters and his press secretary. Janet was doing a good job of deflecting most of the questions. It was a matter of time before the press would become agitated and demand more concrete answers. He knew it was his time to enter, so he walked in and suddenly the room filled with the clicking noises of high-speed cameras. He looked at Janet and said, "Thank you, Janet."

She stepped off to the side, away from the podium. The major took his place behind and pretended to look comfortable. He lifted his head and said, "I have several updates to talk about. Let me start with our missing hunter from Altona. The recent storm has impeded our progress, but we are still looking."

"Major, hello. Kyle Thompson from channel five news. It's been almost a week. At what point do you call off the search party?"

"Kyle, we are not ready to make that decision. The missing hunter's family doesn't want us to make that decision. We still feel that he could be alive and disoriented from the recent winter storm. We intend to double our efforts today and hopefully find him."

"Major, Christine Blue from the Press Republican. Is there any correlation between the missing girl on Forest Home Road and the missing hunter from Altona?"

This question gave the major pause, he had not anticipated it. He responded back, "As of now, we are treating both as separate missing persons cases."

Major Vierra spotted Pete with his hand up. He had been reporting for the local paper, the Adirondack Daily Enterprise, for a couple decades. Longer than the major had been assigned to Troop B. "What is it, Pete?"

"Thanks, Major. There was a statement from one of the hunters on Channel Five News the other night about a deer attack? Can you elaborate on the validity of that statement?"

The press room erupted with laughter. Even the major smiled. "I personally have never seen a deer attack another man. I am an avid hunter and from my experiences in the woods, deer aren't aggressive towards humans."

Several questions started flooding the major all at once. The reporters were trying to be heard, competing against each other. The major held his hand up and after a few seconds, the room became silent. "There has been another hunting incident. In the past forty-eight hours, five hunters from Middletown, New York have gone missing."

Again, the room erupted with blurted out questions. The major raised his hand, but the reporters continued to ask questions.

"People!" Major Viera raised his voice, and the room became quiet. "This is a developing case. Janet will hand out our press release at this time. All we know is that a party of six were hunting near Santa Clara. We have one man in custody and again, five are missing."

The room erupted with questions from the reporters. There were only a handful of them, but they did try to shout over each other, competing for the major's attention.

"Major, have you interviewed the surviving hunter?"

"Is there any evidence of foul play?"

"Are you releasing the names of the missing hunters?"

The major again raised his hand, but the questions continued to come.

"Major, what is the name of the surviving hunter?"

"Can you tell us what you think happened?

Major Viera raised his voice another octave and yelled, "Quiet!"

The press room became silent. But it was an uncomfortable silence. The room was ready to explode with a question that could lead tomorrow's headlines in the local newspapers. The reporters were like racehorses corralled into the starting gate, all anticipating the doors to swing open. Major Viera looked around the room like he was sizing up the competition. He then said, "We are not going to release the names of the missing hunters. We are in the process of contacting their families. We are still collecting evidence and conducting interviews. It is also too early to start drawing conclusions about what happened. We are still hoping to find the hunters."

"Major, a foot and a half of snow just dropped on us in the last twenty-four hours. You're not going to find any bodies until spring!"

The major looked at Christine Blue from the Press Republican for a long time. Before he could respond to her question, he got hit with another one from the Adirondack Daily Enterprise.

"Major, do you think there is a correlation between these missing hunters from Santa Clara and the missing hunter from Altona? And what about the missing girl from Forest Home Road, any connection? Is it possible they were attacked by deer?"

The major turned his attention to Pete and started shaking his head no. He looked at everyone and said, "That's all I have for you today."

Major Viera walked out of the room. A volley of questions were lobbed at him as he fled to the hallway. The farther he walked away, the quieter their questions became. He got to his office a moment later and closed the door behind him. He sat down at his desk and pressed a button on his phone. A few seconds later investigator Morrow answered. "Yes, major."

"Listen, you and Allen get back in there and break that kid! We need something! Interrogate him by the book, just don't physically hit him with one. I don't need a lawsuit against this department. Am I clear!"

"Crystal, major."

The major hung up the phone. He started to develop a mild migraine. The kind that would get progressively worse in the next few hours. He leaned back in his chair and crossed his fingers together behind his head. He closed his eyes. The thought of deer attacking men made him chuckle a little, and he started grinning.

——

CHAPTER NINE

TRANSPORT

John was on his way to the St. Lawrence Psychiatric Center located almost two hours north up near the mighty St. Lawrence Seaway. The small city of Ogdensburg was only a few miles from the Canadian border. His last interview with the two BCI agents hadn't gone well. John had kept slipping back and forth from listening to incriminating questions and fighting man-eating deer in the woods with his brother Darrel.

John's ankles and hands were restrained, and he was sitting in the back of a State Police car. He had overheard the B.C.I. officers talking about the Sheriff's department not having a vehicle available for transport for forty-eight hours. His interviewers were tasked to deliver him to the Psychiatric Center. They had been driving for well over an hour. John had to go to the bathroom but every time he thought to ask to stop, he would lapse back into his nightmare, the one where everyone died except him. Every now and then he would focus on their conversation they were having in the front seat. And they would ask him a question from time to time, but he never responded. They thought he did it. They called him a mass murderer.

"Oh, come on man! He just pissed himself!" Trooper Allen said.

"We're almost there." Trooper Morrow responded.

They were right. John noticed he had urinated all over the seat, his pants, and the floor. He grinned. The way they had treated him, John felt like they deserved it.

"Oh, now he's smiling about it! I told you he's not crazy!"

Trooper Allen looked at John and said, "You're going away for a long-time you bastard!"

John turned his attention away from the man and concentrated on the landscape going by outside the window. They were slowing down. They had entered a village. It seemed to be bigger than the smaller hamlets in the Adirondack Park. They weren't in the Adirondacks anymore.

CHAPTER TEN

——

CLS

The Crime Laboratory System of the New York State Police, or CLS for short, had finished the forensic testing on the bullet and blood samples found at the crime scene in Santa Clara. Major Viera was studying the results in his office. The bullet was definitely fired from the rifle that the perpetrator had used to shoot at George and Phil. The blood samples were inconclusive. They identified four different blood samples that were human. But the other blood samples couldn't be identified.

A confused Major Viera got on the phone with CLS and listened to their explanation. He became even more confused when CLS stated that the blood samples were not deer or cougar. After an exhausting explanation that didn't answer any of his questions, the major decided to give Dr. Yogerra from the Biogen Farm a courtesy call.

"Hello Dr. Yogerra, this is Major Viera. I hope all is well."

"Hello major, what can I do for you?"

"Can I send you over a few blood samples to test?"

"Yes, by all means. What is so special about these blood samples, and why can't your people handle them?"

"My CLS team has identified the samples as human. But there is one type of blood that they can't identify."

There was a pause on the other end of the phone, Major Vierra waited patiently for a response. In a thick European accent Dr. Yogerra said, "My laboratory can easily have the results back to you in a day or two."

"Thank you, Dr. Yogerra." The major hung up the phone. He then made another call to CLS and had the samples delivered to the Biogen Farm, in the care of Dr. Yogerra. As he hung up the phone with CLS, he looked out the window and noticed the snow was falling again. The major had an uneasy feeling settling in and it had everything to do with the Biogen Farm. It was going to be a long winter.

CHAPTER ELEVEN

MAX

The falling snow looked fluffy to Henry. Henry and his best friend Max next to him both stared out the window. Max had his paws up on the top of the couch. Henry was kneeled on the couch with his hands also on top.

"Get that mutt off my couch now!" said Henry's Mom.

"Come on Max, let's go outside."

Henry and his best friend jumped off the couch and headed for the back door.

"Make sure you put your boots on, no sneakers!"

"Okay, Mom."

"And don't forget to put a hat on!"

"Okay, Mom!" a highly agitated little boy responded back.

Henry put his boots on and found his Green Lantern winter hat. Max sat and waited patiently. He watched Henry, wagging his tail the whole time, anticipating the adventure that awaited the two of them. Henry stood up and opened the back door. Max sprinted out before Henry had the door completely open and brushed up into Henry's legs. Henry lost his balance and grabbed the door to prevent him from falling. "Watch out, Max!" he shouted.

He then closed the door and followed his furry friend toward the garage. Max was a chocolate lab that Henry had received as a birthday present when there had been six candles on his cake; and that was four years ago. Now they were inseparable. When Henry would get on the bus in the morning to go to school, Max would sit at the door and wait. He wouldn't leave from that spot until Henry came home after school. Mrs. Moore always knew when the bus was getting close because Max would start pacing and wagging his tail.

The snow was deep, it almost came up to Henry's knees. Henry looked up and noticed that the sky was cloudy. It was too chilly to take his hat off. He could see his breath when he exhaled. Henry looked around and noticed that the trees were full of snow. He was also surprised to see how much snow had accumulated on the roof. He always liked this time of year. Snow meant that Christmas was coming.

Henry bent down to feel the snow. It wasn't packed enough to make a snowball, but he did find Max's tennis ball. It was buried under the recent snowstorm. Max started barking with excitement as soon as he saw what Henry had found. Henry was standing about fifty feet from the garage. He threw the ball and it hit the garage door with a thunderous metallic noise. Max didn't wait for instructions; he quickly located the ball off the rebound in the snow and retrieved it back to Henry. He dropped the ball at Henry's feet and started barking.

This time Henry threw it higher, and it hit off the top of the garage door. Again, it made a loud metallic noise. Max had no problem anticipating where the ricochet was going to go. A few seconds later he had the ball in his mouth and trotted back to his master. His tail wagged the whole time. Henry picked the ball up and again Max started barking with delight. Henry took aim and released the ball to hit up high again. Max sensed where the ball was going to come off the garage door and sprang into action. He leaped up as if he were going to catch the ball in the air, but something leapt higher than Max.

It all happened so fast. It was a deer, and it sprang above Max. Its whole body was above Max in the air, and it caught the tennis ball in its mouth. Before Max landed on the ground another deer drove its head into Max's rib cage. Henry heard Max yelp and watched his dog roll over several times before coming to a stop on his side.

The acrobatic deer that had caught the tennis ball still had it in its mouth. It stood there looking at Henry. The other deer that rammed into Max started walking over toward its prey. Max managed to get to his tummy and lift his head up and look at Henry. He tried smiling at Henry with that puppy face he always had. Another deer came out of the tree line behind the garage from the right and it started trotting over towards Max.

"Yelp!" Max whimpered as the two deer sank their teeth into him. Henry watched in horror, too afraid to move. Max cried and yelped for several moments, it seemed like an eternity as the two deer dismantled him one leg at a time. One of the deer lifted up its hoof and produced a talon-like claw. Henry watched as Max was eviscerated. His entrails spilled out onto the ground and the surrounding snow turned blood red.

The life was gone from Max's eyes. The acrobatic deer was still looking at Henry. Just chewing on the tennis ball that he and Max had been playing with a few minutes ago. Suddenly it spit the ball out toward Henry, it fell to the ground in pieces. The deer grinned at Henry and showed him a mouth full of carnivorous teeth. That was Henry's cue. He ran toward the back door as fast as he could. Without hesitation, he turned the doorknob, opened the door, and stepped inside and closed the door behind him. Henry sat down a few feet from the door. It was a thick door, too solid and hard for a deer to open or break through. At least that's what he told himself. Scratching noises started from the other side of the door. All Henry could think about was that sharp talon ripping Max open. It was now on the other side of the door. Henry got up and ran for the kitchen and screamed, "Mom!"

CHAPTER TWELVE

WHERE ARE YOU

The snow fell about an inch an hour. Craig was on foot. He had walked about a mile from his house toward where they had found Cheryl's truck. His truck.

The temperature wasn't bad, high twenties. He was starting to sweat, he had too many layers on. He unzipped his jacket to about the middle of his chest. Where are you Cheryl, Craig thought to himself. He remembered the fight they recently had about the truck. Specifically, about the stereo Craig had purchased. Cheryl hadn't wanted him to buy the stereo. She had argued that the stereo cost more than the truck. But he wanted the stereo so bad he ended up convincing Cheryl to let him buy it. Suddenly Craig's thoughts were interrupted by an owl. "Hoo, hoo!"

He looked up to where he thought the owl would be, but he couldn't see it. The falling snow was blocking his view. He kept walking. His backpack contained water, flashlight, extra pair of socks, thirty feet of rope and a box of crackers. At the last second, he found a box of crackers and just threw them in there as he was headed out the house. He also brought a pair of snowshoes and his twelve-gauge shotgun. If Cheryl did walk into the woods, he would need them.

Over a foot of snow had just dropped. His mind was racing in several directions.

"Hoo, hoo!" There it was again. This time Craig looked behind him. He couldn't see up into the trees, the snow was falling and it was difficult to see. The owl sounded closer. He was certain that it was an owl. Craig had listened to owls his whole life. He could differentiate between a bird and an owl, especially when they vocalized. Craig shrugged and kept walking. The thought of Cheryl being abducted made him start crying. Tears were falling down his cheeks. He noticed the throbbing in his head. Every time he concentrated on the throbbing, the thought of Cheryl drifted away. This was a different kind of headache. It was deep and the back of his head seemed like it was being crushed in a vice. Craig tried to concentrate on his surroundings. He had driven on Forest Home Road his whole life. But he never walked it, this was new. There was snow everywhere, on the ground and in the trees and it seemed to be falling faster. It wasn't fluffy, it felt like BBs. The kind of BBs one would use in a BB gun. This snow made a sound as it ricocheted off Craig's jacket. It crackled off him as it fell to the ground. Craig noticed the snow making the same noise in the distance as it fell off the surrounding trees.

"Hoo, hoo!" Craig stopped and looked to his right. There was a deer standing about thirty feet away.

"You're not an owl," Craig said.

It just stood there looking at him. Craig reached into

his backpack and pulled out the crackers. He opened them up, and took a few out of the box.

"Are you hungry?" Craig asked the deer.

He didn't expect it to respond. He tossed a few crackers toward the deer. They fell a few feet in front of it. The deer looked at the crackers and then back at Craig. It walked over to the crackers and started eating them.

"You are hungry. Well I'll be damned." Craig started to smile, but it quickly faded. The throbbing was getting more intense. He started to think of Cheryl. How beautiful she was.

"How beautiful she still is!" he said out loud.

He started walking faster. The thought of a deer eating crackers, or even a deer letting him feed it, wasn't important.

"Hoo, hoo!" This time the noise came from his left. He turned and saw that deer again. He was confused, Craig turned around and saw that the deer was still eating his crackers. There were two of them.

"Wow, you guys must really be hungry."

Craig looked at the new deer and said, "I don't have time to feed you also."

Craig continued to walk. He figured he was about a mile away from where they had found his truck. He walked in the middle of the road. It had not been plowed recently and the snow was starting to accumulate. Every step he took, the snow was over his ankles. He noticed that the snow made a crunching sound with each footstep. Craig started to think of the reasons why Cheryl would get out of the truck and try to walk home. Maybe someone ran her off the road. She could have also lost control of the truck and slid into the ditch. Cheryl wasn't good with directions; she could have gotten lost walking home.

Craig's thought process was interrupted by other crunching footsteps in the snow. He looked to his left and noticed a deer about twenty feet away walking with him. To his right he noticed another deer walking with him, again it was about twenty feet away. Craig turned his head and looked behind and to his surprise there was another deer following him. He stopped walking and the deer also stopped. When he started walking again, they also started walking. A funny thought came to Craig and he started smiling. "You all must think I'm Santa Claus."

Of course he didn't expect his newfound friends to respond back. Craig continued to walk. There was something up ahead. It was hard to make out through the falling snow.

"Cheryl, is that you?" Craig shouted.

He started walking faster. The adrenaline started to flow, his heart started to beat quicker. He instinctively started running and then shouted, "Cheryl!"

He slowed down and stopped. It wasn't Cheryl. It was another deer and there was something in its mouth. Craig had to squint his eyes to focus his vision. He was sure that the snow was distorting what he was seeing. He took a few steps toward the deer in front of him, it was still a good twenty-five feet away. An owl was in its mouth.

Craig shook his head and refocused his eyes. Again his brain reaffirmed what his eyes were telling him. The deer had an owl in its mouth. Craig had never seen a deer eat anything other than vegetation and now crackers. He was confused. Suddenly the deer opened up its mouth and the owl dropped to the ground. It grinned, slightly turning its head and opening up to reveal several sharp teeth.

"What the fuck are you?" Craig said out loud.

Craig instinctively raised his shotgun at the deer in front of him. Without warning Craig was hit from behind. He fell forward on his chest and when he hit the ground his shotgun misfired. His back felt like something sharp had just scratched him. Something was on top of his back. Craig knew it was the other deer, the one he was feeding the crackers to.

"Get the fuck off me!" He could feel wet hot breathing on the back of his neck. Craig's mind was racing. He couldn't grasp the situation, he was being attacked by deer. He tried to roll over on his back but he couldn't move. Craig suddenly felt sharp teeth biting down on the back of his neck. They pierced his skin and blood started seeping out.

The deer twisted Craig's neck until it snapped.

CHAPTER THIRTEEN

CRAZY CONDO

The car door opened. One of the troopers looked at John and said, "Your crazy condo awaits!"

They grabbed John and pulled him out of the car. Trooper Allen gave John a parting gift, a punch in the abdomen and he could feel the wind leave his body. They literally dragged him from the car to the front door. John was trying to get his wind back. He was coughing and kicking his feet against the pavement. It was an uncontrollable reaction, John just needed to breathe in air. Suddenly they stopped moving and John fell to the floor on his chest. He took a long, big deep breath. He exhaled and turned his head to notice they were inside a building. Above him he could hear a conversation start to happen between the troopers and another person, it was a female.

"Inmate for transfer." said Trooper Allen.

"I don't see him." said the female voice.

A nice voice, thought John, possibly a girl in her mid to late twenties. Probably blonde hair and attractive, he assumed. Suddenly John felt a hand underneath both armpits, a moment later he was lifted up off his chest and onto his feet. The room was rectangular, and they were standing in front of a desk. There was plexiglass separating them from the female.

"There you are." said the female.

John couldn't have been more wrong about a voice. She was not thin or blonde. No, she was very big and gray. Over forty, closer to fifty. She was dressed in a nursing outfit and her hair was pinned up under a nursing hat.

"Do you have his placement jacket?" asked the nurse.

Trooper Allen slid a manilla envelope underneath the slit in the plexiglass. The nurse transferred it to her side and John watched as she rifled through the corresponding paperwork. A few seconds later the nurse pulled one piece of paper from the rest and put it down in front of her. She then grabbed a clipboard that had a document on it. She started writing on it. After she passed it through the opening in the plexiglass, she looked up at Trooper Allen and said, "Sign and date please."

John watched as she pressed a button on her desk console and started speaking. "Front desk has an arrival."

A door opened behind the plexiglass. John couldn't see it, but he heard it. A loud buzzing sound startled him and even Trooper Allen looked up from the clipboard he was signing. The door to their left opened and two men walked into the room. John noticed the men stop behind him.

"Here you go." said Trooper Allen as he passed the clipboard back under the plexiglass to the nurse.

John felt the troopers letting go of his armpits. He

had to shift more of his weight to his feet to balance. It didn't last long though, the other two men grabbed hold of him the same way. Trooper Allen looked at John and grinned, "I hope you enjoy your stay. It's a five-star accommodated hotel complete with your own crazy condominium."

John turned his head and watched the two troopers exit the front door. He suddenly was walking with the two strange gentlemen toward a different door. He heard a loud buzzing noise again, the three of them paused, and then they went through the door. They didn't say a word. They were both over six feet and dressed all in white. They were walking down a long hallway and it too was painted white. There was black molding where the wall and floor met. Black and white vinyl tiled floor.

They continued to move forward down the hallway. Suddenly they stopped and turned into a room. The next hour John was told to shower, of course he was supervised. He was given a change of clothes, top and bottom, the color blue. Almost like pajamas except they weren't. A pair of white socks, white boxers, and black slippers.

After he was dressed, they brought him to a room down the hallway and sat him down at a table. There were only two chairs at the table. His babysitters, the other two men just stood up away from the table and stared at him. One was beside the door and it was closed and the other stood off to John's right, leaning against the wall.

John started to drift away; he was back in the woods. He watched those monsters tear his brother to pieces. The tears started falling down his cheeks and then he snapped out of it. The door opened up and a strange man walked in holding a clipboard. He walked over to the empty chair at the table and sat down.

"Hello John, I am Dr. David Baumer. I am head of the Psychiatric Department here at this facility. I will be doing your initial screening and I will determine the state of your mental wellbeing."

John noticed that Doctor Baumer was small, about five foot six, mid to late forties. He wore glasses, had brown hair and was balding. He was wearing black pants, a blue button up shirt with a yellow paisley tie. He was also wearing a white lab jacket and the breast pocket had three pens stuffed inside it.

CHAPTER FOURTEEN

SNOWMOBILE WEATHER

Caleb convinced his wife to let him finance a new liquid cooled snow machine. It wasn't easy, she put up a good argument. Diapers and baby wipes and formula were expensive. With the addition of Carter this past spring, the family had expanded to four. He knew she was right. That shit was expensive, basically another car payment when you added it all up. He explained to her that the deal was too good. No money down, zero percent financing for the first six months. And they made your first payment for you. Karen just said, "Whatever Caleb, it's your world." And then she walked away.

He did have to put up with the silent treatment for a couple days. Caleb also had to get her to co-sign. He explained that it was her sled too. That is when she exploded and said, "Who's got time to snowmobile! I'm too fucking busy changing diapers and feeding your son!"

The sled was delivered a few days before Thanksgiving. It was waiting for him in the garage. He convinced Karen to move her car out so that they could put their new snowmobile into the garage. He was tap dancing around her every time the snowmobile subject came up.

If he could, when he could get Karen on the back of that sled just one time, well he knew she would be sold! But that virgin ride wasn't going to be today.

Caleb had to go it alone. See what this machine could do. The conditions were right, over two feet of base snow. The weather was perfect for riding, high twenties and sunny. And the boys, they were all going to be there. His brother Drew said Jessie was in. Chris, and his buddy Tony were coming. Caleb barely got any sleep; he was so excited. Like a boy anticipating Christmas. Waiting the night before to open those presents. He was up at 4:30am. That's when Carter, the baby, started crying. Karen started to get out of bed but he convinced her to go back to sleep. It didn't hurt to get a few brownie points in before he rolled that beautiful beast out of the garage and slid away. So, he fed and changed Carter and rocked him back to sleep. He got dressed and packed a thermos of hot coffee, black, the way it was meant to be.

They were going to Deer Valley. It was a bar and grill around twenty miles outside of town, halfway to Malone. Caleb looked at his watch, it said 5:55am. He wanted to kiss Karen goodbye, but the thought of her interrogating him with a million questions made him walk out the door. He quietly opened the garage overhang door.

He stared outside and filled his lungs with that pristine mountain air. As he exhaled, Caleb turned and looked at his brand-new Polaris crossover snowmobile.

Yeah, Karen wasn't happy about it, but right now it was probably the best decision he'd ever made. The sled roared to life and Caleb quickly drove it outside. He paused for a moment and considered getting off the sled to shut the garage door, but that thought only lasted a nano-second.

Caleb twisted the throttle and he accelerated down Foresthill Ave toward Pine St. The street lights were still on, the sun wasn't up yet. The village was still sleeping. Smoke was rising out of the chimneys from the surrounding houses. A quick right hand turn connected him onto Pine St, and then he headed toward the train track trestle. It was a railroad bridge that spanned across the Saranac River. It was a good fifty feet high, he had to be careful of pedestrian traffic or another sled. He didn't see anyone; he twisted the throttle and flew across the bridge. What a rush.

The Polaris was everything it was advertised to be, fast. He cut across Bloomingdale Ave and stayed on the tracks. A few minutes later he would rendezvous with his posse behind the drug store on upper Broadway. Caleb pulled his sled up alongside his brother Drew's sled. He cut the engine and took his helmet off.

"That there boys is a liquid-cooled, sixteen thousand dollar Polaris," said Drew.

They all had their helmets off. Caleb watched as the boys walked around his sled. He felt a measure of respect emanating from them. This was his first brand new sled. He had been riding for years with these guys, but always with a used sled. A beater, one that always broke down or wouldn't start.

"Doesn't look like you will be needing a tow from me anymore." It was Chris. He was smiling at Caleb.

Caleb knew what Chris was referring to. "Well, I did appreciate it, every time."

Everyone started laughing.

"Front and back racing shocks. A matrix deep snow chassis." It was Tony. He was inspecting Caleb's sled.

Then Jessie chimed in, "Is that an eight hundred and fifty Wolverine?"

Caleb just grinned and took it all in.

Tony continued his inspection. "Looks like a three-point five inch track that helps reduce weight and distribute unwanted load bearing stressors."

Drew looked over at Tony and said, "How the hell do you know so much about Caleb's sled?"

Tony pointed to the sticker on the side and said, "That's what it says on the manufacturer sticker."

Everyone started laughing again. Tony looked at Caleb and said, "To Charlie's Inn, you lead the way."

Caleb put his helmet on and waited a minute for everyone else. He then fired up his machine and twisted the throttle. He shot forward and felt his body move backwards.

It was an eight-mile ride to Charlie's Inn, located out in Lake Clear. The old railroad tracks were a perfect snowmobile road in the wintertime. Caleb wasn't ready to really open up the throttle, not yet. He cruised at around sixty. He looked over to his right and noticed Jessie pulling up alongside him. Caleb grinned and decided to pull back a little more on the throttle. He instantly shot ahead of Jessie, and it stayed that way till they got to Charlie's Inn. Caleb turned his sled off and one by one they all pulled up to him in the parking lot. He took his helmet off and the others followed suit. It was almost like he was the new leader. Caleb smiled and looked down.

"Breakfast!" Tony was pointing at the door.

Caleb looked at the door, he wasn't sure if they were open for breakfast. He noticed the sun was almost up, things were starting to brighten up.

Jessie was at the door reading the sign. He turned and looked at everyone and said, "They're closed. Open at 12:00pm."

"Let's go to the Airport Cafe." Drew responded, he had a smile on his face like he had just discovered gunpowder.

"Let's have venison." Everyone looked over at Chris. He was looking over toward the tree line, off to his right. Caleb noticed a doe. She was standing there about two hundred feet away. Caleb had to blink his eyes; she was big for a doe. Just staring at them, tail up, didn't seem to be afraid. Suddenly three more appeared out of the tree line. They walked up next to the first doe and started looking over toward them. Like they were checking out their snowmobiles.

"It's Caleb's sled they're after." Everyone looked over at Tony and started laughing.

"I'm hungry, let's go to the airport." said Chris.

Everyone got on their sleds and fired them up. Caleb watched the four doe disappear into the tree line. The sound of the engines must have frightened them.

Caleb twisted the throttle and started following the path into the woods that would lead them to the Airport Café. It was a five-minute ride. The county paid to have the snowmobile trails groomed but Caleb was still surprised how smooth the trail was. It must have been done by Mr. Schlebe. He drove the Snow Cat that packed down these trails and had been doing it for years. Caleb noticed the snow that was stuck in the surrounding trees. It was so beautiful. Everywhere Caleb looked he saw white fluffy snow. The nice part about a snowstorm was that the ugliness of the land-scape, like the rocks and exposed tree roots, fallen down old dead trees and stumps would get covered up by white fluffy snow. They came off the trail into the parking lot of the airport. They parked their sleds near the trail and started walking to the café. Caleb was thinking of an omelet, possibly with hash browns and definitely coffee.

"Maybe they want to come to breakfast too," said Chris.

Caleb noticed what he was looking at. The deer, there were four of them. Standing off near the tree line, about one hundred feet away.

"Coincidence." responded Tony.

Jessie looked at the doe and said, "That is just weird."

Caleb watched the deer as he walked to the entrance of the café. They were definitely looking at them. The doe were watching as they walked into the building. Caleb felt unnerved by this. He had hunted deer his whole life and never could he recall a time when he felt this way about deer. The way they were looking at him. He paused, just stopped before he walked in. Drew put his hand on his shoulder and asked, "What's up little brother?"

Caleb pretended to lift up a hunting rifle and aim it at the deer. He then pretended to pull the trigger. As he brought the rifle down he noticed a change in their disposition. The deer tilted their heads at an angle and grinned.

"What the fuck," said Chris.

Before anyone could say anything else, the deer disappeared into the tree line. They all just stood there for a long time, just staring out where the deer just were.

Tony made his way to the door and said, "Get out of my way, I told you I am hungry."

They all followed him into the Airport Café. They found a table and dressed down and became comfortable. The next thirty minutes consisted of breakfast, coffee and some more talk about Caleb's new sled. Caleb liked the café, he had brought Karen out there a few times. The place was a hidden gem only the locals knew about. Portions were big, price was affordable, and the food was good. Everyone was finishing up and there was some discussion about where to go for lunch.

Chris interrupted the conversation and said, "I ain't never seen a deer tilt their head like that and grin."

Everyone stopped talking and looked at Chris. He said, "I'm telling you, it was those same deer we saw at Charlie's."

"You think they followed us?" Tony asked.

Drew smiled and said, "They must be after Caleb's sled. Maybe they work for the bank."

This brought down the house with laughter. Even Chris started chuckling. Fifteen minutes later they exited the café and started walking towards their sleds. Suddenly Tony just stopped. Everyone froze and looked at him. He was looking where they had last seen the deer. Caleb scanned the horizon in all directions, there was no sign of them.

Tony looked at Chris and said, "The deer, they're gone!"

Chris just shrugged and pretended not to be bothered. Soon they were on their sleds and headed toward Lake Clear. Caleb wanted to open up the throttle on his new sled, the lake was the safest place. Frozen, flat and long. They found Route Thirty and followed it to Lake Clear Beach. Caleb drove out on the lake first, then they all followed. He stayed over by the beach at first. After a big snowfall, the lake could have soft ice. He definitely wasn't going to go out near the middle. Not until the below-zero weather in late January would the ice be completely safe. He would stay around forty feet from the shoreline and go in a straight line.

Caleb looked at his brother and then pulled the throttle back all the way. He took off like a rocket, whole body forced backwards. If he hadn't been holding onto the handlebars, he would have rolled backwards off the sled. He noticed the shoreline go by him faster and then faster. He could feel the wind hit his helmet visor and it was loud. He glanced down at his speedometer, it read sixty-five, seventy-five, ninety. Then he had to lift his head back up to check his line of sight. Still had plenty of frozen lake in front of him. He looked back down and noticed one-hundred and three, one-hundred ten. Caleb looked back up, he still had room. One-hundred twenty, he cut the throttle back and turned the sled back around. He was satisfied. Caleb was sure he could go faster, but he didn't want to. One-hundred and twenty, on a snowmobile outside on a frozen lake was fast enough. He cruised back to the others; it didn't take but a few seconds. He pulled up to them, where they were sitting on their sleds.

"Did you break ninety?" asked Tony.

Before Caleb could respond he was interrupted by Drew. "Definitely one hundred, you had to break that."

Caleb pulled his visor up and stated, "One-hundred and twenty!"

Jessie revved up his engine and the rest did the same. The noises from the engines were loud and it almost sounded like a group of musicians laying down a harmonic snowmachine concerto.

They started moving and this time Tony took the

lead. They found their way back on Route Thirty, heading toward Paul Smith's College. From there they would go up to Deer Valley. After a beer or two, who knew? It was shaping up to be a great day. Out of the corner of his visor, Caleb saw movement. It was in the trees, the tree line. He looked down, they were going around fifty. He looked back over and saw a deer, two of them. Caleb watched them for a few seconds. They were so majestic and graceful. Without very much effort, the deer moved through the snow and forest like a ballerina dancing to swan lake. Or was it the nutcracker? Karen loved all that shit and every Christmas morning she would make him watch the stupid princess get kidnapped by the mouse king. Caleb looked ahead to get his bearings. He was following Drew. He looked back over, and they were gone. The deer had vanished into the snow-covered Adirondack forest.

CHAPTER FIFTEEN

WHERE IS MY SON

Major Viera had just gotten off the phone with a very distraught parent. Her son was missing, part of the group of hunters who had been missing out at Butch Fuller's place. In the past twenty-four hours, the major had spoken to all five families related to the missing hunters. Janet, his receptionist, couldn't answer their questions. She also couldn't deal with their grief and emotional outbursts. Troop B's phone was ringing every five minutes, and it was related to the missing hunters. A newspaper reporter or news station was constantly around digging for answers. He told Janet to stop answering their questions. Stick to the company line.

> *"Search and rescue efforts are still continuing at this time. Please be patient, Troop B and the Department of Wildlife and Conservation are doubling their efforts."*

This repeated statement didn't stop the angry parents from screaming obscenities over the phone at Janet. The Major decided to put a robot answering machine to work. The switchboard would direct the phone call to a robot. The robot would simply say:

"Search and rescue efforts are still continuing at this time. Please be patient, Troop B and the Department of Wildlife and Conservation are doubling their efforts."

The major understood this would only buy him some time. Eventually those hunters would be found, dead or alive. Or it would be a long winter and then the bodies would be found in the spring after the snow melted. Regardless, someone had to deal with some very angry parents and family members. He pressed a button on his desk phone and said, "Janet, get me someone from Albany, mental health division."

"Yes sir, major."

The major started to breathe slower. The thought of a press team and a head shrink from the Albany division taking questions from distraught parents and the press made him feel more relaxed.

"Major, you have a call from the Franklin County District attorney's office."

"Okay, patch it through."

Major Viera instantly associated the name Allen Rodstein with the Franklin County District attorney's office.

"Major Viera, this is Allen. Boy have you had a hell of a week!"

The major smiled and asked, "What can I do for you Mr. Rodstein?"

"Well for starters, can you give me an update on our five missing hunters?"

"Still unaccounted for. The snow hasn't helped with our search efforts."

There was a considerable pause on the line between both gentlemen. Major Vierra didn't care about what this guy had to say. He had more pressing issues to deal with.

"My office in Malone has been fielding calls from some very upset parents. They want to know where their sons are. I have been asked that question a thousand times today. These people are headed your way and they have attorneys. Armed to the teeth. They want blood, but mostly answers."

The major didn't have time to deal with this blowhard at the moment. This guy was all about politics.

"I'm staying one step ahead of them. I have a little help coming up from Albany to take care of this mess." responded the major.

"I need something, major! You have to give me something. I have some congressman from down near White Plains asking me questions. Questions I don't have answers to. He's somehow connected to one of the missing hunters. This thing is getting ugly, fast!"

The voice on the other end of the call became silent, as if the silence demanded the major to show his cards. A high-stakes card game and this was the river card. The last thing he needed was more irate parents busting down his door asking questions he didn't have the answers to.

The major said, "I will send over all the evidence we collected so far."

There was another long pause.

"The suspect, what did your boys get out of him?" Allen asked. "Surely, he said something incriminating."

"I will send over the interview transcripts. We did two rounds with the kid. I am currently waiting to hear back from a psychiatrist named Doctor Baumer, he is doing the psych evaluation on the kid."

"Do you think the kid did it." Allen asked.

"I honestly don't know, something happened out in those woods, and I know that boys witnessed it." the major said back.

"I will be in touch. Let me know if anything comes up, I mean ASAP." Allen said.

"Will do Allen."

He hung up on the District Attorney from Malone. His desk phone was blinking, it was Janet.

"Major, I have a call from the Essex County District Attorney's office."

"Patch it through."

Troop B headquarters was located in Essex County. The Franklin County line was only a few miles away in the village of Saranac Lake. Troop B was heading two missing hunter investigations, one in Franklin County and the other in Essex County.

"Major Viera, this is Ken Jordan. I am an assistant district attorney under Mrs. Lauri Seeley. She asked me to reach out to you for an update on the missing hunter from Altona."

Major Viera started thinking about Albany. How fast would they send this PR team up to help.

CHAPTER SIXTEEN

DEER VALLEY

They all followed Tony to Deer Valley. It was a legendary bar and grill a few miles from Paul Smith's College that was a haven for snowmobiles. The parking lot had more sleds than cars. They weren't hungry, seeing that they just ate breakfast. So, everybody had a couple draft beers. The pumpkin spice lager was a popular selection. The place was packed, and it wasn't even noon. Chris recognized a few locals and went over to talk with them.

"Canadians." said Drew.

Tony nodded his head in agreement. It was the accent, most of the people in here were definitely north of the border. The Canadian border was less than a couple hours away. There were a few places in the Adirondack Park that did snowmobile tours. Caleb wondered if these people were part of a tour.

It took around thirty minutes to do two draft beers. Again some more talk about new sleds and possible future sleds.

Tony raised his voice and said, "Let's drink up."

Drew took a hard look at Tony and started to guzzle his draft. He didn't know Tony that well. He was Jessie's buddy. They had been riding snowmobiles together for a couple years now, ever since Jessie brought Tony into the group. The guy always acted like he was in charge. Drew thought he was arrogant. Outside of riding, the only thing they knew about Tony was that he was an Italian from Massena, about an hour away. Tony De-Falco. He always talked about the reservation, it seems he had dealings or some kind of business up on the reservation at Hogansburg.

"Where to next?" asked Jessie.

Caleb downed his draft and placed the mug on the table. He stood up and started heading for the door.

"Chris, saddle up!" Tony called out.

Chris looked over at Tony and gave him a thumbs up. He said goodbye to his friends and started walking toward the door. As they walked outside, Caleb noticed the temperature had warmed up. It was above freezing and there was a slight fog starting to form.

Tony looked around and then said, "Going to be a slower ride to Owls Head if it's foggy."

Owls Head was the next stop. It too was a snow-mobile haven that had a restaurant and bar. It was located a few miles from Titus Mountain.

Chris threw a curve ball at everyone and said, "Hey fellas, I'm going to hangout for another beer. I will meet you up at Owls Head. Probably thirty minutes behind you."

Tony gave him a serious look and responded, "Don't be too long, we're probably going to be there for about an hour, tops."

"Hey, look Chris, it's your buddies." indicated Drew.

Chris looked over to where Drew was pointing and froze in his tracks. There they were, just standing near the tree line about one hundred feet away.

"Three, no I count four." said Jessie.

He was correct. There were four deer staring at them.

"Relax Chris, those are not your buddies." Tony put a reassuring hand on Chris's shoulder and walked to his sled.

Everyone followed in pursuit.

Tony looked back and said to him, "Your other four deer are ten miles back toward Paul Smith's."

Chris looked away from the deer with uneasy speculation. He then said, "See you up at Owls Head."

Chris walked back into the bar, and he didn't like the feeling that was starting to settle in the pit of his stomach. Caleb jumped on his sled, put his helmet on and started her up. She roared to life, they all roared to life. This brought a smile to Caleb, he twisted the accelerator and his sled moved forward. He was third behind Tony and Jessie. His brother Drew was behind him. They were about fifteen miles to Owls Head. It would be a nice ride, not too fast. Caleb noticed the spruce trees, full of snow. All the trees, pine, birch, maple, all full of snow. The trail was groomed, probably a few hours before. The snow was deep in the woods, had to stay on the trail. It would be easy to get stuck in two feet of unpacked snow. Caleb followed

Jessie; they were going around thirty when they caught up to Tony.

He had come upon a crossroads where the trail went in two directions. Tony pointed to his right, which went to Owls Head. Jessie started pointing the other way. Caleb was confused because that way went back towards Deer Valley. Jessie was adamant, he kept pointing. Caleb looked and noticed several deer. There were four of them. They were staring at them, about one hundred feet away. The deer were standing on the trail, almost like they were blocking the way back. Tony signaled for everyone to follow him. Tony turned right and everyone followed. Caleb didn't bother to turn his head to see if the deer were in pursuit. He smiled and thought about bringing some venison home. The thought of spilled deer blood all over his new machine quickly put that idea to rest.

CHAPTER SEVENTEEN

ONE MORE BEER

He walked up to his friends and said, "One more beer."

Chris knew a couple guys in this group. He had played softball with Gary on a travel team the past two summers and they had played in a few tournaments. Gary was a great player and he recruited other real good players. Chris wasn't the best one on these teams, but he could hold his own. He was also acquainted with Ronnie, a corrections officer out of Bear Hill in Malone. Chris worked Corrections at the Dannemora Prison and they both went to the academy together.

The conversation covered everything from softball, golf, and of course the size of the bartender's chest. Eventually they walked over to the dart boards, Chris pulled up a chair and watched his softball buddies play a game. Their conversation continued and Chris noticed that his beer was going down better than his breakfast. He looked back up at the dart game and watched Gary close out Ronnie in a game of dart baseball. He then asked, "Hey Gary, do they still throw knives here?"

Gary walked over to the dartboard and retrieved his darts. He turned towards Chris with a big grin on his face and said, "Do you still throw that pigsticker?"

Chris reached down toward his right hip and un-buckled his knife. He held it up chest high in a non-threatening way toward Gary and responded, "I never leave home without it."

Gary motioned to the door behind him. Chris got up and followed Gary and Ronnie through the door. It led outside behind the restaurant. Chris noticed that the sun had become brighter, it was getting warmer. The three of them trudged over in the newly thick snow to a couple bullseye targets that were about five feet high, three feet taller than the snow. The targets were a four by four three quarter inch plywood with quarter inch cork board on top. They were mounted on the outside wall of the restaurant. Chris had thrown at these targets before.

Gary looked at Chris and asked, "Are we playing 21?"

"Exact or over?" asked Chris.

Gary smiled and said, "Let's play over, I don't have all day."

Gary motioned towards Chris to signal that he had the board. Chris stood in front of the target, behind the line and gripped the blade of his knife with his thumb and two fingers. As he started to follow through with his throw Gary interrupted and asked, "Do you still call that pigsticker Mary?"

"Yup." replied Chris.

The blade flicked out of Chris's hand and rotated through the air two times coming to a stop in the middle of the target.

"Bullseye." said Ronnie.

Chris walked over in the cumbersome snow to the target and retrieved his knife. He looked at Gary and said, "Beginner's luck."

Chris cracked a smile and got out of the way. Gary held on to his knife by the handle. He lined up the target and released a knife with a quick flick of the wrist. His knife rotated a couple times through the air and landed just outside the bullseye.

"Five points." said Ronnie.

Gary retrieved his knife as Chris walked up to the line with Mary.

Ronnie said, "Seven to five. Chris is winning."

Again, Chris grabbed Mary by the blade and sent the knife two rotations through the air. Mary found her target.

"Bullseye again." said Ronnie.

Gary looked at Chris and said, "Nice throw Chris."

"Thank you, sir." Chris responded back.

A moment later, Chris retrieved his knife and got out of the way. Gary then grabbed his knife by the handle and sent it toward the target.

"Bullseye," said Ronnie.

Chris acknowledged the throw by Gary and gave him a thumbs up.

Ronnie updated the score and proclaimed, "Chris is winning fourteen to twelve."

Chris walked up to the line and prepared to throw Mary.

Gary shattered his concentration by saying, "I will bet you twenty bucks you can't hit a third bullseye in a row."

Chris turned his head and looked over at Gary and Ronnie and said, "Make it forty bucks and I'm interested."

"And another twenty whoever wins." responded Gary.

Chris nodded his head yes.

"Just hold on one second. So we're talking forty bucks if he hits this third bullseye and another twenty for the win?" confirmed Ronnie.

The two men looked at Ronnie and shook their heads yes. Before Gary could say something else, Chris released Mary and her aim was true.

"Bullseye!" Ronnie proclaimed.

Gary smiled at Chris and asked, "Come on now, give a man a chance to get even."

With a puzzled brow Chris looked over at Gary and said, "I'm listening."

"I'll bet you double or nothing you can't guzzle a draft beer and hit a fourth bullseye."

Chris cracked a grin and said, "I will have one more beer, but this will have to be the last."

Ronnie got up and ran to the door. He disappeared and one can only assume he was navigating himself to the bar. Gary walked over to Chris and asked, "Can I see Mary please?"

Chris reluctantly handed over his knife to him. It wasn't that he didn't trust Gary, he just didn't like anybody holding her. Gary studied the knife; he turned it over several times in the palm of his hand. The handle was red and there was a thinly wrapped black cord woven around it. The blade was black, and the name *'Mary'* was engraved into it. The butt end of the handle had a black polished stone with a gold star also engraved into it. Gary gripped the handle and then he tried to hold it by the blade; the way Chris held it. He looked confused and said, "I don't understand how you can throw a knife by the blade?"

The door opened and Ronnie appeared holding a draft beer. He walked over and handed it to Chris. Chris looked at Gary and held his hand out, and Gary placed Mary into Chris's hand. Chris walked to the line holding his draft beer in his left hand and Mary by the blade in his right. He looked at Gary and Ronnie and said, "Bottoms up fellas."

It took him about two seconds to down the draft. One second later Mary was rotating through the air and again her aim was true.

Ronnie smiled and looked at Gary and said, "Bullseye!"

"Fuck a rattlesnake!" shouted Gary.

"There ain't no rattlesnakes up in these parts." proclaimed Ronnie.

Gary pointed at Chris and said, "Yeah, well I feel like I just got bit by one."

Gary reached into his wallet and pulled out a C-note. He then looked up at Chris and said, "I'm twenty short."

Chris looked at Gary and smiled. "You got the first round in softball this summer."

He looked at his watch, he was about twenty-five minutes behind. He figured he would get to Owls Head right when Tony was ready to head back. He looked at Ronnie and said, "I have to go. Thanks for the beers."

Gary said, "Remember, second week of July there's a tournament in Massena."

Chris gave him a thumbs up and said, "Pencil me in."

He walked inside and headed for the front door. The restaurant was still full of snowmobilers. He stepped outside and noticed the fog was getting thicker. He took two steps and froze, expecting to see deer, but they were gone. Chris smiled and walked over to his sled. He put his helmet on and started it up. The machine roared to life and Chris accelerated forward onto the trail that would take him to Owls Head. The fog was going to slow him down, it was going to add another ten minutes onto his trip. But it was going to be a nice ride. The trees were blanketed in snow, and it was thick. He definitely wanted to stay on the track. Going off the trail and into the deep snow would cause more of a delay. Trying to dig your sled out of a snowbank by yourself was no fun.

The boys ahead of him had laid down a nice track to follow. Chris came upon a crossroads where the trail went in two directions. He slowed his sled down to a stop. He looked up at the sign and it told him to go right to Owls Head. Chris twisted his head back to the left to look down the trail, and there they were. Four deer, his deer. Just standing, staring at him about one hundred feet away. This is more than a coincidence, thought Chris.

He realized he was alone, his friends were already at Owls Head waiting for him. He had another twenty-five-minute ride ahead of him. Chris accelerated the throttle forward and turned the sled to the right. At the moment he didn't care about the fog, he needed to lose the deer behind him.

The trail opened up straight ahead for about a quarter of a mile. Chris accelerated the sled up to sixty miles per hour. He didn't dare look behind him but he was pretty sure they couldn't run that fast. The trail turned left and he decelerated the sled down to forty-five, but quickly accelerated out of the turn and opened her up to seventy miles per hour. He whizzed by the pine trees on both sides of the trail. Chris had to negotiate a few turns that caused him to slow down, but each time he came into a straightaway, he gunned it. He started thinking about the deer. Why were they following him? He suddenly got irritated and felt stupid. He shouldn't be afraid of four deer staring at him. He would just ignore them like everyone else had. After all, he was in the woods where they lived. It wasn't uncommon to see four deer in the woods.

Chris banked the sled to the right and came out into an opening, the trail opened up on both sides and the tree line had regressed hundreds of feet. It reminded

Chris of a meadow where grass and wildflowers would grow in the summertime. It was about two-hundred yards long and there was a blanket of fog on top of the snow. He could see up ahead where the meadow ended and where the trail entered the pine tree forest. He slowed the sled down as he entered into the pine trees.

Again, Chris started thinking about the deer. Was he afraid of them? Or was it the way they looked at him? They didn't seem like regular deer. Chris noticed movement off to his right. A deer leapt over Chris and his sled. Instinctively, Chris slowed his sled down and turned to his left. He watched as the deer landed in the deep snow gracefully. He was in awe at how athletic it was. Chris didn't know they could do that. If the deer hadn't leapt over him, he would have run it over. Chris turned his head forward to look at the trail only to notice another deer standing less than twenty yards in front of his sled.

With almost no time to react and without hesitation, he turned the sled hard right off the trail. His sled hit something hard underneath the snow and this caused Chris to go over his handlebars. He was floating through the air and a moment later he landed on his back in a deep drift. Chris rolled over and sat himself upright. His helmet visor was all fogged up from the snowbank. He unbuckled his helmet and took it off. The forest was thick with pine trees. So thick that the sun was having a hard time penetrating. The fog was heavy, and it was about waist high. Chris turned his head to locate where his sled was. He could see the handlebars, but the rest of the it was covered in fog. Chris stood up and walked over to where it was and instantly became confused. He was okay, as far as he could tell he had no injuries. Thank God for the soft snowbank he thought to himself. He started to wonder what he hit. He reached down to touch the front of the sled under the fog and felt a hard stump.

"Fucking lumberjacks!" Chris yelled.

Whoever had cut the tree down left the stump too high. Chris wondered what kind of damage this stump had done to his sled. He looked down at the front of his sled to assess the damage, but his vision was blocked by the fog. He started to feel the sled with his hands.

A grunting noise startled him off in the woods. Chris froze, every muscle in his body locked up. Several moments passed, it could have been a few seconds but to Chris it felt like an eternity.

He heard it again, but this time it seemed closer. Chris recognized the sound, it was a deer. He stood straight up and turned around where he heard the noise. About forty feet away was a deer. It was standing in the middle of the trail. Chris figured it to be the same deer that caused him to turn hard right.

"Thanks a lot asshole!" Chris shouted at the deer.

The deer continued to stare at him.

"What the fuck are you looking at?"

As soon as Chris finished yelling at the deer he felt something crash into him from behind. As he fell forward he rolled to his left only to see another deer jump over him. He quickly got up to his feet.

"*Assssssholllllle.*"

Chris looked behind where the sound came from. It was the first deer and it was still staring at him, but this time its head was tilted. Then it slightly opened its mouth and seemed to grin at Chris. It also revealed sharp carnivore teeth. Before he could process the moment another crash from behind sent Chris face first into the ground.

Lucky for him he ended up with a mouth full of snow. He rolled over and got to one knee. He was only a few feet from his sled. He leapt to it and managed to straddle the seat in two strides. Chris attempted to start the sled but it made no noise. Before he could process a variable solution another deer crashed into him, head first from the side and he fell off the sled. Chris got to his feet and turned his head to survey where they were. The first one that had called him an asshole was still standing in the same spot. The other three were to his right and left, all maintaining about twenty feet away. Except for the one that had just knocked him off his sled. It was now directly behind him. Chris thought to himself, deer don't speak and they also don't attack humans. He must have knocked his head when he fell off the sled. Surely there was a logical explanation.

"*Assssssholllllle.*"

Chris couldn't believe his ears or his eyes. But before he could comprehend the gravity of the situation, the first deer started to charge him. Chris grabbed Mary and let her fly toward his attacker. Mary hit her target right between the eyes.

The first deer continued straight past Chris. He twisted to his right as the deer whisked by. He was sure Mary hit the deer. Chris noticed his helmet on the ground by his feet. He bent down and picked it up just in time to see another deer attacking him from the left. He swung his helmet with his right hand and connected with the deer's head. It fell to the ground hard, like it had been knocked out by a heavyweight boxer's right hook.

Chris cracked a smile and tried to pretend he wasn't afraid for his life.

That all changed when he turned back to his right. About five feet away was Mary, looking straight at him. Chris could make out the red handle with the black cord and the perfectly polished stone in the butt end. She hit her mark, bullseye. The first deer stared at Chris with Mary driven deep between its eyes. Chris couldn't even see the blade. The deer tilted its head and said, *"Assssssholllllle."*

The deer was close enough so that Chris could smell its hot foul breath. It smelled like rotten meat.

It then raised up its front right hoof above Chris's head and produced a talon-like claw. The talon came down fast and cut a straight line from the top of Chris's head in a downward motion. Chris instantly lost his left eye. He could feel a warm sensation crawling down his cheek, it was his blood.

CHAPTER EIGHTEEN

WHERE IS CHRIS?

Tony and Jessie partnered up and won the first pool game. Caleb was at the bar buying them a shot of Fireball and Drew was re-racking the balls.

"That will be five dollars please." said the barkeep.

His name was Daunte. He was mid to late forties, balding and wore a thick brown mustache.

"Yo Caleb!" Tony shouted from behind. "Three more drafts."

Caleb nodded and then grinned up at Daunte. "Make it four."

The barkeep turned back around and a few steps later started pouring the draft beers. Caleb admired the decor of the pub. It was rustic. The shelves behind the bar were made of oak and were finished off with a rough-cut edge. The walls and ceiling had a maple-colored wainscoting theme. There were black and white pictures plastered on every wall. Each one depicted snowmobilers, hunters and party goers all smiling or laughing, having a great time, so it seemed. Caleb noticed that some of the pictures had to be fifty years old or more, it was like a time capsule. The pub was packed, every stool and table were full. There were people standing gladly at the bar and they didn't mind waiting for a drink. There was music playing on the jukebox, a song Caleb recognized from the seventies.

"Thirteen dollars all together." said Daunte.

Caleb turned his head from the jukebox back to the barkeep. He put a ten and a five on the bar and said, "Thanks."

Two-dollar drafts were a great happy hour special, and the locals seemed to agree. Caleb grabbed the tray with the beverages and did his best waiter impression on his way back to his pool-playing posse.

"Your drinks, fine sirs." Caleb pronounced in his very best Irish brogue accent.

Tony walked over and grabbed both shots off the tray. He handed one to Jessie and said, "May you be in heaven a half hour before the devil knows you're dead!"

The two men threw the shots back. Jessie shook his head side to side, almost like his GI tract didn't agree with the fireball. Tony acted like it was water. He then grabbed the thickest pool stick that was leaning against the wall and walked to the front of the table. He slid the stick back and forth a few times, each time with a little more momentum. Finally, he sent the cue ball on a mission, one where it would disrupt fifteen other balls on the table and send them into random collisions. Success, the five and three balls followed each other into a side pocket. Tony smiled and lined up his next shot and said, "Two Ball in the corner."

A moment later the Two Ball fell into the corner pocket. Drew looked around the bar and then said, "Where in the hell is Chris?"

Caleb looked at his watch, it had been over an hour since they said goodbye to Chris at Deer Valley.

Tony smiled and said, "Those deer got him."

Beer exploded out of Jessie's mouth; uncontrollable laughter followed. Caleb and Drew looked at each other and both burst out laughing.

"Nice miss Tony." said Drew as he watched the one ball miss the side pocket and ricochet off the bumper wall of the table.

Tony walked back to his chair and sat down. He looked over at Drew, who was in the process of lining up his shot, and said, "Hey, Drew. You suck."

Again, beer sprayed from Jessie's mouth. Caleb and Jessie also laughed. Drew sunk his next three shots before surrendering the table to Jessie. The game lasted another twenty minutes. Then Drew lined up the Eight Ball. It was a long green shot, corner pocket.

"Soft Drew." Caleb whispered.

Drew gave his brother a scowling look and said, "Shut the fuck up little brother, and I never do anything soft."

When they were little Drew would always go first in everything they did. He was a total risk taker, and didn't seem to be afraid of anything. Caleb started to crack a slight smile, he had fond memories of his older brother and their childhood. Drew jumping off Bluff

Island. A seventy-foot cliff free fall into lower Saranac Lake. Caleb to this day would never do that. He watched Drew hit the cue ball very hard, and it struck the Eight Ball harder. The Eight Ball went into the corner pocket and Drew smiled. Caleb continued to watch the cue ball and it was not slowing down. It bounced off the far rail and followed a diagonal path toward the opposite corner pocket. Drew turned his head and started tracking the path of the Eight Ball. Tony started repeating, each time a little louder, "Go! Go! Go!"

The cue ball continued on its path and dropped out of existence into the far corner pocket. Tony looked up at Drew and said, "Hey Drew. You suck."

They all burst out laughing. Tony looked at Caleb and said, "Two more please."

Several minutes later they all had four new draft beers in front of them. Tony and Jessie downed two more fireballs.

Drew was looking at the door while he sipped his draft. Caleb was also expecting Chris to come walking in the pub any second.

Tony looked at everyone and said, "I'm going."

"Let's wait fifteen more minutes." said Drew.

"I'm with Tony, let's hit it." responded Jessie.

Tony stood up and guzzled the rest of his draft. He started heading for the door and said, "Thanks for the beers boys."

Jessie stood up and started following. He stopped, looked back at Drew and Caleb. "Are you guys coming?"

Drew looked at Caleb and then back to Jessie and said, "No, we will be right behind you. As soon as Chris gets here, maybe fifteen minutes."

Jessie gave Drew a thumbs up and headed for the front door. Tony and Jesse walked by the bar. On the way out the door, Tony turned his head toward the barkeep and said, "Thanks Daunte, see you next time."

"Thank you again Tony. Remember, two-dollar drafts on Saturdays." Daunte said back.

The two of them walked out the front door toward their sleds.

Tony looked around and said, "I think it warmed up some more."

Jessie took off his jacket and tied it around his waist. Tony grabbed his helmet and put it on, Jessie did the same thing with his. After Jessie got his buckle strapped, he looked at Tony and said, "I feel kind of shitty not waiting around for Chris."

Tony shook his head no and then said, "Knowing Chris, he's probably already on his way to Charlie's Inn."

Tony started his machine first and then Jessie did the same. Tony took the lead and Jessie followed not too far behind. Within a few minutes they were back on the trail heading back toward home. Jessie assumed the plan was to stop at Charlie's Inn for one beer before they eventually called it a day. The weather seemed warmer, and the trail was packed down hard. Tony was going fast, Jessie noticed. The only time he would slow down is when they came upon some fog. It was easier to go back because they were familiar with the trail. It was a great day riding snowmobiles, Jessie thought to himself. His sled was working well, that was always a concern the first time out for the season.

Up ahead, the trail banked to the right and Tony disappeared around the corner. Jessie sped up and leaned into the curve. He came out of it like a slingshot and the acceleration caused Jessie to move back slightly in his seat. He noticed Tony about forty feet ahead. Suddenly Jessie caught some movement off to his right. He turned his head and noticed a deer.

He admired how gracefully it moved in the thick snow. It seemed to leap up in the air, like it was floating. It would then fall back down into the snow and a second later it would be back up floating in the air again, almost like Santa's reindeers. Tony was slowing down. Naturally, Jessie slowed down too. Tony was watching the deer also, Jessie noticed. A few seconds later Tony accelerated his sled and Jessie followed. The next couple miles were fun. They banked right and left a few times and went fast down the straightaways. Truly, it was a great day to ride. The trail started to enter a thicker part of the forest, where there were pine trees on both sides. Jessie remembered going through this section on the way up this afternoon. Tony suddenly stopped his sled. Jessie almost rear ended him, but managed to squeeze the brakes just in time, coming within a centimeter of Tony's sled.

Jessie lifted up his visor and screamed, "Why the fuck did you stop!"

Tony turned his head back to Jessie and pointed forward. Jessie leaned out to his right so that he could see what Tony was pointing at. It was a deer standing in the middle of the trail. Tony would have hit it had he not stopped in time. It was about thirty feet away. Tony unbuckled his helmet and turned his sled off. He took his helmet off and put it on the handlebars. Jessie turned his sled off. Tony got off his sled and stood there looking at the deer.

"There's something wrong with you, girlfriend." Tony said.

Jessie took a closer look at the deer. It was definitely a doe. One of the biggest female deer Jessie ever saw. He also noticed that there was something sticking out of her head. He couldn't quite make out what it was. Jessie got off his sled and unbuckled his helmet. He took his helmet off and put it on his seat and started walking up toward Tony.

"What the fuck is that sticking out of its head?" asked Jessie.

Tony concentrated on the object and said, "Looks like a polished black stone in the butt end of a handle. Is that a star?"

The deer turned its head to the right.

"Red handle with black twine interlaced." said Tony.

The deer turned its head back and looked straight at Tony and Jessie.

"I believe that's Mary sticking out of the deer's head." proclaimed Tony.

A surprised Jessie asked, "You mean Chris's knife?"

Tony started laughing and then said, "You know it belongs to Chris."

"What's so funny?" asked Jessie.

Tony continued to laugh even louder and harder for several more seconds.

"Hey asshole, what's so fucking funny?" a perturbed Jesse asked.

A few seconds later, Tony gathered his laughter and put it away. "I bet you twenty dollars Chris is pissed off. Imagine this, the fucker is riding and sees this deer. He has a few beers in him and decides to throw Mary at it. Figures he's gonna pull some venison home tonight on the back of his sled. He's out here jacking deer while we're enjoying a perfect day of riding."

Tony started bending over, again, more laughter came out of his body. A few seconds later he lifted his head and said, "Do you know how much money Chris paid for that knife?"

Jessie didn't know how much Chris had paid for Mary. He just knew Chris carried that knife with him everywhere. He also knew Chris was very accurate throwing that knife.

"That there is a custom-built throwing knife that Chris paid over a thousand dollars for. He won't tell you that, he even spins a story that he made the knife himself."

Jessie looked confused, he responded, "Everyone knows Chris built that knife."

"That's bullshit! His wife Donna wouldn't talk to him for over a month, and she told my wife why." a smirking Tony replied.

Jessie was getting annoyed. He waited a few more seconds for Tony to explain why. A few more seconds passed, and he kept staring at Jessie with a grin on his face like he was privy to top secret information.

"Oh, please do tell." Jessie sarcastically asked.

Tony could tell Jessie was getting annoyed.

"So, my wife tells me that Chris's wife Donna, told her that she found a credit card bill from Knife Universe, for a thousand bucks."

Jessie started smiling. Tony turned back around and pointed at the deer and said, "That there is a thousand-dollar throwing knife sticking in that deer's head."

Jessie was still smiling. It was definitely Chris's throwing knife; Mary was stuck right between the eyes of this deer that happened to be squatting in the middle of the trail. The poor thing seemed helpless to Jessie, it just looked at Tony and him. Like it was asking for help but couldn't speak English or communicate with humans for that matter.

Tony continued, "For some reason this doe didn't die when Mary hit it in the head. I bet you Chris drove after this deer trying to get his knife back for a few miles. It just ran away with his beloved Mary stuck in its head."

Tony bent over and started laughing uncontrollably again. Jessie started to make sense of Tony's story, and this caused him to start laughing out loud also.

Their laughter was interrupted by a grunting noise. The two of them stopped laughing and looked up at the deer.

Tony looked at Jessie and said, "I have an idea. Can you imagine what Chris would do if I walked up to him and showed him my new throwing knife?"

Jessie grinned and then asked, "Yeah, and how are you gonna do that? Are you just gonna walk up and pull Mary out of that deer's head?"

"That's exactly what I'm going to do. And I bet you this poor girl wants me to pull that knife out of its head." declared Tony.

Tony turned around and started walking slowly toward the deer. He got about twenty feet away and it grunted again. Tony stopped and said, "Whoa, whoa girl, it's okay."

The deer just stared back at Tony. He slowly started walking again toward the deer. Tony stopped in his tracks about ten feet away from the deer. It slightly turned its head and opened up its mouth only to reveal several sharp carnivorous looking teeth. The kind of teeth you would see in a dinosaur's mouth, thought Jessie. And these teeth were stained with blood.

Jessie's eyes became as big as saucers, he said, "Tony, what the fuck. Let's get out of here."

Tony shook his head slowly yes. The two men

started walking back to their sleds the whole time keeping their eyes on the deer. The deer that had Mary sticking out of its head. Jessie picked up his helmet and straddled the seat of his sled.

"Fuckkkkkkkkk."

The two men looked up at the deer in amazement. Tony was in the process of putting his helmet on when he turned around and said to Jessie, "Did that thing just say – "

Out of nowhere another deer crashed into Tony from his right side and knocked him off his sled. It happened so fast. Tony was lying on his face on the other side of his sled in the snow and before he could get up the other deer was twenty-five feet away slowing down from its brutal assault. Jessie watched as the other deer turned back around and faced where Tony was laying down in the snow. Tony slowly got to his feet. He was holding his right side and moaning in obvious pain.

"Are you alright, Tony?"

Tony seemed to be looking around for his helmet, he seemed dazed and confused. He then turned his gaze from the ground back to Jessie and said, "Are you fucking kidding me!"

Tony was ready to fire back more rhetoric at Jessie but decided to stop when he noticed the concern on Jesse's face. Tony observed that Jessie wasn't looking at him. No, he was looking past him. Tony turned around and stood face to face with the deer and it had Mary sticking out of its forehead. It was looking down upon him. Tony stood over six feet two inches tall and weighed close to two hundred and thirty pounds. He was looking up at this deer and was having a hard time comprehending how tall the doe was.

He couldn't help but stare at Chris's knife. It was a beautiful knife. The star on the handle seemed to be outlined in gold. The deer made a grunting noise.

Jessie watched in horror as the deer turned its head slightly to the side and opened up its jaws exposing razor sharp teeth. The deer clamped a hold of Tony's neck. it raised its head up high, lifting Tony off the ground. This deer had Tony's neck in its mouth and his feet were dangling off the ground by a good foot. Blood was starting to ooze out of Tony's neck on both sides. He reached up with his hands and grabbed a hold of the deer's face. Tony's legs started kicking violently, like he was trying to run somewhere. Jesse knew that that was not going to save him.

"Tony!" screamed Jessie.

The deer violently shook its head and Jesse heard a loud snap. A moment later it opened its mouth and Tony's limp body fell to the ground like a sack of potatoes. The deer turned its gaze onto Jessie. It tilted its head again and slightly opened up its mouth. *"Tooonnnnnnieeeeeeee."*

Jessie's jaw opened in amazement. Without thinking, Jessie turned on his sled and didn't even bother to put his helmet on. He opened it up so quickly that the front end rose in the air like he was doing a wheelie. He took a slight wide berth around the deer that just killed Tony and darted down the trail. The trail that would take him home.

CHAPTER NINETEEN

BLOOD IN THE SNOW

Caleb and Drew were sitting outside on their sleds. They had just finished paying their tab and left the bar. They waited an extra twenty-five minutes, but Chris never showed up.

Drew went first and Caleb followed close behind. It was warmer and there seemed to be more fog. Caleb also noticed that the snow was starting to melt off the trees. But all in all, it was a beautiful day to ride.

Drew was setting a good pace, but not too fast. Caleb didn't mind, they both had a few beers and there was no need to get back at a certain time. And Caleb noticed that the trail was well groomed now that several snowmobiles had used it today. The sun was starting to fall, Caleb figured they had about an hour and a half of sunlight left. Plenty of time to get to Charlie's Inn and have a couple more drafts and then call it a day and go home. No problem driving home in the dark from Charlie's.

The next ten minutes were spent casually riding through twists and a few sharp turns. There were patches of heavy fog where they had to slow down and then they could speed up on the straightaways. Caleb noticed that Drew started to slow his sled down. Drew held up his right arm and Caleb knew that he was going to come to a stop, so he did too. It took a few moments for Drew to figure out why they stopped, then he spotted why. A snowmobile was sitting in the middle of the trail. Caleb wondered where the driver was. Drew turned off his sled and took his helmet off, Caleb followed suit. The two of them got off their sleds and walked up to the unattended sled.

"That's Tony's sled." said Drew.

Caleb noticed the color of the sled, blue with black racing stripes on the cowl. It was definitely Tony's sled, thought Caleb.

Caleb looked at his brother and asked, "Well, where the fuck is he?"

Drew said nothing. He turned his head and spanned his vision in all directions.

He then looked at his brother and said, "Maybe his sled quit. He probably jumped on Jessie's."

"Yeah, I bet you're right." agreed Caleb.

Drew walked over to Tony's sled and sat on it. He looked at the start button for a few seconds and then pushed it. To their surprise, the sled roared to life. Drew turned his head back toward Caleb and said, "Why would he leave his sled in the middle of the forest?"

Caleb motioned to his brother to turn the sled off, so he did. He then asked Drew, "What did you say?"

"Why would Tony abandon his sled twenty miles from Charlie's Inn?"

Caleb shrugged his shoulders; he didn't have the answer either. Drew got off Tony's sled and walked around the front of it. Caleb watched him, he noticed that Drew seemed to be studying the ground on the other side of Tony's sled.

"There's blood in the snow." pointed Drew.

Caleb walked around the sled to where Drew was, and he noticed it too. He looked up at his brother and asked, "Are you sure that's blood? Maybe it's oil, or grease."

Drew turned his head toward Caleb and said, "Oil and grease aren't red. That's blood, little brother."

Drew started studying the ground around Tony's sled. He started walking a few feet away into the woods. Caleb watched him bend down and pick something up, it was a helmet. "Why would Tony throw his helmet into the woods?"

Caleb shrugged his shoulders, again he couldn't answer his brother's question. Drew walked up to Tony's sled and put the helmet on the handlebars.

Drew looked at Caleb, grinned and said, "I bet you they hit a fucking deer."

This made sense to Caleb, it was the only logical explanation.

"Maybe Tony's hurt, and he hopped on Jessie's sled." replied Caleb.

The two of them didn't even bother using their cell phones, there was no service out in this area.

"Let's go find them." said Drew.

They both hopped back on their sleds and put their

helmets on. A few seconds later, Caleb was following Drew down the trail back towards Charlie's Inn. Their pace was much faster. The next few miles were uncomfortably fast. A few twists and turns, and Drew was not slowing down. They were on a mission to find Tony and Jessie.

Caleb noticed a fogbank up ahead and instinctively started to throttle down. He quickly noticed that Drew wasn't, so he turned the throttle more and his new sled caught up to his brother a few seconds later. It was nerve wracking going through the fogbank that fast thought Caleb.

Drew held up his right arm and made a fist. The two of them came to a stop. Caleb could see it and he was sure Drew could too. Jessie's sled was all smashed up.

He must have gone off the trail and hit a tree. Like the sled ricocheted off a couple trees before coming to a stop, thought Caleb.

Caleb and Drew unbuckled their helmets, took them off, and then turned their sleds off. Caleb waited for Drew to get off his sled and then he did the same. He walked up to his older brother who seemed to be studying the crash scene. Broken pieces of snowmobile were scattered all around. Plastic, metal, and rubber were thrown about. This sled itself seemed twisted, almost upside down between two pine trees. Amongst the rubble, Caleb noticed what looked like a jacket. He walked a few feet over to his left and picked it up. "Isn't this Jessie's jacket?"

Drew nodded.

"Where the hell is Jessie? And where the hell is Tony?"

"Over here!" it was Jessie's voice. Drew gave Caleb a confused look. They both started walking to their left where there was a clump of pine trees.

"Up here." said the voice.

Drew and Caleb looked up and saw Jessie about forty feet up in the tree.

"What the hell are you doing up in a tree?" asked Caleb.

"Keep your voices down or they will come back." a very nervous Jessie said.

Drew looked at Caleb and gave him an even more confused look. He then looked back up at Jessie and said, "Jessie what the hell happened to your sled and where's Tony?"

"Why did you guys leave Tony's sled back there?" asked Caleb.

"Keep your voices down!" Jessie responded back sternly.

He was visibly shaken.

Drew raised his voice at him and said, "Jessie, Jessie get your ass out of that tree and come down here and talk to us."

"Jessie why are you up in a tree in the first place?" asked Caleb.

"No way am I coming down there, it's safer up here. Hurry up, get up here now before they come back." explained a highly agitated Jessie.

Drew turned his head toward Caleb with his mouth agape. He whispered so that only Caleb could hear him. "He must have banged his head when he crashed."

"Yeah, but where's Tony?" Caleb responded back to his brother.

Drew looked back up at Jessie in the tree and asked, "What are you talking about, and what do you mean it's safer up there?"

"The killer deer!" Jessie emphasized in a loud whisper. Trying not to be too loud.

Drew looked back at his brother and said, "Oh yeah I think he hit his head, definitely a concussion."

"I didn't hit my head. My head's okay, I'm not crazy. Tony's gone!"

Caleb turned his gaze toward his brother and shook his head no a few times. He looked back up at Jessie and asked, "What do you mean he's gone? Obviously, he's gone because he's not here right now. Why did he abandon his sled? Or for that matter why did he leave his helmet back there in the woods?"

"Mary killed him." Jessie emphasized in a loud whisper.

Jessie started to sob; tears were starting to fall down his cheeks. Drew and Caleb had known Jessie their whole life. They had played baseball together throughout high school. He was a pretty tough kid growing up and Caleb could never remember seeing Jessie cry before today.

"Who the fuck is Mary?" asked Drew.

Caleb watched as Jessie transformed from a quiet tree climber to a statuesque terrified observer. He noticed that Jessie stopped looking at them, he was looking off in the distance. Scanning for something.

And then Jessie said, "It's too late, they're back."

Drew and Caleb turned around to see what Jessie was pointing at. The trail was in the middle of a Pine Forest and there were trees on both sides. Caleb remembered that there was a small clearing about three hundred yards behind them. That is what Jessie must be looking at up high in his tree.

"I don't see anything, Jessie." said Drew.

"Back behind us in the clearing, that's what he's talking about." said Caleb.

The two brothers looked behind them where the trail entered the forest, where they had just come from. Expecting to see something, whatever it was Jessie was referring to. Caleb turned his head and looked at his brother with anticipation, but he wasn't sure what to expect. Drew looked at his brother and then motioned with his right hand up in the tree and said, "Fucking guy has lost his marbles."

Time passed very slowly; it could have been seconds but to Caleb it felt a lot longer. They turned their bodies back toward the tree and looked up at Jessie. Caleb said, "Come on Jessie, there's nothing. Climb down the tree and let's find Tony."

"Behind you!" a frightened whisper came from Jessie.

Caleb and Drew turned around and noticed a deer. Drew turned back toward the tree and looked up at Jessie. Jessie could tell that Drew didn't believe him. He saw the perturbed look on his face.

"Enough, Jessie! It's a fucking doe, big deal. Get your ass down this tree now, we have to find Tony. We are running out of sun li – "

"What's wrong with this picture?" Drew turned around to see what his brother was talking about. He noticed that Caleb was staring at the deer.

A voice up in the tree said, "That's Mary!"

The two brothers stared for a long time at the deer. It was standing fifty feet away.

"The rut season is over, is that some fucked up antler growing in the middle of its head?" asked Caleb.

Drew continued to stare at the deer. "No, I don't think so. That there's a doe, a big one."

"That's no antler. That's Mary. That's Chris's knife sticking out of its head." declared Jessie from up above.

The two brothers continued to stare at the big doe. Drew started to slowly walk towards it. Caleb stayed where he was.

"Where the hell is Chris?" asked Caleb.

"I don't know where Chris is, but I know where Tony is." sobbed Jessie.

Drew stopped about thirty feet away from the deer and turned his head back towards the tree and said, "Get down out of that tree and tell us where Tony is."

Before Drew could turn back around the doe attacked him. Jessie and Caleb didn't have time to verbally warn Drew what was about to happen, and it ran him over. It happened so fast. Drew fell on his back and the deer whisked by Caleb. It stopped about thirty feet away and turned around and looked at Caleb. It didn't take long for Drew to get back to his feet. He brushed himself off and looked back at his attacker and asked, "What the fuck just happened!"

"Well big brother, you just got run over by a doe." responded Caleb.

"A big doe that has a knife sticking out of its head." Drew answered back.

"That's Mary!" Jessie screamed.

The two brothers concentrated their gaze on the knife. The sunlight was penetrating the pines in a few spots and one solid ray beam suddenly hit the deer. It was like a spotlight suddenly appeared. The brothers noticed the black polished stone and red handle with black twine.

"Yup. That's Chris's knife." said Drew.

Jessie screamed, "That motherfucker killed Tony."

The deer twisted its head to the side and slightly opened up its mouth revealing sharp, jagged, bloodstained teeth. The kind of teeth you would see in a monster's mouth.

Caleb turned his head to Drew and said, "I think I know what happened to Chris and Tony."

Drew looked at his brother and said, "I'm not sure what happened to Chris and Tony, but we can't wait around here to find out."

Caleb was scared. He and his brother had been hunting deer in these woods their whole lives. But this was different, this creature wasn't a deer. No, it was a monster.

Drew shouted up in the tree, "Jessie we gotta go now! Get your ass down from that tree and jump on the back of my sled."

Jessie hesitated for a few seconds like he was working out a plan in his head.

"Jessie, I will leave your ass up in that tree if you're not on the back of my sled in ten seconds!" Drew again shouted up in the tree with a sterner warning.

Jessie started to climb down the tree. The monster jolted past the brothers. It was on an interception course with Jessie, thought Caleb. Jessie didn't even notice and jumped the last fifteen feet to the snow. Before his feet hit the ground, the monster crashed into his back.

Jessie did a backward roll over the deer and landed awkwardly on his shoulders. His body did a half twist, and he came to a stop on his back. He immediately started moaning in obvious pain. Before the monster turned back around, three more deer came out of the pines. They were big also, noticed Caleb. They stopped about ten feet away from Jessie. The two brothers were frozen, they didn't dare move. A guilty feeling started to creep into Caleb's soul. He wanted to help Jessie, but he was terrified to move.

"Jessie get up." Drew was pleading with him.

A few seconds later, Jessie managed to get to his feet, his back was facing them. The monster walked up to Jessie and brought its hoof up high in the air. Jessie was about six feet tall, but the brothers could still see this deer standing on the other side of him. In a swift action, it brought its leg down and made contact with Jessie.

"Ahhhhhhg!" a blood curdling scream escaped from Jessie's mouth.

The brothers could see what appeared to be blood droplets splattering all around Jessie. His body twisted and he fell to the ground face first. They could see the top of his head. Caleb noticed that Jessie was starting to lose his hair. That thought quickly faded away when Jessie lifted his head up and looked at them, right in their eyes. Even from this distance, about fifty feet away, they could still see the horror in his eyes. Caleb started crying, he couldn't hold it back. The tears were already flowing down Drew's face.

"Come on buddy, get up. Get on the back of my sled." Drew was pleading again with his lifelong friend.

The two brothers started slowly walking backwards toward their sleds. Jessie got to one knee. The deer did nothing. It was like a cat and mouse game, where the cat plays with the mouse just before it kills it. The brothers were helpless, there was nothing they could do, and they knew it. Caleb noticed Jessie was bleeding all the way down from his chest to his stomach. It looked to be a huge slash that cut right through his shirt. He tried to stand up but lost his balance and fell back on his chest. Blood was just pouring out of him. The deer did nothing, they just sat and watched him.

"Come on buddy, you can do this." Drew got the words out, but it was with a mixture of crying involved.

Jessie got up to one knee again, and he was balancing on his right arm. With a look of worry and concern, like when an exhausted but determined marathon runner tries to finish running twenty-six grueling miles, he stood up. The brothers started to smile as they continued moving backward slowly and methodically toward their machines. Jessie took one step forward and blood continued to pour out of his stomach.

"You got this Jessie." an optimistic Caleb said.

A sudden change to Jessie's face, Drew noticed. A look of hope. Jessie took another step forward and he almost lost his balance.

"That's it Jessie, a few more steps." shouted Drew.

Jessie took another step and again the deer did nothing.

"He's gonna make it." said Caleb.

Two more steps, a smile from ear to ear on Jessie. The brothers reciprocated with a smile back at him, but their smiles were full of pessimism. Jessie took two more steps with confidence and looked at Drew who was about thirty feet away and said, "You sit in the back, I'm driving."

The smiles quickly faded from the brothers faces and Jessie noticed it. Two deer quickly caught up to

Jessie from behind. Suddenly Jessie fell forward on his face and screamed in agony. Caleb noticed a slash mark from the bottom of Jessie's neck, all the way down to his ass. Caleb and Drew could do nothing. The two deer bit down on Jessie's ankles. Again, Jessie started screaming in agony. They lifted their heads up, turned their bodies back toward the direction they came from and started trotting towards the monster that had Mary sticking out of its head. Jessie lifted his head up and made eye contact with the brothers. Pure horror filled his eyes. In a last-ditch effort as the deer dragged him farther away, he screamed, "Drewwwwwwwwww!"

The scream seemed to last forever but within a few seconds it started to fade away and Jessie disappeared into the pine trees. The brothers were frozen statues. They couldn't hear Jessie screaming anymore. It was just them and the monster, and she was about forty feet away just staring at them with Mary sticking out of her head. She started walking towards them very slowly. When she got about twenty feet away, she stopped. She turned her head slightly sideways and opened her mouth. The brothers had seen her do this before, they knew what she was hiding in her mouth. They also had a good idea what was happening to Jessie. What also happened to Chris and Tony. The monster looked right at Caleb's older brother and said, *"Drewwwwwwwwww."*

It was still saying his name when the boys jumped on their sleds, fired them up and took off down the trail. Within a few seconds they had the sled up to sixty and their speed was increasing. No slowing down for turns or fog. Here we go again, thought Caleb. Drew was driving recklessly. Caleb was having a hard time keeping up. There was movement off to his left, he thought he saw a deer. He turned his head back and couldn't see Drew's sled in front of him.

A hard left bank turn, Caleb slowed the sled down and then accelerated into the turn and shot out like a missile. His long hair was flowing behind him and the wind was smashing into his face. They hadn't had time to put their helmets on. Hell, they hadn't had time to even pick them up, they'd simply left them back there on the side of the trail. He spotted Drew about two hundred feet up ahead. Drew turned his sled hard right, and at the last second he rolled off his sled before it crashed into a tree. It was a deer that he was trying to avoid. Caleb accelerated his sled and made a beeline for the deer that was starting to walk over toward where Drew was lying in the snow. Within a couple seconds Caleb crashed into the deer and it rolled over the top of his sled. He ducked his head at the last second behind his windshield. He pulled his sled up beside his brother and said, "Get on."

Drew climbed on the back of Caleb's sled and they accelerated like a rocket down the trail, leaving the other snowmobile smashed against the tree. Caleb couldn't understand where all the deer were coming from. He wasn't sure if it was the same deer that just attacked Jessie or if they were different? He was pretty sure they weren't the same deer that attacked Jessie, that is unless they could run sixty miles per hour?

"Faster, go faster!" Drew yelled into Caleb's ear.

Caleb twisted the throttle more; he could feel his body fall back into his brothers behind him. He glanced down at the speedometer: eighty-five. Drew kept looking over his right and left shoulder and he had a death grip around his little brother's waist. He was a dead man if he fell off the back of this sled, and it wouldn't be from the fall.

"You have to go faster!" Drew was screaming.

"I'm not gonna crash like you did!" Caleb screamed back at his brother.

The next few miles Caleb negotiated turns and straightaways, slowing down and accelerating. The whole time Drew was constantly looking to his right, left, making sure there weren't any monsters.

"Left up here!" screamed Drew.

Caleb could see the turn up ahead, it would take them back toward Charlie's Inn. He started to slow down. Instinctively, Drew turned and looked behind just in time to see a deer with razor sharp teeth about to pounce on him.

"Go straight, punch it!" screamed Drew.

There were four deer blocking the trail. Caleb twisted the throttle hard. The sled started to rise in the front and they sling-shotted down the trail toward Deer Valley. It was a long straightaway. Drew looked over Caleb's shoulder at the speedometer, the needle was passed one hundred miles per hour. Caleb's eyes were watering from the force of the wind blast on his face. At the end of the straightaway Drew screamed, "Slow down little brother, stop!"

"Are you fucking kidding me, I'm done stopping!" Caleb responded.

"They're gone, stop the sled. They're gone! I said they are gone!" Drew screamed back at his brother.

And to get his point across he started squeezing his midsection to the point where Caleb was going to have trouble breathing. Caleb started to slow the sled down. He could hear the high pitch of the engine wind down to a slow murmur. He stopped the sled but kept it idling. They both turned their heads behind them and checked the trail. There was no movement, nothing. Caleb turned his body and looked at his big brother and said, "We must get to Deer Valley. It's the shortest distance. They have a landline."

Caleb was breathing very rapidly. He was trying to process the information his brother was giving him. He knew he was right; it was hard to get bars on a cell phone even at Deer Valley.

"We're going to have to run along route thirty." Caleb said.

Drew agreed and said, "Only for a few miles, just be careful of traffic."

Caleb started to accelerate the sled. Drew looked

over his shoulder behind him, and he thought he could see movement.

"Faster Caleb!" he screamed into his little brother's ear.

The next five miles were the fastest Caleb ever drove a sled before. His mind was racing. He started to think about his wife Karen. Her long velvety brown hair. Those brown eyes of hers that could see right through to his soul. How she always stuck up for him, no matter the situation. They banked left and went through a small thicket of clumped up bushes on both sides of the trail. Fog seemed to be patchy in some areas.

Caleb started thinking of his daughter, Nora. She was going to start kindergarten next fall. She idolized him. Nora always got mad when he spent alone time with her mother. This made Caleb grin.

"Route Thirty up ahead!" screamed Drew.

Caleb nodded and proceeded to where Drew was pointing. They came out of the woods and turned left onto Route Thirty. Caleb stayed on the left soft shoulder of the road. He started thinking about his newborn son. How happy he was when Karen delivered him. To be blessed with a daughter and a son, a man couldn't ask for anything more. Possibly, a brand-new snowmobile. Caleb started giggling, but his brother didn't hear him. He sped up to eighty. Caleb had to be careful, he wasn't driving on a lakebed that was flat and smooth. Meacham Lake was on his left, and there was a thin row of trees in between Route 30 and the lake. On the soft shoulder of the road, it dipped down sometimes. So, Caleb had to slow down sometimes, and this did not make his brother Drew happy. Up ahead, they were approaching a fogbank. It was still a good mile away, and it covered the whole road.

"Deer!" shouted Drew.

He started shaking Caleb's left shoulder and was pointing off into the woods.

Caleb turned his head to the left and saw movement in the trees. He couldn't focus his vision on the movement too long because he was driving very fast. The fogbank was getting closer. Caleb couldn't see over it; it was too tall. It looked like a thick white cloud that belonged way up in the sky. But for some reason it was sitting in the middle of Route 30.

Caleb felt his brother pulling on his left shoulder again. He started to turn his head but noticed Drew's left arm to the side of his ear pointing straight ahead. A second later Caleb noticed what Drew was pointing at. Three of them standing on the left shoulder of the road in front of the fogbank. It was like they were waiting for Caleb and Drew to surrender.

"We're not stopping. Punch it!" screamed Drew into Caleb's ear.

Caleb felt Drew pat his left shoulder two times. He twisted the throttle back as far as it would go. The brothers both felt the acceleration of the new snowmobile. They could feel the wind hit their faces and with every second it only intensified. Caleb had to squint to maintain his vision. They were about a quarter mile away from the fogbank. The sled was continuing to go faster, Caleb glanced down at his speedometer and noticed that the needle was buried at one-hundred and twenty miles per hour. The deer weren't moving. He could hear Drew trying to say something, but he couldn't understand his words. They were a few seconds away, the fogbank was getting really close, and those deer weren't budging. His family started to flash in front of him. Karen holding his son and Nora standing next to her. Caleb quickly brushed back the memory and focused on the deer in front of him. He turned the sled to the right just missing the deer. They shot into the fogbank like a ballistic missile.

CHAPTER TWENTY

DON'T SCRATCH MY BABY!

Phillip pulled out of the Mobile Mart on Broadway and started heading toward Paul Smiths. He was uncomfortable driving his new car. A used Coupe 911 Turbo 930. Against the advice from his wife, he decided to purchase it now. She told him to wait until springtime, especially after the recent storm. She was right about one thing; this car was terrible driving in the snow. He just couldn't wait until springtime and there was no promise that the vehicle would still be for sale, or available.

The car itself had low miles, less than fifty thousand. Phillip had looked for this Porsche for a long time. It was black with no rust, 1984. Every time he'd found one, he got outbid, it needed too much work, or the price was too high. But not today, he bought one in Saranac Lake and was driving his new baby home back to Syracuse. Normally it would be a three-hour drive. But in these conditions, it would take considerably longer.

His wife had reluctantly agreed to drive him up this morning to make the purchase. He wasn't surprised that she didn't wait for him. It would be a day or two before the silent treatment wore off. Phillip knew she would eventually appreciate the Porsche. He got lucky, a call from a friend tipped him off about the vehicle and where it was located. The previous owner wanted fast cash, and Phillip was more than happy to provide him with it. Within a couple miles he reached the outskirts of Saranac Lake and drove by the hospital. The speed limit changed to fifty-five miles per hour. He accelerated up to fifty and a few miles later came upon a slow-moving snowplow. It was going around thirty-five miles per hour but that wasn't the biggest concern Phillip had. The thing was throwing sand and salt all over the road in front of him. He had to get by this monstrosity.

Phillip pulled his new toy over to the left and started to pass when he noticed another car about a quarter mile ahead approaching in the opposite lane. He quickly tucked his baby back behind the monstrosity. He tried to patiently wait for the other car to pass. It seemed to take forever; he knew it was approaching. His gaze was focused on the sand and salt in front of him. Splashing and bouncing in front of his baby, bouncing off his Porsche. Phillip became irate and screamed out loud, "Don't scratch my baby!"

The car finally went by, and Phillip pulled out to pass again. It was a no passing zone, double line. He started driving down a hill and Phillip did not see any other vehicles coming in the opposite direction. He wondered why the snowplow wouldn't pull over and let him go by.

"Fuck it!" Phillip screamed.

It was perfect timing; he reached down and turned the volume up on the stereo. The drums and bass provided background for the lead guitar; it was a song he really liked. The stereo and the speakers worked fine, thought Phillip. It had a CD player in it, and he would have to replace it with a more modern stereo with Bluetooth capability down the road.

The Coupe 911 Turbo 930 nosed out into the left lane. Phillip punched the gas pedal to the floor and the Porsche shot forward. Phillip leaned back into his seat and a moment later he was parallel with the snowplow. He turned his head and smiled at the driver who seemed to be mouthing a few colorful metaphors at Phillip. He wasn't exactly sure what the guy was saying, but Phillip was sure it wasn't flattering. He noticed that the driver of the snowplow was pointing his finger forward. Phillip turned his head back to the road and his heart sunk to the floor. He had less than a few seconds to get back over in the right lane before he was involved in a head-on collision with a truck.

"Ohhhhhh baby!" Phillip screamed with exhilaration as he pulled his new toy back into the right lane ahead of the snowplow in time.

The opposing truck flew by with its horn blazing. Phillip was sure he saw the driver holding up his middle finger. His heart was pounding as he slowed the vehicle down to around fifty again. The adrenaline was an insane rush. If he could only bottle it up and sell it, he'd be a billionaire.

He started to come back down off his high. Phillip was in a good place, the car felt right. He flew by Donnley's Corners and headed straight toward the small hamlet of Gabriel's, at least that's what the sign said.

He slowed his baby down to forty, and even at this speed it didn't take him long to exit the town of Gabriel's. There would be several more small towns to go through before he got his new toy back home. Phillip wasn't in too big of a hurry, he just didn't want his baby to get scratched by sand or salt throwing snowplows. They would be the biggest hazard on the way home. A few moments later he cruised through a place called Easy Street. It was located on a hill a few miles before Paul Smith's College, and it was about a mile long. Phillip wondered what was so easy about this street, or how this place got its name? Again, he had to slow his baby down.

At the end of this place the speed limit kicked back up to fifty-five again. The snowbanks were high off the soft shoulder. It was quite a storm that had come through the Adirondacks, thought Phillip. Before he departed, to come to Saranac Lake he had checked the extended forecast, and it called for more snow. He figured he had a short window to get up and grab the Porsche before this region got snowed in for the winter. His wife still thought he was crazy.

Phillip took a right at Paul Smith's College and started heading north on Route Thirty. He had traveled through the Adirondacks a few times. When he'd been a kid, his parents used to take him to Fish Creek and go camping. Everyone always said how beautiful the region was. Phillip didn't have a clue what they were talking about. All the trees and mountains, rivers, and ponds, saturated with lakes every few miles, definitely not his preferred place to live. Most people have fond memories of going camping with their parents. Roasting marshmallows and going fishing. All Phillip seemed to remember about the camping days with his family was the insane black flies. Bug bites everywhere! Sleeping on the ground in a damp moldy-smelling sleeping bag. Creepy crawling insects all over the place, especially on the ground where he was told to sleep. Camping was for the birds, not his cup of tea.

A sign up ahead read, *'Barnum Pond.'* The road took a sharp left turn, and Phillip noticed a large body of water to his left. About a mile up, Route Thirty started to straighten out. Phillip felt claustrophobic, huge pine trees on both sides of the road and nothing else. His turn was a few miles up, NY Four-Fifty-Eight. The GPS wanted him to go Route Three, up through Tupper Lake, Cranberry Lake, Star Lake–too many lakes, Phillip thought to himself.

He decided to go up through Potsdam and then over towards Watertown. It would take a little longer, but at least he would be traveling through more civilized areas. This stretch of road was a long straightaway, Phillip estimated three to five miles. He noticed pockets of fog up ahead. They kind of just hovered over the road. It was creepy, like a horror story where something bad was lurking in the woods.

Phillip slowed down as he entered the fog. Within a few seconds he exited it and sped back up to fifty-five. He looked in his rearview mirror and examined it again. It was thick and looked heavy. A few movies that shared the same name started to replay in Phillips' mind. One could always imagine a monster or two always lurking in the fog. He brought his attention back to the road and noticed a sign up ahead. It said, *"Meacham Lake straight, NY Four-Fifty-Eight left, one mile."*

The snow was melting and there was a considerable amount of water in this area on top of the road. Phillip decided to slow down and then a deer ran across the road and Phillip had to turn the wheel to miss it. He yanked it right and immediately started hydroplaning on the saturated road. He was in an uncontrollable right spin. His hands clutched the steering wheel with a death grip, and he clenched his teeth so hard he thought they might break. He closed his eyes and started screaming so loud that he drowned out the music playing on the stereo. Phillip expected to crash any second, possibly into another car or off the shoulder and into a tree. He kept spinning and screaming. At any moment the car was going to flip or stop violently. He wasn't sure how many times he spun around, but finally the car started to slow down and it came to a stop. He could still feel his heart pounding in his chest. After a few seconds he opened his eyes and slowly released his grip on the steering wheel. To his amazement, he was still alive.

Phillip looked around and noticed he was in the middle of Route Thirty in a jack knife position. The front end of the vehicle was pointed directly across the road to where he was headed, NY Four-Fifty-Eight. Phillip started laughing. He couldn't believe his luck. His baby was unscratched, and he was unharmed. He noticed that the music was still playing. The song was fading out, it was at the end.

Phillip suddenly heard another noise. It was coming from his right, outside the car. He turned and looked out the passenger side window. It was a high-pitched noise, like an engine, but not a car engine. It was getting louder, and it seemed to be coming from the fog bank to his right. He couldn't quite put his finger on what thing made that kind of a noise. Phillip spotted movement across the road to his left. There was a pack of deer, and they were running into the fog. He counted four, maybe five. It was almost like they were headed in the direction of the strange noise, thought Phillip.

The next song on the stereo started playing. He hadn't heard that song in years, another golden oldie. The deer were gone, they disappeared into the fog. The high-pitch noise was also gone, replaced by drums, bass and a guitar from the car stereo. Phillips' eyes became big as saucers. He finally understood what was making that noise.

A snowmobile burst from the fog, and it was headed straight for his baby's passenger side door. He punched the gas pedal with his right foot to avoid the collision, but he forgot that his left foot was still pressing the breaks to the floor. He didn't realize that he had pressed the break with both feet. He hadn't had time to recover from his spin. His wheels started spinning water back out behind and it didn't take long for his tires to meet the asphalt. White smoke started bellowing up from the chemistry that happens between car tires and asphalt.

A moment later the snowmobile crashed into his Coupe 911 Turbo 930.

The impact caused the passenger side window to explode inward. Glass fragments filled the cockpit and bounced in several directions. Phillip took his foot off the break and his baby darted across Route 30, but it was no longer facing NY 458. The collision turned his vehicle enough that he accelerated the Porsche across the road and into the snowbank off the soft shoulder. The airbag deployed and the engine shut off moments after the snowbank impact.

Several seconds passed before Phillip opened the door. He surveyed the damage to his new toy and after a moment, rage started bubbling up into his psyche. He wasn't even concerned with his health. He was bleeding, he could feel warm liquid running down his forehead. He didn't care. He was on a mission. Phillip looked across the road and located the snowmobile that just broadsided him.

"Where are you!" he screamed out loud.

He waited a few seconds but heard no response. He was walking toward the snow machine. Phillip couldn't locate the driver. He started replaying what happened and he realized that there wasn't a driver. It burst from the fog without one. Phillips thoughts were interrupted by voices, or was it screams? He tried to listen more attentively.

"Help meeeeeeee." A voice, it was coming from the fog.

Phillip raised his voice back at the fog and said, "Hey asshole, are you the one that doesn't know how to drive a snowmobile!"

A few seconds went by, and he became impatient and screamed, "I hope you have good insurance! Besides my car, I'm hurt badly. You're going to be paying for my medical bills for a long time!"

Phillip turned back around to look at his Porsche, but this just depressed him more.

"Help meeeeeeee." a voice said again from the fog.

"Help you? You must be kidding me pal."

Phillip reached into his pocket and pulled out his cell phone. There were no bars.

"No service! Well, that's just perfect!" he screamed.

Something came out of the fog. Phillip stopped and studied it. It was a deer. Not the same one that caused him to spin out, no. This one was bigger, much bigger. And it had those things on top of its head, thought Phillip. He couldn't quite remember what they were called. He started counting them.

"Thirteen, fourteen, fifteen and sixteen!" Phillip said out loud.

He was amazed at the sure size of the creature. Maybe it was a moose, thought Phillip. Whatever it was, it was majestic. He watched as it strolled ever so effortlessly over to the snowmobile. When it got there, it simply stopped and sat down behind the machine and started staring at Phillip. He noticed it had a red tint to its fur.

Philip wasn't afraid. He had seen deer before, mostly on television, but not up this close. He remembered that he had his camera packed in his bag. He turned around and walked to his car to get it. After a minute, he retrieved it and started walking across the road to take a picture. The massive red deer was still sitting behind the doomed snowmachine.

Phillip stopped in the left lane of Route Thirty and raised his camera up. He aimed and focused so that the massive red deer came into perfect clarity. This picture would win him a Pulitzer. The majestic beast tilted its head and slightly opened its mouth. Phillips' heart started to beat faster again as he noticed the sharp carnivorous teeth. He quickly snapped a few pictures and then slowly lowered the camera down. He didn't dare move. Behind the beast he noticed that the fog seemed to grow thicker. Phillip started to remember the genres that were synonymous with this scene. Monsters lived in the fog and someone always got eaten. The monster on the other side of the doomed snowmachine stood up from its sitting position, staring at Phillip the whole time.

That was his cue to exit.

"Help meeeeeeee."

Phillip stopped breathing for a few seconds. He was trying to comprehend what his ears just heard. But before his brain could process the fact that the majestic red deer with sixteen points and dinosaur teeth just spoke, an eighteen-wheeler emerged from the fog and plowed into him.

It hit Phillip with forty tons of force at full impact at over seventy miles per hour. He was dead before he hit the ground. For a few seconds afterward, pieces of Phillip rained down all over Route Thirty.

The big red majestic deer watched the semi-truck slam on its breaks and slide off the right shoulder of the road. The truck tipped over on its side and skidded along the snowbank for another one hundred feet before coming to a stop. Big Red grinned and then let out a loud holler. A few moments later, four does appeared out of the fog, one with Mary sticking out of its head, and the animals started following their Alpha toward the crashed semi-truck.

CHAPTER TWENTY-ONE

IT'S A MATCH

Dr. Yogerra had a problem in front of her. The blood samples that Major Vierra had sent over for her to distinguish, identified traces of human and animal. If a Forensic Science Technician were to examine the samples, they would identify the human samples but would have no idea what the other blood samples were. Some type of animal, or probably a new species of animal, not yet discovered.

Dr. Yogerra had seen this blood signature before. She knew it well. She helped create it along with her boss under the protection of The Weller Group.

The group was a multi-billion-dollar Fortune 500 company that had influence in several major sectors such as robotics, nuclear medicine and prosthetic devices. The defense department of the United States had its own top secret weapons testing laboratory created by Dwight D. Eisenhower in the late fifties called DARPA: Defense Advanced Research Projects Agency. Advanced prototype weapons technologies were presumed to be in the works at this facility.

DARPA had an annual budget in the multi billions. Because The Weller Group had its tentacles in several contrasting and diverse companies, Dr. Yogerra didn't need a budget.

She answered to one person, her boss. She did his bidding. No angry congress people or senators to deal with. Didn't have to show where the money was being spent. This meant she had access to the best technology, the best science and the best equipment.

Dr. Yogerra looked at her computer screen and focused on the blood samples. She lined them up, side by side and said out loud,

"It's a match!"

She sat back in her chair and took a deep breath and then after a few seconds, she let it out slowly. She could feel a small headache start to form at the front of her head.

The Biogen Farm had two landlines. One connected it to the business world and the other was a secure line that connected it to The Brain. That was the name of Dr. Yogerra's boss. Or that was what everyone at The Weller Group referred to him as. She would never call him that. She never heard anyone directly call her boss that. She was certain that would lead to a death warrant. She simply called him sir.

Dr. Yogerra looked at the red phone on her desk. It was intimidating. Especially when she had to convey to her boss that Mother's blood signature was infused with indigenous deer in the Adirondack Park.

Why a red phone, she wondered? Why did he insist she communicate with him with a red phone? It was so old school, it conveyed a message that the world was being destroyed, we must call the president. When her boss wanted a secure line, this was the means by how they communicated. Old fashion tech, that's how The Brain preferred to talk when the information being shared was deemed vital.

Regardless, she had to make the call.

The pressure in the front of her head was increasing by the minute. Why not a black phone, she thought. Black was her favorite color. She looked at the red phone and noticed its features. No buttons, just an old-fashioned handheld banana that had a mouthpiece to talk into and a speaker up by the ear. But before she could pick up the red phone, she had to call him on her H.C.I. to let him know she needed to discuss vital information. He would then tell her what time he would call her on the red phone.

Holographic Cloud Interface technology was invented by The Weller Group and not yet shared with the world. Only a select few people in the company had this device. A computer chip had been implanted into Dr. Yogerra's brain. She could access the world wide web by just thinking about it. She could also access satellites, and this technology allowed her to talk to other recipients who also had an H.C.I. unit installed in their brains. All she needed to do was look up above her left eye to turn it on. A video screen would appear above her. She would then think of the name of the person she wanted to call. A moment later the connection was made, much faster than cellular technology.

It was like a video call with no physical screen needed. A moment later he appeared above her left eye. "Hello, Dr. Yogerra. This better be important."

With a thick German accent she responded, "Oh, it's vitally important!"

The Brain seemed to stare at her for several seconds, nothing but silence.

"I will call you immediately." he said.

Her H.C.I. went dark. She took another deep breath, but before she could slowly exhale, the red phone started blinking. She picked it up.

"What is so vital that you have to interrupt me?" the voice on the other end said.

"It's Mother."

There was a long pause on the other end. "Continue" he said.

"I have found her signature in the indigenous deer population."

Again, a long pause. "What are the hypotheticals?"

She knew he would cut right to the chase. The Brain didn't care how or why, he just wanted to fix the problem. The pressure was now starting to affect her sinus cavities.

"Only one possible contamination." she responded.

"Please do share." he said back with much arrogance.

"There was an accident involving our van and a deer. The van, company van was transporting a sample to the airport. They hit the deer, and the van rolled over."

"What do you mean?"

"It turned over on its side."

There was another long pause from the voice on the other end. She started to finish her story. "When I showed up the sample was leaking onto the ground. We incinerated the sample that leaked out."

"Why do you think the deer was contaminated?" he asked.

"*Dumm, dummkopf!* The driver–he told me that the sample didn't contaminate the dead deer. But the only logical conclusion I can make is that the driver was wrong."

"Did you see the deer?" he asked.

"I never saw the dead deer." begrudgingly she responded back.

The voice on the other end went silent for a long time. She knew he was thinking. After almost a minute he started talking again.

"So, our company van was transporting a sample from Mother, the vehicle hit a deer and rolled over on the side of the road. We can only presume that the sample leaked onto the deer. How long ago did this happen?"

"Drei, three years." she responded.

"How fast has mother nature been working?" he asked.

She knew what he was leading to. She collected her thoughts and responded, "We have heard rumors of depleted wildlife in the park"

"But that is not the primary reason we are talking

on the red phone, having this vital conversation, is it?" he asked.

"Recently, we have had some hunters go missing." she said back in her thick German accent.

Laughter echoed through her earpiece. He was laughing uncontrollably. She had never heard him laugh before. The laughter continued for some time. She was confused by his reaction. She was even concerned for the consequences of her actions. People disappeared all the time from The Weller Group. She herself was responsible for making people within the company go missing. The laughter started to subside, and he asked, "Just how many hunters are we talking about?"

"Four, five or six." she said.

"I need you to bring me up to speed on what has been going on up there over the past three years. I need to know the politics of that little town. What the authorities are thinking and all the random accidents that have been happening. I presume we have a short timeline to come up with a solution before the Council of Five gets involved."

The Council of Five sat upon the board of directors of The Weller Group. The Brain wasn't afraid of them, but they technically were his superiors.

"Let's talk this time tomorrow. I expect a detailed report." He hung up the call.

She leaned back in her chair and took a long deep breath again holding it in for a few seconds. She then exhaled slowly. She reached inside her top drawer and pulled out a pack of Russian cigarettes called Prima. She took one out and lit it. Her head felt like it was in a vice. She took a long drag and watched the end of the cigarette turn bright orange. After holding the smoke in her lungs for a few seconds she slowly expelled the toxic gasses. She had a long night ahead of her. A detailed report was what The Brain was going to get.

CHAPTER TWENTY-TWO

WAR ZONE

Route Thirty was closed down for over ten hours to deal with the semi-truck crash. A car and snowmobile were also involved. Major Viera got the call from Trooper Barret. He described it as a war zone. An eighteen-wheeler turned over on its side. A smashed-up Porsche and a slightly damaged new snow machine. Cars were backed up in both directions. The phone kept ringing with irate drivers not appreciating the rerouting back towards Tupper Lake; nor appreciating the extra hour drive. The major was in the process of getting updated before he held a press conference with the local news affiliates. He picked up his radio.

"Barret, this is Major Viera. What's going on out there? Over."

"Copy that, Major. Route Thirty is clear. Semi is being towed to Allistor's Garage. Over."

The accident happened after 4:00pm and it was now 8:00am. The investigation was hindered because the sun went down and the semi was partially blocking the road. To add to all the mayhem, a fog bank had settled upon the area. The best thing to do was close the road.

"Barret, what's the status on the truck driver? Over."

"Still M.I.A. And we still can't find the driver of the

snowmobile. The coroner is picking up pieces of the other guy all over the place. It's bad, Major. Over."

"Your relief will be there around 10:00 am. Go home and get some sleep. Over." said Major Viera.

"Copy that, major. Over."

The major started thinking of how spread thin his department was. Two different missing hunter investigations. Now an accident has closed Route Thirty down.

His thought was interrupted when his secretary Janet knocked on his door. "Excuse me, major."

"Yes, Janet."

"Nine-one-one just received three calls in the last ten minutes about missing snowmobilers." she said.

They were both interrupted by a loud voice down the hall. "Make it five. Five missing snowmobilers now!" Trooper Hanlin shouted.

The major had a puzzled look on his face. He then looked at his secretary and said, "Janet, cancel my press conference and get me the chief of police from Saranac Lake on the line. We're going to need more help."

CHAPTER TWENTY-THREE

DR. BAUMER

John was laying on his back looking up at the ceiling. He was in his room. He thought to himself, three days or possibly four. Maybe it had been four days since the state troopers dropped him off at this place.

The room was small, approximately six by eight feet. At least that's what he paced out. No sink or toilet, just a small window with bars. He couldn't even open the window. His bed had one mattress and it was too soft for him. A pillow and blanket and two sheets. It definitely wasn't the Hilton.

His back and ankles were bothering him, they were itchy and he couldn't stop scratching them. He could see a rash starting to appear on his ankles and just above on his lower leg. That's where the monsters chomped down on him and dragged him back into the woods. John assumed that his back was also breaking out in a rash.

At any moment now John would hear the familiar footsteps getting louder as they approached his room. He was getting used to the daily routine. They would wake him up, take him to the bathroom and then usher him down for breakfast in the cafeteria. After breakfast he would be escorted to the bathroom again and it didn't matter if he had to go or not. Then he went back to his cell. A meeting before lunch with Dr. Baumer and another trip to the bathroom before they took him back to his room. Another meeting with Dr. Baumer before dinner and then back to the bathroom before bedtime. John assumed it was around 3:00pm. The sun had dropped below his window, and it was after lunch. That's the thing about this place, there were no clocks anywhere. It's almost like time didn't exist to these people.

John suddenly noticed he was scratching again. It was like his hand and fingers were acting independently from the rest of his body. He wasn't even thinking of scratching and yet he was scratching his lower legs. He couldn't quite reach all of the itching; it seemed to be strategically placed on the part of the back where your fingers couldn't reach. He started thinking of the woods where it happened. Where he lost his childhood friends and his best friend, his brother. He remembered getting to the edge of the forest and seeing the hunting camp. That incredible feeling of relief. He had made it out alive. He'd beaten those fuckers.

And then suddenly that sharp pain and pressure on his back that caused him to fall face forward onto the ground. Then he started moving backwards, being dragged back into the forest. He was done, no more second chances. They would tear him to pieces like they had his brother. He remembered trying to break free. Twisting his body right to left. The monsters continued dragging him further to his doom. John remembered seeing a small branch to his left, he reached for it, touched it but couldn't get a hold of it. His descent continued. He remembered that helpless feeling consuming his whole soul. When the ride stopped the monsters would eat him, like they did Billy.

Then his right hand slid on top of a rifle. He knew what it was before he saw it. He twisted over onto his back and pointed the rifle at the left one. He pulled the trigger and shot it in the ass. It let go of his left ankle and this caused the other monster to stop, but it still had his right leg. He pulled the trigger again, but nothing happened, and that's when the other deer let go of his right ankle and started charging him. John remembered turning the rifle around and driving the butt of the weapon square into the forehead of the monster. It staggered back. John remembered getting to his feet and pulling the bolt back. But before he had time to aim, it charged and drove its head into his stomach and knocked him down. He somehow got to his feet and turned the rifle around like a baseball bat. He made contact, hitting the bastard in the ribs. They disappeared back into the woods.

He was still swinging the rifle; he wasn't sure if they were gonna double back. He hated these things. John had never felt a hatred for anything this deep before in his entire life. They were evil. And then Phil showed up with the other guy. Yeah, the other guy who was about to get knocked down from behind. John aimed the rifle and shot that fucker just in time. They thought he was shooting at them. John smiled as he sat on the edge of the bed and recalled the nightmare. He saved that fucking guy's life; he still thinks he tried to kill him. He started shaking his head side to side. He was sure that Phil believed him.

John laid back down on his bed. He didn't interact with any other inmates; or clients as the staff called them. John could hear their footsteps from a distance, it was time to go have a meeting with Dr. Baumer before dinner. It was a long hallway from John's room to where the double doors separated the rooms from the office. John had noticed the double doors were always locked. Whenever someone went through them a loud buzzer went off first. The footsteps were louder, they were almost at his cell.

"Hello John, we're here to take you to go and see Dr. Baumer," Mr. Rason said.

Mr. Rason was an African American guy. He was about five foot ten and a little overweight at about two-hundred and thirty. He had big arms; the guy definitely worked out. He looked to be in his late twenty's early thirties. He was the one consistency John had in his life over the past several days. Mr. Rason was always there. John thought the guy must sleep at this place, maybe he lived here. John sat up on his bunk and dropped his legs so that his feet touched the floor. He turned his head and gazed over at the door that was locked from the outside. There was a small window and John could see Mr. Rason smiling back at him. "On your feet, we mustn't keep the good doctor waiting."

John stood up and took a step back away from the door. The door slowly opened up and John was greeted by two guards. He recognized Mr. Rason, but he had never seen the other guy before.

"Hi John, I'm Mr. Ryan. I'm going to help you get to your meeting with Dr. Baumer."

John didn't even acknowledge the new guy. He slowly walked towards the door and the two men gave John a wide berth as he exited out into the hallway. John started walking towards the double doors. Same routine, Mr. Rason was in front a few steps ahead and the new guy was behind John. A few moments later they arrived at the double doors. John watched as Mr. Rason swiped the electronic key eye with his badge. A loud buzzer broke the silence and the three men walked through the double doors. A few moments later, after a right and then a left-hand turn, they arrived at the good doctor's office. The three men stood outside and waited to be invited in. John could see Dr. Baumer sitting at his desk. He was on his computer typing something. The orderlies just stood there quiet like John.

Dr. Baumer said, "I will be right with you gentlemen in a minute."

A minute went by, and then another. Still Dr. Baumer continued typing at his computer, ignoring the fact that there were three men standing outside his office in the hallway waiting for him. This bothered John. For several days now he'd told his story, exactly in detail what had happened. Nobody cared. It didn't matter how many times he told them about his brother being ripped to shreds by those monsters, nobody cared. They all thought he was crazy. He knew what was going to happen next, Dr. Baumer would invite him in. He would then start a recording device and take out a pen and pad and start taking notes. Suddenly Dr. Baumer stopped typing and rolled his chair away from his desk a few feet. He looked up at John and said, "Hi John, come on in please."

John walked in first and then the other two orderlies followed behind. He walked over to the open chair across the room and sat down in it. Mr. Rason and the other orderly stood on each side of John's chair. They never left him alone with Dr. Baumer.

"John, can you tell me about the talking deer again?" asked Dr. Baumer.

John could feel his blood start to boil. How many times did he have to revisit the nightmare of his childhood friends and his own brother being torn to shreds by these monsters?

"Dr. Baumer, it's obvious you don't believe me. I'm done. I need to talk to my mom, please I need to talk to my mom now!" John raised his voice another octave.

"No need to raise your voice, John. If you help me, I can help you. If you want to talk to your mother, then you must help me finish my report. Will you help me finish my report, John?" the doctor asked.

John desperately wanted to talk to his mother. He knew he had to play the doctor's game. The thought of his mother being alone without his father or his brother, John knew he had to see her. John exploded out of his chair. He was on his feet before the orderlies could react.

"I have to see my mother now!" John screamed and started heading for the door.

John's sudden reaction caused Dr. Baumer to fall backwards in his chair. John reached the door and desperately tried to open it, but it was locked. Within a few seconds Mr. Rason and the other orderly had John face down on the floor. John could feel pressure on his upper back, he couldn't move. Mr. Rason had his knee in John's back. This caused him to want to itch more.

"Get off me! I must see my mother. Get the fuck off my back. Let me go now!" John was screaming.

"Hold him still, gentlemen." said Dr. Baumer.

The doctor had managed to get to his feet and grabbed a sedative that had already been prepared on his desk. He calmly walked over to John and stuck the needle into his deltoid muscle.

In a calm cool collective voice, Dr. Baumer said, "Perhaps after dinner, John, we can try again."

John could feel his muscles and his mind start to fade away. It didn't take long. He knew what was going to happen next. This wasn't the first time Dr. Baumer had to jab a needle into his arm. He could still hear Dr. Baumer talking to Mr. Rason, but their conversation was drifting away by the second. *"Take Johnnn backkkk to hissss roommmmm."*

John was starting to drift away, farther away from Dr. Baumer. Within a few seconds he had arrived in that special place far away in his mind. There was no comfort here either, the nightmares would come, where his lifelong friends were torn to pieces. Where his brother and himself were battling too many monsters with blood-stained carnivorous teeth. The nightmares always started with that voice. The monster's voice:

"Help meeeeeeeeeee."

CHAPTER TWENTY-FOUR

CHIEF REUGER

Chief Reuger had just gotten off the phone with a concerned citizen. Jack Ransom's basement had been invaded by rabbits.

The village of Saranac Lake didn't employ an animal specialist, so the police department always fielded calls from concerned citizens regarding animals in the village. When Chief Reuger was growing up, the village had a dog catcher. That position had been phased out decades ago. Most of the residents tied up their dogs. There was a leash law on the books in the village and it was very rare to see a dog running loose. It was a more common sight to see deer or rabbits or an occasional fox roaming around. Raccoons were known to get into people's garbage. And an occasional black bear would be looking for a late-night snack. Like the raccoons, the black bears went after people's garbage.

Anytime there was a problem with these types of critters roaming around the village, the Department of Environmental Conservation was called in to deal with this type of issue. They had a separate department that dealt with wildlife management within the Adirondack Park. Over the past year the police department had been getting flooded with calls from citizens complaining about animals.

"Chief, I have Mrs. Moore on line three. She's calling again about her dog." Deputy Knowles was standing at the door of the chief's office.

Chief Reuger had a puzzled look on his face.

"You remember, the crazy mother that called last week and said their family dog got attacked by deer."

The chief nodded. He looked up at Officer Knowles and said, "Tell Mrs. Moore to contact the Department of Environmental Conservation."

"Okay, Chief."

The chief started thinking about all the complaints filed the past year from local citizens. The most common one dealt with missing dogs, in the hundreds. When he started rolling that number around in his head, it didn't make sense. Hundreds of dogs have gone missing over the past year. He wondered where the hell they had all run off to. Like there was a big posse of domesticated dogs running loose in the Adirondack Mountains. That thought put a smile on the chief's face and he started chuckling to himself.

"Chief, Major Vierra is on line two." shouted Deputy Knowles.

Chief Reuger pressed line two. "Hello, Major Vierra."

"Chief, have you heard about the missing snowmobilers?"

"Just the missing snowmobiler involved with that

crash out on Route Thirty yesterday. Have your guys found a body yet?"

"No, and in the last fifteen minutes there have been multiple nine-one-one calls complaining about five missing snowmobilers." replied Major Viera.

With a puzzled look on his face, Chief Reuger asked, "Where are these snowmobilers missing?"

Major Vierra replied, "Just getting the details now. I will fill you in later. I'm spread thin, can I borrow some of your men."

"I got no problem with that major, but who's gonna pay the overtime?"

"I'll find the money, just call those guys in. Hang tight, I will call you back in thirty minutes." stated Major Vierra.

"Okay major, my boys could use the extra cash."

The major hung up the phone. Chief Reuger started thinking about his department's working relationship with Troop B. The village police and the state troopers got along well, but Chief Reuger and the rest of the Saranac Lake Village Police Department felt resentment towards the difference in salary. The state troopers, after a few years on the job, made over one hundred thousand annually. A person could work thirty years as a police officer in the village of Saranac Lake and not even come close to that salary. The troopers mostly stayed patrolling the roads. The SLPD dealt with patrolling roads, but they were also responsible for other things like domestic disputes, petty crime, assault, narcotics, burglary. It seemed like his boys did more and got paid less compared to the average state trooper.

CHAPTER TWENTY-FIVE

ANOTHER PRESS CONFERENCE

The major walked into the room. It was full of reporters, more than usual. When he got to the podium, they didn't even notice him. The chatter in the room continued.

"Excuse me." said the major

The room continued to buzz with several conversations happening all at once.

"Excuse me!" shouted the major, this time a lot louder.

The room started to quiet down. Several hands went up.

"I will answer all of your questions after." said the major.

Most of the hands dropped but a few remained raised. The major despised reporters. But taking the promotion had meant that he would have to liaison with the news media. With the increase in salary came that responsibility. He accepted that but he still didn't trust reporters.

"Let me get started. We have called off the search for the missing hunter from Altona. There's only so much that can be done after several days of looking. Our efforts were confounded by the recent snowstorm that dropped over two feet of snow on the area. We still hope and pray that Mr. Caulfield is found safe. Our department is still open for any leads or information that can be useful to our investigation and help bring Mr. Caulfield home safely."

The major was interrupted with several questions from the reporters. Several more hands raised up. The usual reporting core was present. Peter represented the Adirondack Daily Enterprise. Other local papers like the Plattsburgh Press Republican and the Lake Placid News were also present. Channel Five News out of Plattsburgh was also represented. The major also noticed four new reporters and he couldn't read their credentials hanging around their neck.

"Again, let me finish and then I will take your questions, thank you." stated the major.

He waited for all the hands to slowly go back down. He had to stare at one gentleman whose hand remained raised. Finally, even that one went down.

"We are still searching for Miss Peterson out on Forest Home Road. We believe a possible domestic dispute may have taken place and we're hopeful that Miss Peterson will contact us in the near future."

The room was about to explode with lots of questions. The reporters were doing their best holding back.

"We are vigorously still searching out in Santa Clara for the missing hunters. This investigation is still ongoing, and we are still collecting evidence. A psychological evaluation is being conducted on Mr. John

Fuller. As you know, he is the lone survivor of the hunting party."

The major paused for a second, then scanned the room. It must have been torture to the reporters; he knew they wanted to ask their questions. They hated waiting for him to finish. He wanted to smile, to laugh out loud. To tell them all to go to hell. The truth of the matter was, he hated them and he liked making them wait.

Then the levee broke and the first question hit him, "Major, has he confessed to killing his brother?" asked Peter from the Adirondack Daily Enterprise.

That opened up the floodgates. Several questions came flying at the major at once. The major held up his hand and waited for the reporters to stop asking questions. This took several seconds. When the room went quiet, he started again.

."Yesterday, at approximately 4:00pm, there was a multi-vehicle accident on Route Thirty and Four Fifty-Eight. A tractor trailer collided with a Porsche, and a snowmobile was also involved. There was one casualty. Route Thirty was closed down for several hours and traffic had to be rerouted through Tupper Lake and Ellenburg Depot."

The major pointed his very large right index finger at Peter. "Don't do it Pete. I will answer your questions when I'm finished."

Peter nodded like he'd just been caught with his hand in the cookie jar.

"I also have breaking news."

A murmuring started to slowly erupt around the room amongst the reporters.

"We have opened up an investigation into five missing snowmobilers."

That news brought the house down. Questions exploded from every direction in the room. The reporters were like kids trapped in a candy store. There was no decency. Toss their higher education degrees out the window: it was a dog-eat-dog world. The loudest question seems to always get answered first.

Without warning, a noise so loud and offensive filled the room, and this caused all of the reporters to cover their ears. It also stopped them from yelling and screaming loud questions at the major.

The major had a blow horn in his hand. The kind you would see at a high school soccer game, it would have compressed air and an orange horn screwed onto the top. The room went silent. The major cracked a half smile, it worked perfectly.

"Now if you could please raise your hands and ask your questions in a civil way, I'll do the best I can at answering them. Pete, I will let you go first."

"Thank you Major. Has Mr. Fuller confessed to murdering his brother?"

"No. We did extensive interviews with Mr. Fuller, and it was clear to us that the man was having some form of a mental breakdown."

"Yes, hello major, Kyle Thompson Channel Five

News. Don't you think it's a little early to call off the search for Mr. Caulfield?"

"No Kyle, we have limited resources. We have a search team out on Forest Home Road and one out in Santa Clara. We did a thorough job of interviewing that hunting party and investigating the surrounding areas."

The major was picking out familiar faces from the crowd.

"Yes major, can you describe the domestic incident that possibly happened with Miss Peterson." asked the reporter from the Lake Placid News.

"During our investigation we concluded that there may have been an argument between Miss Peterson and possibly a family member. So, we're hopeful that she's just cooling off in a safe space with family or friends."

"Major, do you know the identities involved in the vehicle accident last night out on Route Thirty?" asked an unidentified reporter.

The major had never seen this reporter before. He looked at him and asked, "Where are you from?"

"Watertown Times, sir. Joe Hunt."

"Mr. Hunt, aren't you a little out of your jurisdiction? What's a small paper like yours doing reporting two hours away from home?"

Laughter burst throughout the room.

"There just seems to be a lot of bad things happening up in this area lately, major." responded Mr. Hunt.

The major took a step back from the podium. He'd thought he was prepared for their questions. But it felt like he just got socked in the stomach. He stepped back up to the podium and said, "There have been a lot of strange things happening. But I assure you, my department here at Troop B is working tirelessly to help find these missing people."

The reporters were silent. It was like they could sense the strain and immense pressure shouldered by the major. After a few moments, Mr. Hunt asked his question again. "Major, if you could respond about the identities involved in the accident out on Route Thirty yesterday, please."

"At this time, we're not going to release any names. We still have to reach out to next of kin."

"Major, Christine Blue Press Republican. How many people were involved in last night's accident and how many fatalities were there?"

"Hello Chris. There were at least three people involved, and there was one fatality that we know of at this time."

"Major, Kyle Thompson Channel Five News."

"I know where you're from, Kyle."

The reporter from Channel Five News looked a little embarrassed. He then asked, "Major, what hospitals were the survivors of the accident on Route Thirty from last night taken to? Are they in Saranac Lake General, or were they shipped out to Burlington?"

"At this time, we don't know where they are." the major said.

The room became quiet for a moment. It was like the

reporters couldn't understand the information that the major had just shared with them. The quiet moment soon passed, and another flurry of questions exploded.

"Major, Vic Gordon, Lake George Gazette."

The room was still bubbling with voices. The major was having a hard time hearing the reporter ask the question. He held up his air horn and that caught the attention from everyone in the room. The noise disappeared. Again he cracked a half smile.

"Who are you again?" asked the major.

"Vic Gordon, Lake George Gazette."

The major looked puzzled.

"We're out of Saratoga, sir." the reporter explained.

"Well, at least you're closer than Watertown is." responded the major.

Another short burst of laughter filled the room.

"Where do you think the survivors are?" asked Vic Gordon.

The major stood speechless. He didn't know how to answer the question. Before he could even respond another question hit him, "Major. Are these five snowmobilers' local boys? And how long have they been missing?" asked Christine.

"This is a developing investigation. We're not sure if these boys are out playing cards somewhere or sleeping one off at somebody's house." the major responded.

This was not going well and he knew it. His head was starting to throb. He had to end this now. "That is all for now, as new information comes in we will share it – "

"Major. Do you think there are deer involved?" interrupted Pete.

The major had already turned his body and taken one step towards his office when Peter asked his stupid question. It had been a long couple of weeks. The pragmatic part of him wanted to walk out the door, down the hall to his office and sit down at his chair. He needed to pop two aspirin, turn the lights off and close the door for thirty minutes. No calls Janet, that's what he would tell her. But the major didn't listen to his pragmatic side and turned back around to face the reporters. He turned his gaze to Peter, the longtime reporter from the Adirondack Daily Enterprise and asked, "Come again, Pete?"

The room was quiet again. All the reporters were looking at Pete, and his next question did not disappoint. "Do you think the missing hunters and the missing girl out on Forest Home Road were attacked by deer?"

An uncomfortable feeling came over the room and everybody could sense it. Suddenly, the major burst out laughing, and this caused other people to start laughing. Within a few seconds everybody in the room was laughing.

"Very funny. Very funny. I'm serious, I'm telling you there's something going on." stated Pete.

Everyone in the room could tell Pete was annoyed. Everybody just kept laughing, even the major. After several seconds the laughter started to subside. The major looked at Pete and said, "No!"

And then he started laughing again. This was like a chain reaction and everybody else followed the major to the laughing party. It turned into a gut-wrenching laugh; the major was trying to hold himself up at the podium. Other reporters were literally bent over laughing. The major turned around and walked out of the room. He walked down the hall and headed to his office. He could still hear laughter coming from the press room. He turned the lights off and sat down behind his desk. He found two aspirin and used the half drank coke that was left over from lunch, to wash them down. He pressed a button on his desk phone and said, "Janet, hold all my calls."

CHAPTER TWENTY-SIX

THE BASTARD LEFT TOWN

Dave Peterson was sitting at the bar at the Belvedere Restaurant. He had just been slapped with a restraining order to stay away from his daughter's boyfriend. That happens when you coldcock the bastard in the face and knock him out on his kitchen floor in front of the state troopers. It hadn't stop him from riding by his daughter's house to see if she had come home. Her boyfriend, the asshole, was lucky he hadn't been home.

Dave's heart sank low. He had such high hopes his baby girl would be in her house. His whole life he'd struggled with a short fuse, always letting his temper get the best of him.

Dave started smiling and thought, boy was it worth it. He started thinking of how his fist made contact with that jerk's face and how he watched him fall backwards and hit the floor. He never liked his daughter's boyfriend. Thought he was a piece of shit, white trailer trash.

"Mr. Peterson, can I get you one more?" asked the bartender.

Dave looked up at the bartender and nodded. He started thinking of Craig Bronson, and why his daughter got mixed up with him in the first place. He had gone to school with Craig's father and was a year ahead of him. Billy Bronson was his name.

Dave had played sports and was popular, but Billy came from the other side of the tracks. The guy hung out with a shady crew of people, outcasts of society. He couldn't even remember seeing Bill in school after eleventh grade. Dave was pretty sure the guy quit school at sixteen.

He remembered coming home on leave from the navy a couple years after high school and hearing about twenty-something Bill Bronson knocking up a fifteen-year-old, Tanya Brown. The guy should have gone to jail, but no one said anything. Everyone in town knew who the father was, but the girl's family stayed quiet. Nine months later Craig Bronson was born. And his piece of shit dad, Billy, didn't stick around to help raise him. That piece of shit went on to father three more kids from three different girls in town.

"Here you go, Mr. Peterson." the bartender dropped off a draft beer for him and walked away.

Dave didn't even look up. He reached out and grabbed the draft and took a swig. It was nice and cold, the way a draft beer should be. Dave could never understand how the old timers could drink warm draft beer at room temperature.

He remembered his father and his grandfather in the VFW (Veterans of Foreign Wars). They would take him down there when he was little and let him play bumper pool. Dave thought it was the greatest thing because he would always get to have Shirley Temples and Adirondack Shrimp, also known to the world as a crunchy corn puff. But those two would sit there with five or ten other guys and sip warm draft beer. Dave remembered the older men shaking salt in their drafts also, another concept he never understood.

Dave's train of thought was interrupted by the TV. He looked up and noticed the news was on. Something about missing snowmobilers. He turned his head toward the bartender and said, "Hey Welchie, can you turn that up."

"No problem, Mr. Peterson."

It was Channel Five News and they were reporting about five snowmobilers that had been missing over a week. Dave recognized four out of the five, they were local boys. The newscast went on to say they were seen eating breakfast at the Airport Café the morning of their disappearance.

"Five snowmobilers don't go missing." said Ralph.

He was sitting a couple stools down from Dave. Younger man in his thirties, five foot seven with black curly hair. He sported a black goatee. Dave knew the man's whole family. Ralph worked at the local fuel company delivering fuel oil, just like his father did before him.

"Maybe they fell through the ice." said Jason, who was sitting on the other side of Ralph.

Dave knew Jason also. Matter of fact, Dave knew more about Jason and Ralph's families than they even did.

"No, you're both wrong." claimed Scotty. "Those fellers are probably shacked up with a few bitches, plenty of booze, playing the mother of all card games."

Everybody in the bar started laughing. Even Dave cracked a smile. He also knew Scotty. Dave pretty much knew everybody in town, and he liked it that way. It was a great place to raise kids. He just couldn't understand how his beautiful daughter could go missing in the Adirondacks, God's country.

He could feel his blood start to boil. He was sure that piece of shit Craig had something to do with Cheryl's disappearance. He had a death grip on his draft beer glass. Without warning the glass broke and small fragmented pieces flew up in the air.

"Fucker! I know the bastard left town!" Dave screamed out loud.

He garnered the attention from everybody in the bar. Nobody said a word for what seemed like an eternity.

Scotty tried to lighten the mood, he looked over at the bartender and said, "Welchie, throw me a clean rag, and get Mr. Peterson another draft."

Everyone noticed that Dave's hand was bleeding, but his glass was in much worse shape.

"Here you go Mr. Peterson." Welchie gave him a clean rag and put a fresh draft in a new glass down in front of him. Welchie then proceeded to clean up the mess in front of Mr. Peterson.

Dave was embarrassed, he'd let his temper get the best of him again.

The boys in the bar went about their business and pretended nothing had happened. Dave wrapped the clean rag around his hand and reached across with his other hand and picked up the newly poured draft beer.

"It was Big Red that got him." said Sully at the end of the bar.

Perfect timing in the delivery. He waited till the TV was in between broadcast news and a commercial. Everybody in the bar heard what he said, and everybody stopped what they were doing and looked at him.

"Who the fuck is Big Red?" asked Scotty.

"I've heard of Big Charlie, if that's who you mean, but I heard he was dead." stated Ralph.

Before Sully could respond, the broadcast news came back on.

"Turn that shit off, I want to hear who the fuck Big Red is." screamed Jason.

Welchie turned around and reached up and turned the TV off that was located above the bar. Everybody fixed their gaze on Sully.

"He's the one who killed Big Charlie." responded Sully.

"Well, where's this fucker from? I hope he kept the rack." said Scotty.

Ralph looked at everyone and said, "This is the first time I've heard of this."

Jason interrupted next and said, "I always knew a

fucking out of towner would bag big Charlie, this sucks!"

Sully's eyes got big and round, he looked at everyone in the bar and stated, "Weren't no hunter that bagged big Charlie!"

Welchie started rolling his eyes and shaking his head no. He looked at Sully and said, "Come on Sully, stop with your bullshit again."

Sully suddenly stood and slammed his fists down on the bar. He shouted, "I tried to warn those boys!"

Scotty looked at Welchie and asked, "What's he talking about?"

"The six guys that went hunting out to Santa Clara a couple weeks ago."

"You mean the guys that are still missing?" asked Ralph.

"Yeah, they were in here partying it up the night before, before they went out. And Sully tried scaring them with some bullshit story."

"Big Red got them, too." Sully interjected.

Dave Peterson stood up at the bar and glared at Sully. He had known this man his whole life. Went hunting with him. He always thought of him as a good man. The whole bar stopped and looked over at Mr. Peterson.

"What about my daughter!"

Sully dropped his eyes to the top of the bar and then responded without lifting his gaze, "I'm sorry Dave, she's gone."

Dave stood up and threw his new beer glass at Sully

causing draft beer to expand in the air, everyone got a little wet. Sully ducked out of the way and the glass shattered into pieces behind him against the wall. Dave immediately made a beeline for Sully. The first bar stool that was in his way flew off to his right. He then lowered his shoulder into Ralph, and this caused Ralph to fall backwards into the bar. Before Dave took another step towards Sully, Jason and Scotty grabbed him. They had to use all their might to stop him from attacking Sully.

"You fucker! She's not gone. What do you know! Where's my daughter!" Dave was determined to get to Sully.

It took a long time for the boys to calm Mr. Peterson down. After a long minute they convinced him to go back to his barstool. When Dave started walking back, Welchie looked at Sully and said, "I'm sorry Sully but you gotta go."

Sully stood up and grabbed his jacket off his barstool.

Dave looked at Sully and said, "Sully, sit down."

Everybody in the bar looked quite surprised and Sully was confused.

"Sully, please sit down, I'm sorry." said Dave.

Sully put his jacket back down on top of his bar stool and sat down on top of it. There was an uncomfortable silence that seemed to last forever. No one dared to say anything for some time. And then Mr. Peterson lifted his head up and looked over at Sully and asked, "Who is this Big Red you're talking about?"

Sully buried his face in his hands and then said, "You're not gonna believe me Dave, nobody ever believes me. They all think I'm crazy, everybody in town laughs at me."

Welchie looked over at Dave and swirled his finger around his temple that made a reference to Sully being crazy. Dave looked at Welchie and said, "Let him talk."

Sully lifted his face from his hands and looked at Dave and said, "There are monsters in those woods. Nobody will listen. I told those boys not to go into the woods. You've heard my story, Dave, just like everybody else in town. Those things tore Pat up to pieces. His stomach was split open down past his belly button. I had to help push his intestines back inside him."

"What monsters are you talking about?" asked Scotty.

Sully glared at Scotty and responded, "The new deer, they are the monsters!"

Scotty looked at Jason and Ralph and made a motion like it was time to go. He looked at the bartender and said, "Hey Welchie, settle us up."

A couple of minutes later the boys said their goodbyes and walked past Dave out the door. Each of them put a soft hand on Mr. Peterson's shoulder when they walked by him. Not a word was said for several minutes. Welchie started to clean things that didn't need cleaning just to stay busy. After a while Dave looked back up at Sully and said, "So tell me about this Big Red."

Sully's eyes got really big and his face started to display a wise grin.

"Biggest buck I've ever seen, over four, no, probably five hundred pounds. Has a red tint to his fur. A sixteen-point rack that looks like a tree. He's the ringleader, the alpha."

"How do you know this–"

Sully immediately raised his voice and interrupted Dave, "I've seen him. And that's when Pat got attacked,"

Dave was trying to contemplate everything Sully was telling him. He was sure that it was a made-up story, but he was still intrigued, and he never knew Sully to be a liar.

"Let me ask you this, Dave, how many deer have you shot and killed in the last three years?" asked Sully.

Dave started thinking about hunting the last few years. How unlucky he was and then said, "I got a six-pointer a couple falls ago."

"Dave, that was over four years ago. I was hunting with you and the Martin boys on the back side of Moody Pond."

Dave started thinking back to when he shot the deer. He remembered, Sully was right, it was over four years ago.

Sully raised his voice higher and said, "Dave, nobody has shot and killed a deer in over a year. If you don't believe me, call up the D.E.C. and ask them how many tags they handed out last fall."

That can't be right, thought Dave. He could call up

the Department of Environmental Conservation and ask a few questions. He could probably go online and check their website to see how many deer were killed last fall.

Sully then asked, "Dave, do you and Sue still have that dog–Golden Retriever? What's her name, Maple?"

"No, she ran away last summer, never came back."

"My dog ran away last summer too." said Welchie.

Sully looked at both of them and said, "My dog ran away last spring, and never came back home."

Welchie then asked, "So, what you're saying is that this Big Red and his harem of deer are eating all the dogs."

Sully grinned at the bartender and said, "Dogs, cats, raccoons, rabbits, foxes and everything else. There are no more normal deer left in the Adirondacks. They killed all of them too."

Welchie gave Sully a confused look and asked, "Who killed the deer?"

"The more dominant species wiped out the lesser, the weaker normal deer are all gone."

"Where did this new dominant species of deer come from?" asked Dave.

Sully looked at both men and stated, "I think they started showing up in the last few years. Don't know where they came from, but they're here to stay. Mark my words, when their food supply starts running out in the woods, they're going to come to town. We are not at the top of the food chain anymore!".

"It's an interesting hypothesis, Sully. The hunting the last couple of years has not been good, I'll give you that. My dog just ran away, probably is loved by another family somewhere else. If anybody knows what happened to my Cheryl, it's that no good boyfriend of hers. That bastard left town and I'm gonna find him. They can take that restraining order and shove it up their asses. I got to go."

Mr. Peterson stood up and walked out the bar without paying his bill.

Welchie didn't dare call after him as he walked out the door.

Sully looked at Welchie and said, "I will pick up his tab."

CHAPTER TWENTY-SEVEN

A DETAILED REPORT

Dr. Yogerra sat by the red phone in her office patiently waiting for it to blink. She didn't get much sleep during the night; she'd been too busy putting together a detailed report. Most of her time was spent waiting for other people to report back to her. She had questions out to the Department of Environmental Conservation, the Bureau of Criminal Investigation out at Troop B, several police departments across the Tri-Lakes which included Tupper Lake, Saranac Lake and Lake Placid. The village governments from Tupper Lake, Saranac Lake and Lake Placid. Most of these municipalities didn't open till after 8:00 am, so Dr. Yogerra sent her minions out to gather up the information. Dr. Yogerra also had her assistants comb through archives from the local media sites such as the Channel Five News Station, and the local newspapers in the Tri-Lakes region. Sitting in front of her was a detailed report, put together by her assistants. Suddenly the red phone started to blink. Dr. Yogerra picked it up and said, "Hello, sir."

"Please share with me your detailed report." the voice on the other end demanded.

Dr. Yogerra started sharing statistics and information

from the Department of Environmental Conservation. "The last census taken on specific animals in the Adirondack Park was over ten years old. But D.E.C. officials did go on the record and report that wildlife numbers in the park had decreased sharply over the past two years. Specifically small game like rabbit, pheasant, geese, turkey and ducks. They also stated that the fox populations were below average for the first time in over two decades. The coyote population seems to be migrating south out of the Adirondacks."

She stopped for a few seconds and then said into the red phone, "There is a big red flag."

"I'm listening." her boss said back to her.

Dr. Yogerra started reading the report again. "The most alarming statistic is the deer harvest report. Every year New York State compiles a deer harvest report which includes all deer killed legally by hunters. These hunters have tags and are only issued so many per season. Three years ago hunters legally killed over twenty-eight thousand deer in the Adirondack Park. This year's deer harvest report was considerably down to four thousand seven hundred tags."

"I wonder what happened to the other twenty-four thousand deer if the hunters didn't kill them?" asked her boss in a sardonic way.

There was silence for a few seconds.

"Continue." he demanded.

"There have been fifteen people reported missing in the Adirondacks over the past two years. A woman was reported missing ten days ago. Her truck was found in a wooded area not far from the village of Saranac Lake. There have been two incidents in the last couple weeks involving missing hunters. One hunting party claims they were attacked by deer and one of their members was dragged off. That person is currently missing. The other hunting party included six men from down near New York City, Middletown, is currently missing five hunters. The lone survivor is locked up in a psychiatric ward in the town of Ogdensburg about two hours away."

"I'm curious, has this survivor spun any wild tales of deer attacks?" asked her boss.

"Nothing in the local press so far. They have only reported that he is being evaluated at a psychiatric hospital. But one of my assistants had a discussion with a state trooper who interviewed this sole survivor. That trooper claims this guy is *verruckt*, mad. How do you say? Mind not working."

"I understand your translation Dr. Yogerra. What other details did the trooper provide?"

"A story about his brother and *freundes* being attacked and killed by predatory deer."

"This news is amazing." stated The Brain.

Dr. Yogerra spent the next ten minutes discussing local politics, the major industries fueling the local economies and the local police agencies. For all she knew, The Brain was sleeping. She finally was interrupted by his voice on the other end. "Yes, yes yes. I don't give a damn who the chief of police is in the village of Lake Placid."

Dr. Yogerra hesitantly responded back, "I'm sorry sir, but you did want a detailed report."

She was getting nervous. Her German accent was getting thicker.

"Tell me what they're thinking. What theories are behind the missing people?" demanded The Brain.

Dr. Yogerra continued, "They are in, how do you say *zhe*, denial. The authorities don't believe deer are responsible. They believe a mountain lion is."

"Destroy the blood sample. Tell them you have identified Puma Concolor. The cougar of the Americas. It must have migrated from the west." her joyfully boss stated.

"If they ask for the samples back, what do I tell them, sir?" asked Dr. Yogerra.

"Your very clever doctor, you will think of something. Have one of your assistants leak this out to the local press. This will buy us time and give me a chance to study our new creation. Mother will be happy." stated The Brain.

CHAPTER TWENTY-EIGHT

PUMA CONCOLOR

Major Vieira was having a meeting at Troop B headquarters in Ray Brook. ENCON officers Phil and his partner George were there, representing the Department of Environmental Conservation. Representing the Bureau of Criminal Investigation were investigators Morrow and Allen. Major Vierra looked over at Investigator Allen and asked, "Where did you find the other sleds again?"

"The snowmobile trails that run from Paul Smiths up to Titus Mountain. Two crashed into trees, one hit a stump, and the other was just in the middle of the trail." responded Investigator Allen.

"Can you be more specific, location wise? I know those trails well, I have a sled and frequently ride out to Deer Valley, all the way up to Owls Head." explained the major.

Investigator Morrow looked at his partner and then back at the major and said, "Sorry major. We found one sled about five miles from Deer Valley, it was about a mile in the woods from Route Thirty. Seems the rider went off the trail and hit a stump. There were a lot of tracks, but we couldn't identify them. We took pictures. We found another sled closer to Route Thirty about a mile north. It was damaged, hit a tree. Closer to Owls Head we found the other two. One was tangled in a clump of Cedar Trees, damaged badly. The other was about five miles in from Owls Head and there was nothing wrong with it. Helmet was on the handlebars."

The major seemed to be lost in thought and this made the two investigators nervous.

Investigator Allen then interjected, "It was like the driver parked it, took his helmet off and walked away."

The major looked at Investigator Morrow for what seemed to be a long time, and then asked, "Are we certain that the sled at the crash site involved with the Porsche and semi is the fifth sled?"

Investigator Morrow responded, "Yes. That is a brand-new sled, and it belongs to Caleb Darring. He is the little brother of Drew Darring. Both reported missing."

"Phil, I'm going to need you to look at the tracks that were found around these sleds. I just received news back from the Biogen Lab that we have a cougar problem. They confirmed that one of the blood samples found out in Santa Clara was identified as a cougar." explained the major.

George shook his head and said, "I can't believe it! Those things are out west of the Rockies."

"Major, did C.L.S (Crime Lab Service) also identify a cougar from the blood samples?" asked Investigator Morrow.

"No, their results were inconclusive, and that's why we sent them out to a better lab." explained the Major.

"You know, we did have Darrel, the older brother of John, radio us and tell us that their buck they shot got jacked. That happened the night before they all went missing." Phil recalled.

The major raised his voice and asked, "How come I'm just hearing about this now Phil?"

"Sorry. I've been busy on three different search parties from Forest Home Road out to Santa Clara. Not to mention studying tracks at several of those crime scenes."

"I get it Phil. We're all overworked and understaffed right now. But that is important information. Investigator Allen, get a statement from Phil after this."

"Yes, major." responded Investigator Allen.

The major looked at his other trooper and asked, "Investigator Morrow, have you put together a timeline of events yet?"

Morrow shook his head yes and said, "Should be done in the next forty-eight hours. We still have to interview the bartender that was working at Deer Valley and the waitress at the Airport Café."

The major looked at his officers sternly and said, "You got twenty-four hours. I must talk to the press tomorrow. I also have district attorneys, parents, politicians, and lawyers that all want a piece of me."

CHAPTER TWENTY-NINE

UNCONFIRMED SOURCES

Dave Peterson and his wife were driving back from the emergency room, after getting seven stitches in the palm of his right hand. Seemed the broken glass from the night before at the bar had caused more damage to his hand than he'd previously thought.

This morning after waking up, his wife had convinced him to go get it looked at. She'd even offered to drive him. He tried to talk her out of it, told her it would be a waste of time to sit around and wait for him to be seen by a doctor. One never knew how long of a wait it would be in the emergency room. But in the end, she won out. She insisted on doing the driving.

As they pulled out of the hospital parking lot and took a left-hand turn toward town, Dave turned the radio on. It was tuned to the local channel, WNBZ. Older music was playing and Dave recognized it. A sudden broadcast interrupted the song.

"Breaking news! Unconfirmed sources are reporting that mountain lions have recently been discovered in the Adirondack Mountains. There is evidence that suggests that the missing hunters out on Santa Clara may have crossed paths with a Mountain Lion. Again, unconfirmed sources are reporting that evidence suggests the missing hunters from Santa Clara may have crossed paths with a Mountain Lion. Stay tuned for more breaking news. You heard it first from WNBZ, keeping you up to date on breaking news in the Adirondacks. Now back to the music."

The radio started playing the song again. Mrs. Peterson pulled the car over to the soft shoulder and stopped the vehicle. She looked over at her husband. Dave could see the tears rolling down her cheeks. She asked him, "Is this what happened to our baby girl?"

He reached over and hugged his wife. She started crying loudly. He gently rocked her and said, "No honey. No! Cheryl is fine. We will find her."

Mrs. Peterson violently broke out from her husband's gentle caress and looked him in the eyes. "You find her! Go find our little girl. Do what you must. Promise me!"

"I promise you. I will find our baby girl." Dave said back to his wife. He gently pulled her back and wrapped his arms around her.

CHAPTER THIRTY

A DEAL GONE BAD

Major Viera was having another meeting with his B.C.I. officers, Allen and Morrow. ENCON officer Phil was also present. The major was getting briefed on the missing snowmobilers. They had compiled a brief dossier which included their names, origins, employment history, credit history, extended family, arrest records and social media history. Jesse Miller had a D.W.I. conviction a few years prior and Chris Haynes had a few speeding tickets. But the name that stuck out on the list was Anthony DeFalco. He had served time in the Bare Hill Correctional Facility up in Malone. Seems Anthony, or Tony, got caught peddling meth up towards Massena several years ago.

"Phil, can you tell us anything about the tracks around these snowmobiles?" asked the major.

"We have identified boots worn by the snowmobilers and, again, some type of animal track consistent with the prints we found at Butch Fuller's hunting camp. At first glance I would say it was made by a really big deer. But closer inspection reveals a much wider print and an extra dewclaw on the back."

The major looked confused.

"Listen, think of a deer having four toes. Two big

ones in the front and two smaller ones in the back. Well, these tracks have five toes, two in the front and three in the back." said Phil.

"So does it resemble a cougar print?" asked the major.

Phil grinned at the major and said, "It looks more like a cougar print than a deer print. And if it is a cougar, there's more than one."

The major shrugged his shoulders and asked, "Suggestions?"

Phil pointed his finger at the major and said, "You're going to be getting a call from my boss. She is talking to Albany as we speak. All I know is that if there are Mountain Lions hunting in packs, we have a huge problem on our hands. Major if you don't need me, I have another meeting to go to."

"No, all set Phil and thank you."

Phil stood from the table and excused himself, exiting the room.

Major Vierra waited for him to leave the room and then said, "Let's piece together this timeline of events."

Investigator Morrow proceeded. "Four local boys, brothers Drew and Caleb Darring, Chris Haynes, and Jessie Miller meet up with Mr. Tony Defalco from Massena at Kinney Drugs around 7:00am. They ride out to the Airport Café and have breakfast. A credit card receipt from Jessie Miller has them at Deer Valley around 11:00am. The bartender says that Chris Haynes stayed longer while the other four left after 12:00pm.

Sometime around 1:15pm, Mr. Haynes leaves."

"Were they drinking?" asked the major.

Allen shook his head yes and responded, "According to the bartender and the itemized credit card receipt, yes. Two, possibly three beers each."

The major looked at his investigator and said, "Continue, please."

Morrow looked at his partner and then back at the major and then replied, "The other four end up at Owls Head around 12:45pm. A Mr. Dauntee St. Marie identified Caleb, Drew, Jessie and Tony. He was tending bar and said the four of them drank several drafts and downed quite a few shots."

"So, we're talking drunk snowmobiling." inquired the major.

Morrow and Allen glanced at each other and then back at the major. They responded by nodding yes.

"Okay, continue." said the major.

Morrow spoke next, "Tony and Jessie left first, sometime after 2:00pm. Then the brothers left after 2:30pm. Mr. Haynes never showed up to Owl's Head."

"Theories?" asked the major.

Allen chimed in, "A Mr. Talon Cree reported finding Tony's sled. Mr. Cree is from the Hogansburg Indian Reservation. This sounds like a drug deal gone bad."

"We know Mr. Tony DeFalco is a convicted felon as a drug dealer." interjected Investigator Morrow.

The major pondered on this idea for a few seconds and then asked, "You guys think he's running drugs on and off the reservation?"

"We did some digging. Mr. DeFalco is no stranger to Hogansburg. He spends a lot of time in the casino up there." added Investigator Allen.

The major then asked, "What about this Talon Cree?"

"We made an attempt to interview him but–"

"Let me guess, he's back on the reservation." interrupted the major.

Both troopers looked at the major and nodded their heads yes.

"Where are the bodies?" asked the major.

"Route Thirty runs parallel to those snowmobile trails. They ambush them in the woods, sled them out to the highway, load them up into a van and they're gone. Probably buried on the reservation." stated Investigator Morrow.

Investigator Allen then asked, "Major, can you ask the police on the reservation to cooperate with us."

The major started thinking about how hard that would be. Any crime affiliated with the reservation was investigated by their tribal police. A joint investigation was unheard of.

CHAPTER THIRTY-ONE

TIME TO MAKE SNOW

Whiteface Mountain had hosted skiing events for the 1932 and 1980 Winter Olympics. It also annually provided a boost to the local economy during ski season from December through early April. The season was always at the mercy of Mother Nature of course. But this year the early snowfall jump-started everything. Eddie was in the process of turning on pump number five. The water valve was open, and the compressor was a go. It was time to make snow.

Eddie Duprey had been employed by the Olympic Regional Development Authority for four years. He started off making ice at the bobrun. He didn't like that job, right away they had him working the graveyard shift from midnight to eight in the morning. Always wet, always cold. But what really pissed him off was the attitude the bobsledders had. They acted like they were better than everyone.

After one season dealing with them, Eddie had volunteered to transfer to Whiteface Mountain. It was a bigger venue; he didn't have to deal with the skiers. Eddie could do his job and not be harassed by the paying patrons of the mountain. He grabbed his radio and said, "I'm ready to go to station five. Over."

There was a pause, he waited for a return message.

"Okay, Eddie." responded Mark. "I'm just making sure the generator's up and running. Over."

He was positioned up before the mid station, waiting for the green light to turn the snow making machine on. Mark radioed back and said, "Go ahead, Eddie, throw the switch."

Eddie turned the snow blowing machine on, and instantly heard the fan start to run. A few seconds later snow started blowing out onto the trail, it was like magic. Eddie was always taken back by the beauty of the machine-made snow.

The snow was instantly falling on the ski trail over a wide area, which always made Eddie feel like he had just accomplished something. He liked this job; it was better than manning the zipline in the summertime. The venue, Whiteface Mountain, tried to generate money with tourists in the off-season by providing other alternatives to skiing. There was a zipline, a mountain bike trail, and the gondola lift which many visitors used for a view of the fall foliage.

He needed to sit and wait for a few minutes to make sure that the machine was working properly, and then he had to go up past mid station and check on station six. The best time to turn the machines on was when the temperature was below freezing, and that usually meant at nighttime. Tonight, it was hovering around twenty-three degrees. Perfect snowmaking weather.

Eddie sat down watching the snowfall over the ski

trail. The machine was angled at about forty-five degrees. After about thirty minutes, he would have to reposition the machine. The next few hours he would go back and forth between five and six and keep on positioning them as they produced snow onto the ski trails. The job wasn't hard, it was just more positioning the machines and then waiting.

Eddie had a hot thermos full of coffee. He liked his coffee sweet; some would say Eddie always had a little coffee with his cream and sugar. He maneuvered his body so that he made a natural lazy boy recliner in the snow behind him. He opened his thermos and started pouring himself a cup. He watched the steam evaporate up above him as he filled his cup. It was a beautiful night. Clear sky, lots of stars. Eddie took a sip from his cup and was startled by how hot the coffee was. "Ouch, fuck that's hot!"

He'd almost burned his lips. It was a new thermos that his mother bought for his birthday back in October. Tonight was his first time using it and it kept the coffee hotter than he expected. Eddie's attention was shifted from the hot coffee to an echo in the woods behind him. *"Hotttttttttt."*

Eddie smiled. That must have been his voice echoing back at him, he thought. Or possibly an owl. The machine was so loud he'd barely heard it. His mind must be playing tricks on him.

He concentrated on the machine as it threw snow onto the trail. He wondered if the machine created perfect snowflakes like Mother Nature did.

Eddie suddenly noticed that the machine had stopped producing snow. He wasn't startled at first, the fan was still going, he could hear it running. Sometimes this happened, there might be too much air and not enough water mixed in the compressor. The machine usually fixed itself.

Eddie waited a few seconds, and then before he stood up, he decided to wait a little longer. He could diagnose what the problem was while sitting down and sipping his hot coffee. It was either a compressor or a water problem. The fan was working so that wasn't the problem. He really didn't want to get up. He'd made a really comfortable seat and his coffee was perfect other than being a little too hot.

"Eddie, what's up with station five? Over." It was Mark on the radio.

Eddie lifted his radio and said, "It just stopped making snow. Let me check it out, over."

Mark was his supervisor, and he could look up from down below at the bottom of the ski hill and see if station five was blowing snow. Eddie sipped more of his coffee; it was still too hot.

He stood and walked to the machine. The fan was operating perfectly. There seemed to be air flowing to the fan. It was a water problem. He followed the hose from the machine backwards about fifteen feet. The hose was thick, had to be in these conditions so that it would be able to withstand the cold winters in the Adirondacks.

From his peripherals, Eddie saw something move on his left. He looked up and was startled to see a deer about fifteen feet away. It didn't have antlers. Must be a doe, he thought. Just standing there looking at him.

Growing up in Lake Placid, Eddie had been around deer his whole life. His father and uncle were big hunters. They used to take him out when he was younger. He'd stopped going the last few years. Just kind of drifted away from his father, something that twenty-year-olds do. But even when he did go hunting, he had never been this close to a deer, and it didn't seem to be afraid of him. It was just standing there looking at him.

To Eddie, it seemed unusually large. He wasn't afraid of the deer; his mind was telling him that. That invisible voice inside a person's head, it always talks to them and only they can hear it. Nobody was afraid of deer. The only time anyone was concerned about deer was when people were driving. They seemed to love getting hit by cars. But there was something unnerving about this creature and Eddie sensed that it was definitely not afraid of him. Eddie took a step towards the deer expecting it to run off, but it stood its ground. He was surprised that it remained motionless. It just stared at him, almost like it wanted to attack. Eddie looked down and noticed that the hose in front of the deer was leaking water badly. He picked up his radio and said, "Hey Mark, I think I found the problem, over."

"Copy that, Eddie. Can you fix it? Over."

"I have a leaking hose. Over."

"Impossible. That's a brand-new hose. Over."

"Well, it's leaking regardless of how new it is. Over."

Eddie watched as the water gushed out of the hose back toward the deer. It just stood there unfazed by Eddie or the water.

"Can you fix it?" asked Mark. "Over."

"Don't know. It's a pretty big leak. There's a deer standing next to it. It's almost like the motherfucker bit into the hose. I know it's not possible. I'm just saying. Over."

"Shut the fuck up! Really? What's it doing now? Over."

"It's looking at me about fifteen feet away like it wants to pick a fight. Over."

Eddie heard Mark laughing on the radio. He started to laugh out loud himself.

"There's no way a deer could chew through that hose! Over." Mark responded.

"I know. Let me check the hose out and see if I can patch it. Over."

Eddie took three steps toward the deer expecting it to run off, but it didn't. He stopped about twelve feet away and looked at the deer. It tilted its head and slightly opened up its mouth, revealing sharp teeth. Eddie was confused. A deer wasn't supposed to have carnivorous teeth.

Eddie felt something crash into him from behind. He landed face first in the snow. He rolled over onto his back and was surprised to see another deer looking down on him. It didn't wait for him to make the next move. The deer lifted up its leg and produced a sharp talon. Eddie was trying to process what was going to happen next when the deer ripped open his jacket from his chest to his waist with a downward strike. Before he could shout out something, anything, it did it again. But this time he was bleeding. The cut ran deep into his belly. Eddie lifted his head to examine the damage, and that's when he felt pressure on his head. The kind of pressure that a combination of teeth and a vice would make. Eddie brought both his hands up immediately to where the pressure and pain was coming from. He felt the long slender face of the other deer, it was behind him. But now it was clamping down on his head with its mouth. The mouthful of sharp dinosaur teeth. Eddie felt his head twist violently to his right. The last thing he heard was a crack.

CHAPTER THIRTY-TWO

THE BUCK
THREE YEARS EARLIER

Humans don't understand or know much about how deer interact with their environment. Their speech consists of a few grunts, they are mostly silent animals that are built for speed and agility. Their acute vision and hearing are perfectly adapted to sprint away at a moment's notice, whenever they feel frightened. One can only assume that deer categorize other animals as threatening or nonthreatening. Through the lens of a deer, animals either kill or run away. The threatening animals are called killers, and the nonthreatening animals are called dashers. Nobody knows if deer can count, but it is assumed that they can distinguish between two and four legs. A rabbit might be a small four-legged hopping dasher. A fox could be a small four-legged killer. Although a fox wouldn't frighten a deer, a coyote however would. It is a pack animal, and even though it's a small four-legged killer, enough of them could take down a deer. Domesticated dogs could be interpreted as small to medium size four-legged killers and they also ran in packs. A deer would interpret a human as a two-legged killer that ran in smaller packs.

Deer would also decipher distance in the measurement of deer lengths. Thirty feet to a human might be six deer lengths to a deer.

Three years earlier, a six-point buck was in hot pursuit of several doe. He was a young buck, around two and a half years old. He has scent glands on his hooves, legs and head and through his sense of smell, he can distinguish between the sex, vitality and social rank of other deer. It was the rut season, and this buck instinctively followed the females. We will call him Happy.

It was midday, and snow was falling. Out of all the threats in the woods, the *vrooms* and two-legged killers were the worst. The two-legged killers carried *booms*. The buck, Happy, remembered his sister getting killed by a *boom*. He'd been with his mother and sister grazing when there was a noise. They'd looked up to see a few two-legged killers about thirty deer lengths away; too far to be a threat. Happy remembered one of the killers lifting up what looked like a branch. There was a loud *boom* and then his sister fell to the ground next to him. It was like she'd fallen asleep, but he knew she wasn't sleeping.

After running away and hiding in the thicket, Happy and his mother watched as the two-legged killers came upon his sister. He had never forgotten how they tore out her insides and dragged her away.

Happy refocused on the doe he now pursued. He couldn't see them, but their scent was all around. He decided to let them know where he was with a loud series of snorts. Happy hoped the doe would stop or circle back to him. He listened for some time. He didn't hear any response. There might be another male close by. If there was, he would have to do battle.

Happy suddenly froze and his tail stiffened. He recognized the noise, and it was getting louder, closer.

Vrrrroooooooommmmmmm!

It was gone, went by, he knew what it was. A killer. He walked forward several deer lengths and stopped when he got to the edge of the forest and came upon The Nothing.

On the other side the forest started again, but he had to cross The Nothing to get to it. There were no trees, no bushes, no dirt or marsh in The Nothing. It was a hard place where nothing grew and where large loud killers sped by.

It would take him more than ten deer lengths to cross. Happy looked both ways, his tail now straight up. He lifted his right leg and stepped upon The Nothing. It was smooth, flat, and different. It didn't feel like the ground. He wanted to run but wasn't sure in what direction to do so. His mother had been hit by one of the killer *vrooms* crossing The Nothing. When the *vroom* hit her it didn't stop, just kept going. She had flown through the air from the impact and landed on the ground beside The Nothing, with a bad noise. He'd tried to make her get up, but she was gone, no more. He remembered waiting for a long time, hoping she would get up, but then the four-legged killers showed up, several of them. They chased him away and tried to catch him. He kept running and that was the last time he ever saw his mother.

Happy listened but he didn't hear any *vrooms*. He also remembered that they could come from either side. He started to turn back around; he didn't want to cross The Nothing.

There was a bleating sound. He stopped. It was the other doe and she was on the other side of The Nothing. He quickly turned and started sprinting across The Nothing in the direction of the call. Before he got halfway across, a *vroom* appeared from his left. Happy had no time to react, it crashed into him, and he rolled over the top of it. Everything went black.

CHAPTER THIRTY-THREE

RESURRECTION

They had hit a deer and the van flipped over coming to a stop upside down. Joe was complaining about his arm, but Troy convinced him to help him drag the dead deer out from the middle of the road. They left it behind the van, Troy thought that it was a good idea that they had proof that they did hit a deer.

The green ooze found the mouth and nose of Happy and penetrated the open orifices. It quickly made its way into his brain and jump-started his central nervous system.

Happy started to hear sounds from other animals. He recognized the two-legged killers. They'd made the same noises when they took his sister. He started to move his legs, which twitched with muscle spasms. The taste in his mouth burned. Like some of the plants he ate but stronger. He could smell the killers, and their scent was not unpleasant. Their noises were getting farther away.

Happy opened his eyes, disoriented. His vision was different, clearer. He suddenly stood up. The killers didn't notice him, they were moving away from him toward a *vroom*. It was motionless in The Nothing. Happy remembered what the killers did to his sister, how they tore her open and spread her insides out onto the ground. That was not going to happen to him. He dashed toward the tree line and disappeared into the woods.

He started galloping fast, faster than he'd ever gone before. The trees were moving past him in a blur. He galloped over a downed tree and sailed through the air farther than he ever had. He needed to get far away from the killers, so he soared through the trees and over the streams. He kept running without getting tired. Everything seemed different, better. Happy could smell the animals hiding in the bushes. He couldn't see them, but he knew they were there. He kept running. His energy seemed to be increasing. The more he ran, the stronger he got. There were noises coming from the trees all around him. He looked up and knew what it was immediately, a tiny four-legged dasher. It was high up in the tree and normally he wouldn't be able to see it. But he could see it now, sitting on a branch chewing on a nut. He focused back on the trail.

Happy glided over a stump with ease and when his hooves hit the ground he accelerated up to top speed. Up ahead he noticed water. He slowed down and stopped at the edge of it. He looked around and took in the surroundings with his new senses, the much-improved senses. There were several different flying creatures. Some were up higher in the trees. There were also the tiny flying biters. They usually swarmed him from all directions. It wasn't safe to stand still for very long when they were around. But today, they left him alone. He could see them and there were a lot of them close by, but still they left the buck alone.

He caught movement off to his right. His tail stayed down; he stayed perfectly still. It was a small four-legged dasher, the furry kind that hopped. Happy watched as it hopped over to the edge of the water and started drinking. The dasher noticed the buck but didn't run off. The dasher had never felt threatened before by deer, it had no reason to be. It was about three deer lengths away. Happy felt his eyes concentrate on every detail of the dasher. He noticed its thick fur, fluffy tail, big eyes and ears. Happy turned his head to the side and slightly opened up his mouth. He didn't know why he was doing this; he had never done this before. Every muscle in his body seemed to explode at the same time. He moved so quickly that the dasher didn't have time to react. He scooped up the dasher in his mouth and clamped down. He came to a stop and realized that the dasher was moving violently in his mouth. Happy could feel the dasher's legs moving as it tried to get away. He opened his mouth and watched the dasher as it hit the ground running. Within two hops, it was gone back amongst the bushes.

Happy kept his gaze on where the dasher had gone; he knew where it was. It had stopped behind a bush, about ten deer lengths away. It was breathing fast; it was afraid to move. He couldn't see it, but he could hear it. The dasher was afraid of him.

Happy drank from the water and then escaped back into the forest.

He would spend the next several hours running throughout the forest. He started to home in on his new abilities. He could see farther and hear better. But he really enjoyed how fast he could run and leap.

After many hours he stopped and heard something off in the distance. His nose picked up the scent. It was faint, but he knew what it was. Like a rocket, Happy accelerated in the direction of the doe. A few moments later he burst out of the tree line onto a meadow and saw them. There were four of them and one buck. They didn't notice him yet; they had stopped to graze.

Happy focused his vision on the other buck and every muscle in his body listened. Without slowing down, he made a straight shot for it. The buck was about seven deer lengths away with its head down grazing. Happy lowered his head and drove his antlers into the side of the bigger male at top speed. The sound of cracking ribs filled his ears. He could also hear the air escape from the big male as it lost its balance and started to fall. The doe lifted their heads in time to witness their alpha roll over twice. A moment later the buck staggered back to its feet. It looked at Happy, and the two bucks just stared at each other for several seconds. Happy turned his head and opened his mouth. The ten-point buck turned around and trotted away towards the tree line. Happy understood the significance of the moment, he had just won his first battle.

He spent the next couple hours mating with the four doe, they belonged to him now. The sun was falling, and it would be night soon. Happy led his harem into the woods and they found a bush to bed down in for the night.

That night, he had strange dreams. He was eating plants, but they didn't taste right anymore. Clover leaves and beech nuts were his preferred favorite, but in the dream, he didn't eat them. Instead of foraging, he was chasing down small dashers, catching and eating them like they were beech nuts. Besides the dreams, Happy slept well for the first time in his life. He wasn't afraid anymore. For the first time in his life, he wasn't a dasher. Instead of running away when he heard a noise, he would investigate where the sound came from.

In the morning, he opened his eyes to the warmth of the sun that penetrated the forest canopy and gently painted his forehead. All his attention suddenly concentrated upon his mouth. There was pain around his jaw. He looked down where his front hooves were and noticed several smooth white stones. He used his tongue to explore the inside of his mouth, he realized where the white stones had come from. Happy had emptiness in his mouth in several places. But in some of those empty places, there was something else. It felt like another stone, a much smaller one. But it was pointy, sharp like a thorn in the berry bushes. His mouth was full of sharp thorns. He looked around. The doe were still sleeping. The bushes and the grass were wet with morning dew.

Happy stood quietly and walked over to where there was a small circle of water on the ground. He stood at the edge and looked down. He was not surprised to see another deer looking back at him. He knew that when he looked down upon water, sometimes another deer would look back at him. Happy looked at the other deer in the water. He slightly turned his head and noticed that the other deer did the same. Happy changed significantly at that moment, he had a revelation. He realized that the reflection was his.

Happy opened his mouth and saw pointy stones. The same kind of stones a four-legged killer would have in its mouth. Happy stood there admiring his mouth full of pointed stones, his thought was distracted by a distant sound in the bushes off to his left. All of his muscles coordinated in the direction the noise emanated from. This reaction was still alien to him. It was like he wasn't in control of his body.

Happy focused in that direction. He knew what the creature was that was hiding. It was a four-legged small dasher. The furry kind that hopped. The same type that he'd caught by the water. He couldn't see it, but he could hear it breathing. Fast, faster, it was about to go. The hopper flew out of the bush about five deer lengths away, but before it hit the ground, Happy had already closed the distance. It collected its weight on its back legs and sprang back into the air. He intercepted it mid-flight and clamped down hard with his new pointed stones. The hopper jolted one time and then ceased to exist.

Happy came to a stop and felt the sensation of fluid bathing in his mouth. It was warm and salty and he liked how it tasted.

He studied his kill but was confused. He wanted to eat it, like a chestnut, but it wasn't a chestnut. Happy kept picking up his food and clamping down on it in his mouth. After a while, the juices were gone from the four-legged dasher. He shook his head violently and tore the pelt from the leg of the dasher. He studied it, where it was exposed. Happy smelled the leg and then chewed on it. It came apart in his mouth. He smiled.

CHAPTER THIRTY-FOUR

PRELIMINARY EVALUATION

Major Vierra was having a zoom conference call with Dr. Baumer. The district attorney from Franklin County, Mr. Allen Rodstein, was present in his office.

"Doctor, surely you must have some pertinent information that you can share with us. I have four sets of parents that are wondering where their sons are. They need answers." asked Mr. Rodstein.

"At least some indication of where the bodies may be?" demanded Major Vierra.

"Gentleman, if I may– "

The good doctor tried to answer but was interrupted by the district attorney.

"Doc, I'm ready to go forward with a grand jury, but I must have something. This punk must have incriminated himself by now. How many hours of interviews do you have recorded with this creep?"

Dr. Baumer raised his voice above both men and shouted, "Schizotypal disorder!"

The major and district attorney both glanced at each other in bewilderment. This lasted a few seconds. They then focused their gaze back to Dr. Baumer.

The good doctor lowered his voice and said, "John Fuller is suffering from a psychosis. He believes his brother and friends have been eaten by monsters."

Mr. Rodstein grinned. "Monsters?"

"Yes. He continues to tell a story about some form of mutated deer. They are bigger, stronger and possess canine teeth."

The district attorney laughed. He looked over at the major and expected to see the same response, but the major wasn't laughing.

"Doctor Baumer did John talk about a cougar?" asked the major.

The doctor looked puzzled and shook his head no.

"Maybe he meant a big cat, like a leopard or a big bobcat?" inquired the major.

"No. He's convinced that there's a pack of monster deer with dinosaur-like teeth in the woods. John Fuller truly believes that his brother and childhood friends were torn to shreds by these monsters."

Mr. Rodstein stood up and his head and chest disappeared from the view of the computer screen. He screamed, "This is bullshit! This mass murderer is trying to get away with homicide. Not in my county!"

"Mr. Rodstein, I assure you that John Fuller is suffering from a form of psychosis. He is delusional and frightened for his own safety." Dr. Baumer raised both his palms up and continued, "He is a danger to himself and others."

"That's the first thing you've said I agree with. He's a danger to others. The freak is a serial killer! I promise you; I'm going to put him away for life!" the D.A. pointed back at the screen.

"Mr. Rodstein, I'm not saying you're wrong." said a more measured Dr. Baumer.

The district attorney sat back down. His chest and face became visible again.

"All I am laying out for you at this time is that my patient is suffering from a mental disorder. I don't believe his stories, but I do believe John Fuller is insane!" commented Dr. Baumer.

"He can't be tried if he's crazy." an irritated Mr. Rodstein said.

There was a long silence penetrating the zoom call, it lasted several seconds.

Rodstein looked over at the major and was surprised by what he saw. Major Vierra had a very concerned look on his face. He was in deep thought.

"Major, what are you thinking?" shouted Rodstein.

Major Vierra snapped out of his train of thought and looked over at Mr. Rodstein and replied, "None of this makes sense. The kid is the best lead we have."

"So we're all in agreement then. John Fuller did it. He killed his brother and his friends. Doctor, how long can you keep him up there?" asked Mr. Rodstein.

"My preliminary investigation has deemed John Fuller as suffering a psychosis or a schizotypal disorder. I have no plans on releasing him. We need to study him more. With time and counseling, we may unravel this mystery yet,"

"I may bring you in front of a grand jury to testify on behalf of the county." explained Mr. Rodstein.

"I will gladly testify that my patient is mentally ill. Gentleman I too have a full itinerary today. If there is no more to discuss, I bid you farewell."

The moment Dr. Baumer left the meeting, Mr. Rodstein glared over at the major and said, "I can't do shit right now because your guys didn't collect any bodies!"

The major looked over at the district attorney and replied, "You go out there and try and find five bodies in two feet of snow!"

"I have a congressman breathing down my neck. I told you one of these boys is connected. This is out of my hands now. The heat is going to get turned up and you're sitting in the frying pan!" stated Rodstein.

The major looked across his desk at the district attorney again and said, "When I find a body, I will let you know!"

Rodstein stared back at the major and asked, "What were you talking about a big cat for?"

"There might be cougars on the loose in the park." replied the major.

"Let me tell you something major. There's only one big cat that's in the park and he's coming up from White Plains. Congressman Robert Cummings from the Seventeenth District."

The major looked at the district attorney and said, "You have a nice day."

The district attorney stood and walked out of the major's office. Major Vierra stood up and walked to the door. He closed it. Shut the lights off and walked back to his desk. He picked the phone up and pressed the red button. Janet picked it up on the other end. "Yes, major."

"Hold all my calls!"

Major Vierra put the phone down and sank back in his chair. He started thinking of Peter. The reporter from the local newspaper. The one that had asked about the carnivorous deer. Again, the major smirked. He couldn't help it. It was impossible, had to be. Then his smirk started to fade when he thought about the missing hunter from Altona. The one that supposedly was attacked by deer. The girl missing up on Forest Home Road. And Sully, his story about his hunting buddy, Pat. His head started to throb. He tried not to think about missing hunters. The major took a long deep breath and then exhaled slowly. He was going to have dreams tonight when he went to bed. Bad ones, the kind that have monsters.

CHAPTER THIRTY-FIVE

CONNECTING THE DOTS

Chief Reuger was on hold with the Olympic Regional Development Authority, better known as ORDA. They oversaw all the Olympic venues in the region. His cell phone told him that he'd been waiting for over eight minutes. A repeating voice menu would cycle through every thirty seconds explaining the different activities and upcoming events on the calendar. CAN/AM hockey tournaments, adult pond hockey, World Cup bobsledding and holiday price cuts to tickets at Whiteface Mountain. He had already heard this information over ten times. The chief was interested in Whiteface Mountain, not to go skiing but to talk to his nephew's supervisor.

"Hello, this is Mark Yeffler, how can I help you?"

Finally, a voice on the other end, thought the chief. "Hello Mr. Yeffler, this is Chief Reuger of the Saranac Lake Police Department."

He paused a few seconds, to let his credentials sink in. The voice on the other end remained silent for a few more seconds and then asked, "How can I be of service, Chief Reuger?"

"I'm trying to find my nephew, Eddie. You're his supervisor, am I correct?"

There was another pause on the other end. The chief was going to wait and let Mr. Yeffler speak next.

"Eddie Duprey. Yes, I'm his supervisor."

"Well my sister-in-law tells me he didn't come home from work the other night."

"We're as dumbfounded as you are, chief."

"What do you mean?"

"Well last I talked to Eddie, he was making snow up on pump five. He told me that there was a leak in the hose and we were discussing how to fix it."

"Okay, then what? My brother tells me he didn't come home. Hasn't been seen or heard from in over two days."

"That's the best I can do." said Mark Yeffler.

The Chief wasn't ready for Mark Yeffler to be short on the phone with him. "What do you mean, that is the best you can do?" the chief said back with a more aggressive tone.

An irate Mark Yeffler responded, "Hey, you're the police. Hell, you're the chief of police! You tell me why your nephew walked off the job in the middle of his shift. Left his jacket and thermos. Then no call, no show the next night?"

"This doesn't make sense. The weather was below freezing the last two nights. Why would my nephew take his jacket off and walk off the mountain when it's freezing?"

"Not my wheelhouse, chief. All I can tell you is that we've been running short-handed the last couple nights. I can't afford to fire Eddie right now. When you do hear back from him, tell him to call me."

The chief wasn't paying attention to Mark. His thoughts were headed down a very dangerous place. A place where people freeze to death when they're not dressed appropriately in the wrong elements. A place where several unanswered questions had to be answered. Where was Eddie? Why did he take his jacket off? Why did he walk off the job?

"Chief. Chief Reuger, are you still there?" the voice on the other end asked.

Chief Reuger focused back on the conversation. "Yes. I have one more question. Did you report this to Troop B?"

"What? That one of my employees took his jacket off and walked off the mountain? No, I didn't know that was a crime?"

"Where's Eddie's jacket now?"

"We have it."

"Okay, hold on to it. I'll be over today to grab it. Thank you, Mr. Yeffler, and sorry about my nephew's actions."

He was about to hang up when the voice on the other end said, "Hey chief, one more thing. I don't know if it matters, but one of the last things Eddie told me was that he saw a deer."

"A deer?" the chief repeated.

"Yeah. Eddie said he found the leak in the hose. The hose that feeds the snow maker. He said there was a big deer standing by the hose, like it had just bitten it and made the leak."

"Is that even possible?" asked the chief.

"No way." Mark said. "Those are new hoses. Three inches thick. They can operate in twenty-below weather. There is no way a deer could chew through it."

"Did he say anything else?" asked the chief.

"Eddie also said that the deer looked angry, like it was going to attack. His words were, like it wanted to pick a fight." He paused and then said, "Yeah, that's what Eddie said."

"Well, I'm sure Eddie didn't fight any deer on Whiteface Mountain the other night."

Chief Reuger heard laughter on the other end and then responded, "Okay, see you this afternoon."

He hung up the phone. His mind started racing. His nephew had a history of boozing too hard sometimes. Eddie getting drunk on the job and walking out into the woods was a possibility. Eddie also liked to smoke marijuana, some of the local's referred to it as the Devil's Lettuce. The chief picked up his cell phone and dialed Major Vierra's number.

"Chief Reuger, what do I owe the pleasure of this call?" Major Vierra answered.

"Do you have a minute?"

"To be honest, no. I have a congressman on his way up from White Plains to tear me a new one. Five missing hunters still unaccounted for out in Santa Clara, two DAs barking up my ass for evidence, a missing girl out on Forest Home Road, several missing snowmobilers and the press is having a field day with me."

"You might have another." responded the chief.

"What now?"

"My nephew makes snow at Whiteface Mountain. He walked off the job two nights ago, and nobody has seen or heard from him since."

"I don't understand how that's a crime?" asked the major.

There was silence and then the major started talking again. "C'mon chief. I have real problems going on. Kid will probably show up in a day or two. Out on a bender, probably got in a fight with his boss."

"Major how cold has it been the last week?" asked the chief.

The major quickly responded back, "Cold enough for me to start my wood stove, and I wasn't prepared to do that for another couple weeks."

With a higher pitch to his voice the chief said, "Eddie took his jacket off and walked down the mountain while the weather was below freezing."

"What?" responded Major Vierra.

The chief continued, "His supervisor said they found his jacket almost up at mid station. Why would he take his jacket off and walk down the mountain in freezing temperatures?"

"I got nothing. I can send a trooper out and start an investigation, it's just that we are really short staffed. Dammit chief, my department is spread all over the

Adirondacks. We're still cleaning up that mess out past Paul Smith's. The one with the semi and the Porsche." proclaimed the Major.

The chief responded, "I got this."

"I am really sorry to hear about your nephew, and I'm still certain he's going to show back up."

"I have already talked to his supervisor at Whiteface Mountain, a fellow named Mark Yeffler. Let me poke around and I will report back to ya major."

"Thank you chief, keep me posted."

"Major, one more thing. The deer attack story seems to be raising its ugly head again."

There was an uncomfortable silence on the other end of the call. It might have only lasted a few seconds, but the chief could sense its unpleasantness.

"What do you mean?" asked the major.

"This Yeffler guy, my nephew's supervisor, said that Eddie saw a deer up at pump five, a big one, where he was making snow."

"Okay, not unusual in the Adirondacks." responded the major.

"Yeah, the weird part is that my nephew told the Yeffler feller that the deer might have bitten a tear in the water hose that feeds the snow making machine."

The major asked, "I don't think a deer could do that, those hoses must be pretty thick."

"You're not wrong. According to Yeffler, those hoses are three inches thick. But that's not the most bizarre thing he said to me."

The major shook his head and asked, "Let me guess. The deer attacked your nephew?"

"Not exactly, but according to Yeffler, Eddie did say the deer looked aggressive."

The major started laughing and then said, "Lot of that folklore seems to be spreading around these days."

"Ok major, thanks for taking my call."

The major responded, "Keep me in the loop."

They both hung up the call.

"Knowles, get your ass in here pronto!" screamed the chief out at his subordinate.

Jeremy Knowles came into the chief's office supporting a look of bewilderment.

"Sit down." demanded the chief.

Officer Knowles sat down. To the chief, he was just a kid. Had red hair and freckles. Drove an older Dodge Ram truck and was born and bred locally. The chief knew his whole family. Jeremey was in his mid-twenties, did community college for two years and then signed on to the force. Chief Reuger liked the kid. Took him hunting and fishing. Took him under his wing so to speak and steered him away from some of the others. The others referred to a few bad apples in the department. Chief Reuger had cleaned up the village police department during his first few years. Even managed to end a couple careers. Another officer transferred out, down toward Saratoga, and the chief was happy to see that one go. The last few years the department had recruited some young bucks, and Knowles was one of them.

"What's the name of that lady from a few weeks back. You know, the one who complained about several deer attacking her dog?" asked the chief.

"Mrs. Moore."

"Did you ever go out and interview her?"

"Billy and I both did."

The chief sat there staring at his junior officer and then said, "So, out with it!"

For the next few minutes, Jeremy spun a story of several deer attacking a family dog. Moore's little boy had been playing in the back yard near the garage and then three deer appeared out of the woods and dismantled the dog in front of the boy.

The chief gave his officer a concerning look and asked, "What do ya mean, you guys didn't find anything?"

"We saw blood in the snow, or at least that's what it looked like. But that was it." responded Jeremy.

"So, you think this dog chased the deer into the woods, never came back?"

Jeremy shrugged his shoulders and said, "The boy wouldn't talk to us. His mom said he wouldn't come out of his room. That's the story she told us. If you ask me, it sounds like the kid plays too many violent video games."

The chief stood up from his desk and walked up to the whiteboard on the wall. Jeremy watched as he grabbed a black dry erase marker and started writing.

"What are you doing chief?"

Colt looked at his junior officer and said, "Let me see if I can connect the dots."

Jeremy hung on every letter the chief wrote on the whiteboard. He was full of anticipation.

"Sully!" the chief said as he wrote the name on the board.

He looked at Jeremy and asked, "Does that name ring a bell?"

Jeremy smiled and then said, "The hunting accident a couple years ago. They never found his partner."

"What story does Sully always spin?" asked the chief.

"That his partner was attacked by deer." replied Jeremy.

The chief started writing another name on the board and then said out loud, "Greg Callifield."

Jeremy's face lit up and he said, "Missing hunter from Altona."

"Bingo. And what did his hunting partner Burt Carpenter say happened." asked the chief.

Jeremy turned his eyes upward toward his right, like he was searching for the answer and then his face lit up again, he said, "Mr. Carpenter said that the Callifield guy was attacked by – "

"By deer!" shouted the chief.

The two men looked at each other for a moment. The chief started writing more on the board. Jeremy read it out loud. "The Moore dog."

The chief turned around and asked Jeremy, "What common denominator can we find from the three on this list?"

"They all have supposedly been attacked by deer." proclaimed Jeremy.

The chief wrote one more name on the board. Eddie Duprey.

"Hey wait, why is Eddie's name on the board?" asked Jeremy.

"Grab your jacket, we are going for a ride to find out." said the chief.

"Cheryl Peterson!"

The chief and Jeremy didn't notice the man standing in the doorway.

"Mr. Peterson. Hello sir." said Jeremy.

"Hello, Dave." said the chief.

Mr. Peterson glanced at Jeremy and then responded to Chief Reuger, "Hello Colt."

Only a few people called the chief by his first name and only a few people could get away with that, in the village. Colt Reuger was a big man, John Wayne size. He stood six foot three and weighed over two-hundred and fifty pounds. An imposing figure, especially to the law breakers in the small community.

Mr. Peterson said, "You can add my daughter's name to that list."

"How long have you been standing there Dave?" asked the chief.

Dave pointed his finger at the chief and said, "There's something wrong going on in these woods and you know it."

The Chief put both hands up in the air and said, "Now hold on Dave. We're just speculating. Looking at the picture through a different lens."

Jeremy knew his place; he was going to let these two men go at it.

"I found this about two miles from where my daughter went missing." said Dave.

He tossed a backpack on the chief's desk.

"I also found this twelve-gauge shotgun next to the backpack." He then put the shotgun on the chief's desk.

The chief and Jeremy looked puzzled. Chief Reuger grew up with Dave Peterson, they played high school sports together. They even played little league baseball together. Colt considered Dave a friend but over the years their career paths had taken them in separate directions.

"Dave, what am I looking at?" asked the chief.

"That backpack belongs to my Cheryl's deadbeat boyfriend, Craig Bronson."

"And the shotgun?" asked the chief.

"I know you recognize it. It's mine!"

The chief lifted it up off his desk and examined it. He did recognize it. He had gone duck hunting several times before with Dave.

"Look chief, I went out to check on Cheryl, see if she came back home."

The chief looked at his life-long buddy and asked, "Isn't there an order of protection against you? To stay away from Craig Bronson?"

Mr. Petersons face turned red as he clenched his fists tight and shouted, "They weren't there! When I knocked on the door, nobody answered so I let myself in."

"Dave, you do understand the consequences of your actions?" asked the chief.

"Yes, but he wasn't there! So, I noticed tracks, walking, boot tracks leading away from the house. Too big to be Cheryl, had to be Craig's. So I followed them."

Jeremy watched as Dave tried to explain the story to the chief, but the chief didn't even try to hide his disdain for the whole conversation.

"He was headed in the direction of where Cheryl abandoned her vehicle. After a little more than a mile, they veered off into the woods. And that's where I found the pack and my twelve-gauge."

"What was your shotgun doing with Craig Bronson?" asked the chief.

"That asshole didn't have my permission to use my gun! I gave that to Cheryl a few years back."

The chief just kept shaking his head side to side in a small motion. At this point, he wasn't even making eye contact with Mr. Peterson, Jeremy noticed.

Chief Duprey suddenly lifted his head and looked at Jeremy and told him to, "Go open up number two."

Jeremy stood and walked out of the room. The chief of police in Saranac Lake looked at Dave Peterson and said, "Come with me."

The chief walked out of his office and Mr. Peterson followed suit. The two men walked through a door that separated the check in desk from the back of the station. As they continued to walk, Dave kept on talking. "I think something has happened to the Bronson boy."

Mr. Peterson noticed that they were heading back towards the jail cells.

"Colt, I don't have time for this sightseeing tour! We need to go back to your office. You need to examine the backpack."

The chief walked into jail cell number two and Mr. Peterson followed him in. The whole time he continued to talk to the chief. "The pack has a tear in it, it's ripped up bad."

The chief walked back out the cell and closed it on Mr. Peterson, and then looked at him and said, "Is that so?"

Dave finally realized what had just happened. He gripped the bars with both hands and then looked up at the chief and said, "Hey, what the fuck is going on?"

"Mr. Peterson you broke the order of protection that was issued by Franklin County for you to stay away from Craig Bronson."

Dave started to look around the cell, he was having a hard time contemplating his predicament. He looked up at the chief and shouted, "He wasn't there, I told you this!"

"Just cool off Dave. I will go out and find Mr. Bronson. I need to talk to him anyway."

"He's gone! Just like Cheryl!" screamed Dave.

"Is there anything you would like to confess to me now Dave?" asked the chief.

"Confess? What are you talking about?" Dave screamed back at the chief.

The chief motioned to Jeremy and the two of them walked back out to the front of the station. They left a very irate Mr. Peterson who continued to yell in their direction.

CHAPTER THIRTY- SIX

FEDERAL BUREAU OF INVESTIGATION

Major Vierra was having a meeting in his office at Troop B headquarters in Ray Brook with two men from the Federal Bureau of Investigation. He was expecting Albany to send up help, but instead these guys showed up. The two listened to the major for about five minutes and then Agent Barret interrupted him and said, "At this point, you are to turn over everything to us."

The major didn't like these guys already. Arrogant, clean cut and squared away. He'd expected this but they acted so smug, like they weren't even listening to him. Agent Mason was over six feet, blonde hair, didn't talk. Just stared. The other guy doing all the talking was taller. Possibly six foot two or more, black hair, well-built physique. Both had short military haircuts like the state troopers, but they wore suits, like in the movies.

"Everything? I have multiple investigations going on. Can you be more specific?"

Agent Barret grinned at the major and said, "The snowmobilers. I'll need everything you have."

"Have you made any requests with the tribal police?" asked the major.

The two agents gave each other a puzzled look.

Agent Mason looked at the major and said, "If you're

referring to the Saint Regis Mohawk Tribal police, that information is confidential."

The major looked at the quieter agent and said, "So you do talk."

Agent Barret interjected, "Major, we were informed by your superintendent that your department would fully cooperate with our investigation."

"And we will." responded the major.

Major Vierra stood up from his desk and walked by both agents to the door. He stopped and turned back toward them and said, "Agents, please follow me."

The three men walked out of the major's office and down the hallway toward the press room, unbeknownst to the agents. The major opened a door and ushered the two gentlemen from the FBI into a room full of jackals and hyenas. Major Vierra walked in last. Flashes and clicks started happening as the room, where reporters were packed wall to wall, erupted with voices and questions.

The two agents froze. Maybe it was the flashing lights, or the crowded room full of reporters. Major Vierra walked by the two statues and took control of the podium. He stood there for a few seconds and let all the reporters' questions reflect off him. He knew that he wasn't going to be responsible for answering these questions. The flashing lights kept flickering, cameras kept clicking and the questions kept coming.

"Major, what about the women missing on Forest Home Road?"

"Major Vierra, any comment about the missing snowmobilers?"

"Major, the missing hunter from Altona, have you stopped looking for him?"

"What about the missing hunters out in Santa Clara?"

"Hey major, who are the suits?"

The major seemed to smile. It wasn't a full-on happy smile, no, it was an almost smile. One of release, gratification. Like when a pressure valve on a hot water heater releases steam when the pressure gets too high. He turned and looked at the two arrogant FBI agents, and then back at the room full of jackals and hyenas and said, "Press corps, may I please direct your attention to the FBI!"

The major took two steps to his left and turned his body sideways and swept his arm out to introduce Agent Barret and Agent Mason. More flashing and clicking happened. It was like a rock concert introduction minus the guitar riff. The two FBI agents just stood there, frozen amongst the cacophony of pulsing light and mechanical clicking. An uncomfortable silence resumed until the major said, "Agent Barret, the podium is yours."

The major was pointing at the microphone built into the podium, where he addressed reporters on a weekly basis. But recently, the timetable had turned into a near daily basis. Agent Barret gave Major Vierra an unemotional response and accepted the invitation. He walked forward and took center stage. Within a few seconds the room transitioned from loud mechanical camera clicking and flashing to a sudden silence. Agent Barret stood in front of the microphone for a brief period wherein he seemed to be scoping out all the people in the room, like a rabbit right before his escape.

"Hello. I am Agent Barret, and this is my partner, agent Mason of the Federal Bureau of Investigation."

Suddenly the room forgot who Major Vierra was. It instantly focused on Agent Barret.

"Agent Barret, why is the FBI here?"

"Agent, can you tell us what happened to the hunter from Altona?"

"Agent Mason, where are you from?"

"Why is the FBI in the Adirondack Park?"

The questions were fast and many! The agents hadn't had time to prepare, they weren't ready for this and the questions kept coming. Agent Barret looked over at Major Vierra in a plea for help. Major Vierra felt like walking out of the room and leaving these two to the sharks, and he would have, but it was the one look of help that Agent Barret had sent. His arrogance is fading thought the major. A small victory, it felt good. The Major nodded his head at Agent Barret. He raised his hand and shouted, "Enough!"

The room became silent. They knew Major Vierra, the reporters understood his rules. The major walked up beside Agent Barret and then pointed at a reporter.

"Hello Agent Barret, I am Kyle Thompson from Channel Five News. Can you tell me why the FBI is involved with these investigations?"

The agent paused for a second, the room was standing on thin ice anticipating the response. Hands were already raised hoping to get the next question.

"Yes. We've become involved because of the missing snowmobilers. There might be probable cause of illegal drug trafficking happening in Franklin County. This county also involves the Hogansburg Indian Reservation, and there might be a connection."

Agent Barret pointed at a female reporter with her hand raised.

"Hello, Christine Blue from the Press Republican newspaper. What about the other missing personnel?"

The Agent looked over at his partner. Both kept a poker face.

Agent Barret looked back at Christine Blue and said, "Not our interest. We are only here to investigate the missing snowmobilers and their proximity to the Hogansburg Indian Reservation."

He pointed to another reporter.

"Hello, sir, I'm Joe Hunt from the Watertown Times. This area in the last few months has seen almost fifteen people go missing. Can you give us any closure or clarity on what has happened? Possibly if The FBI is also involved with those investigations?"

"Troop B and Essex and Franklin Counties are conducting thorough investigations upon those missing people. The FBI, again, is only here to find out the correlation between the Hogansburg Indian Reservation and the missing snowmobilers." responded Agent Barret.

Suddenly a louder voice penetrated the room. Major Vierra instantly located the source, it was a new reporter, one he had never seen before. "Excuse me, agent! Surely the bureau is also going to investigate the other missing persons in the park. This is a small state trooper barracks up here. Even combined with the local village law departments, they are in over their heads."

Agent Barret looked confused. He stared at the new reporter for a few seconds. The room had become silent. It was like all the other reporters were thinking about the question just raised in the room.

Major Vierra broke the silence and asked, "Excuse me sir, who are you? Where are you from?"

The major's voice was more of an accusation than a question.

The new reporter looked at the major and said with the utmost confidence, "Phil Silverman from the Albany Times."

The major seemed to take an invisible dagger to his heart. The problems in the Adirondack Park that his department were responsible for were starting to leak outside the blue line. He knew it was only a matter of time before everything would become national news. The major also started to wonder who else was involved? Why were these things happening on his watch? His mind suddenly was intruded by an unsuspecting thought: The BioGen Farm and Dr. Yogerra. A gray feeling came over the major but before he could be fully engulfed, the feeling was interrupted by a question.

"Major, no disrespect towards your department, it's just so strange to see all these missing persons happening up here in the park." said Phil Silverman.

"You're a bit out of your jurisdiction, aren't you Mr. Silverman?" asked the major.

Phil Silverman started pointing at another reporter across the room and replied, "Why don't you ask Mrs. Pierce from Channel Three News out of New York City."

A low murmur grew throughout the room. Everyone looked over at Mrs. Pierce and her cameraman at the same time.

"Hello, Major Vierra. Donna Pierce, Channel Three News. Can you comment on how your department is going to work with the bureau on these investigations? Also, is there any correlation with all these missing people, or do you believe it's a coincidence?"

Before the major could respond, the room erupted again with several more questions. The gray feeling was getting worse. It was now enveloping the major. Flashing and clicking culminated with competing questions that started to rise to an uncomfortable level. The major looked at the air horn resting on the shelf inside the podium. He reached for it and lifted it up above his head. He pressed the button on it. Immediately a loud obnoxious ear-splitting noise engulfed the room. It was powerful enough to drown out all the noise. A few seconds went by and the noise stopped, and then the room became quiet.

The major looked over at Agent Barret and asked, "Do you want to answer that?"

Agent Barret stepped back up to the podium and responded, "The bureau is only interested in the missing snowmobilers and their proximity to the Hogansburg Indian Reservation."

The room started to erupt again. The major was ready, he started to raise the air horn over his head. The reporters all quieted down. The room became silent again.

"That's all for today. Troop B will issue a statement to all your agencies on our investigations currently going on. We will also inform your departments when our next Press release meeting will take place. And that will–"

The room once again erupted with questions. The major raised his bullhorn again and stared down those reporters with a violent gaze. It worked. They withdrew their questions. The major started to smile again, another small victory.

"What about the deer attacks! Those missing people! Your department is sitting on evidence."

The major was blindsided by this question from the other side of the room. He knew who it was, that voice. He turned in the direction and saw Peter from the Adirondack Daily Enterprise. The major pointed at him and said, "Not fair Pete!"

There was an uncomfortable silence in the room,

but the major knew it wouldn't last. He made eye contact with the agents and he walked toward the door behind him. The agents followed. The room exploded again with clicking, flashing, and questions. Some of the questions seemed to be directed towards Peter. The major shook his head in disapproval.

They were walking down the hallway toward his office. The noise from the room started to dissipate, but it was still loud, even with every step they took away from it. Major Vierra noticed that he was still holding the air horn. They arrived at his office, he opened the door and invited the agents in. The major closed the door and sat behind his desk. They could still hear noise emanating from the press room. Major Vierra leaned back into his chair and looked at the two agents. They stared back at him.

"Deer attacks?" asked Agent Barret.

Again, the major started thinking of Dr. Yogerra and the BioGen Farm. He responded, "Welcome to my world."

CHAPTER THIRTY- SEVEN

ANTIBIOTICS

John couldn't stop itching, his back felt like it was on fire. It was infected. The rash had spread all over his body, including his head and face. They had tried creams, sprays, Benadryl and even antibiotics.

It was getting worse.

John was itching so much that they had strapped his arms down to the bed. They tried a few times to wheel his bed down the hall to Dr. Baumer's office, but the meetings proved to be unproductive. The past week they seemed to entirely concentrate on treating his rash. This meant that John had remained heavily sedated and strapped to his bed in his room all day.

John was okay with this. He liked being sedated.

He was in a dreamlike state without actually sleeping. And he didn't want to go to sleep, no, that was the last thing John wanted to do. In the sleep world, or the dream world, that's where John had to relive the nightmares over and over again. Watching his lifelong friends and his brother being torn to shreds by monsters with sharp teeth and claws. There was no empathy in the eyes of these creatures, no remorse. They enjoyed what they did. They were the perfect killing machines.

John's train of thought was interrupted, his fingers itching the sheets of the bed he was tied to. His whole body from head to toe felt like it was burning up. The itching was worse than any pain he had ever experienced before in his life. He balled up his hands into a fist then clenched his teeth together, every muscle in his body contracted and John let out a scream. The scream echoed off the walls in his tiny room and when he was finished, the straps that bound him to the bed were no more.

John sat up and swung his legs over the side of the bed until his feet touched the floor. He somehow broke the straps right in half, they looked like pulled garden weeds dead on the floor. He was confused on how he did it. John became startled by a pounding on the door, "Yo, Johnnie are you all right?" asked Mr. Rason.

The door opened and three men walked into his room, one of them being a confused Mr. Rason.

"What the fuck! John! How did you break your straps?"

"Watch out, he probably has a knife!" shouted one of the orderlies.

John felt another wave of itching rush over his body and grow in intensity. All his muscles cramped up at the same time. He stood up with clenched fists and screamed again at the top of his lungs.

"Grab him!" shouted Rason.

The other orderly just stood there almost frightened to react.

"Come on! Help me!" Mr. Rason again said to the orderly.

They each grabbed one of John's arms and tried to force him back down onto his bed. Mr. Rason tried pleading with John,

"Come on now John, you need to sit down on your bed."

The two men struggled but John was not moving. Another intense itching sensation came over him and again he screamed at the top of his lungs.

"John, Johnnie please, put us down." begged Mr. Rason.

John opened his eyes and realized he had both men lifted off the ground, one in each hand and their feet were dangling like they were trying to touch the floor. John turned his head to see the other orderly, the third guy standing in the doorway. He had his phone out and was videotaping the whole incident. John dropped both men. They lost their balance and fell backwards against the opposing wall when their feet hit the floor. They both had a look of terror in their eyes. To them, John was the monster. John looked at Mr. Rason and screamed, "Get out!"

The three men got out of John's room and closed the door behind them. John could hear the door lock. For the next several hours John did a lot of screaming and physically abused his room. The staff didn't bother coming in. Besides the screaming, there was banging and kicking and punching noises emanating from his room. John would settle down and be quiet for a short period of time and then he would explode into a rage of screaming and physical violence.

The three men stood outside John's room for a long time, just listening. Mr. Rason tried calling Dr. Baumer for some time and eventually the doctor finally returned his call. He was brought up to speed on John's condition. Dr. Baumer instructed Mr. Rason to not let anyone go into the room and that he would be there in the morning to evaluate John.

CHAPTER THIRTY- EIGHT

THERE IS SOMETHING WRONG WITH THAT DEER

Chief Reuger and his deputy were on their way back from Whiteface Mountain. The chief was disappointed. He'd made plans to talk to his nephew's supervisor, but the guy never showed up. He had taken his nephew's jacket and thermos before driving back towards Saranac Lake. His thoughts were drifting toward his nephew Eddie.

"God, I hope he's on a bender." said the chief.

Jeremy turned his head toward his boss and said, "I did see him playing pool last week."

The chief turned his head towards his junior officer and asked, "What day and where?"

"Tuesday last week. It was league night. At the bowling alley in Lake Placid."

Jeremy twisted to look in the back seat. The chief watched Jeremy grab his nephew's jacket through the rearview mirror. Jeremy pulled it up to the front seat and started inspecting it. "This thing's all torn up."

The chief looked over at his deputy and asked, "What do you mean?"

Jeremy lifted the jacket up by its shoulders and displayed the front of it to his boss. It looked like slash marks. Three to four of them from the chest down toward the bottom of the jacket thought the chief.

"Do you think this could have been done by a knife?" asked Jeremy.

A scenario started to form in the chief's mind. One where his nephew gets attacked by a perpetrator with a knife.

Jeremy then said, "This could be a blood stain. Or maybe coffee."

The chief gave his deputy an annoying look, his blood pressure spiked for a few seconds and then started to come back down.

"Hey, what did Dave Peterson say about the backpack again?" asked the chief.

Jeremy looked puzzled.

"On the way out of the jail, what did Dave yell at us again? Something about the backpack he recovered from Forest Home Road. The Bronson kids."

A light bulb seemed to turn on in Jeremy, he responded, "Oh yeah. I think he said it was torn up."

The two men looked at each other and said nothing. The chief turned his gaze back to the road and accelerated the village police car. Ten minutes later they arrived at the police station. As they got out of the car the chief looked at Jeremy and said, "Grab the jacket and the thermos."

The two men walked in the back door of the station and started heading for the chief's office.

"Chief, I got Mrs. Doty on the phone and she's complaining about a missing dog." said Deputy Rose at the front desk.

"That's not our department, Deputy Rose. Tell her to call the DEC."

"I know, chief, it's just that she's the fourth person to call in today about a missing dog."

The chief ignored him and walked into his office, followed by Jeremy. He walked over to the shotgun on his desk and inspected it. It had recently been fired; the chief could smell the gunpowder residue.

"That has to be over thirty dogs reported missing this past month!" said Jeremy.

"Dogs run away all the time." responded the chief.

Jeremy watched as the chief put the shotgun back down on his desk. He then bent over and picked up the backpack. The chief held it up and they both noticed a couple big slices all the way down the face of the backpack. The chief looked at Jeremy and said, "That ain't no knife."

Chief walked by Jeremy, out of his office past the front desk to the back where the jail cells were. Jeremy followed closely behind. A few moments later the chief was standing in front of his old pal.

"Unlock this cell, deputy." the chief said to Jeremy.

"I have to go get the keys from Deputy Rose."

The chief looked at his deputy and shouted, "Hurry up!"

Jeremy quickly scooted up front. Dave Peterson stood on the other side of the cell about four feet away from the chief of police. The two men were just staring at each other, waiting for the other to talk first. It was a test of wills. Whoever talked first would lose face. The chief knew he had to lose, so he broke the silence and said, "Dave, I need you to take me out to Forest Home Road and show me where you found the shotgun and the pack."

"How in the hell can I do that in this cell?" an irate Dave Peterson asked.

Jeremy interrupted the conversation, and the chief stepped aside to allow his deputy to unlock Dave Peterson's jail cell. The chief stepped in front of the cell and Jeremy got out of his way. The chief slid open the door and said, "You're right, that pack is torn up. I also have my missing nephew's jacket, and it's torn up too. What do you really think is going on in the woods, Dave?"

"I don't ever want to give up looking for my little girl, but I know deep down inside I'm never gonna see her again."

Jeremy and the chief watched as the proud, tough guy Dave Peterson crumbled in front of them and started wailing in cell number two. The chief stepped forward and hugged his lifelong friend. Jeremy watched his boss console the man who just lost his daughter. Mr. Peterson continued to cry a little longer. And as quickly as he started, he changed his persona, and the tough guy returned.

He looked up at the chief and said, "Follow me."

A few minutes later the three men exited the police

station from the back door. They all piled into the police car. It took them about fifteen minutes to get out to where Mr. Peterson had found the pack and the shotgun.

The chief parked the police car on the side of the road. They followed Mr. Peterson into the woods. The chief noticed that someone had already walked into the woods, and he assumed that it must have been Dave's footprints, but there were also other footprints. It also looked like it could have been a game trail. They walked about four hundred feet into the woods from the road when Mr. Peterson said, "It was here that I found the pack and my shotgun."

The chief stepped over to where Dave was pointing. He noticed two imprints in the snow. One could have been a backpack, and the other was definitely a shotgun. The three of them were startled by an owl noise and they looked over to the right where the noise had come from.

Jeremy was pointing straight at it, "There's something wrong with that deer."

Standing about sixty feet away was a deer. The chief focused in on it and noticed something wrong with its head.

"What the fuck is sticking out of its forehead?" asked Mr. Peterson.

"Is that a knife?" asked Jeremy.

The chief focused his bad vision on the deer again and this time he could see a knife sticking out of the forehead, right between the eyes.

Jermy couldn't believe what he was seeing. He then asked, "How is this fucker still standing?"

"That looks like one of those fancy throwing knives." said Mr. Peterson.

The chief couldn't help but think of the idiot who had thrown a knife at this poor deer.

"Probably some drunk asshole. These guys give hunters a bad name." stated the chief.

"What should we do, chief?" asked Jeremy.

The chief looked at his deputy and said, "We have to put her down."

The three men stood there and stared at the deer, but they couldn't stop looking at the knife sticking out of its head.

Dave Peterson looked at the chief and responded, "Asshole or not, that's a hell of a throw."

Colt and Jeremy shook their heads and agreed with what Dave Peterson said. As the chief started to un-holster his pistol, they noticed the deer tilt its head and slightly open its mouth revealing razor sharp pointy teeth.

"Chief, that's fucked up!" shouted Jeremy.

Chief Duprey caught a blur out of his peripheral vision. The blur then ran Jeremy over, it was another deer. The thing didn't even slow down after it made contact with Jeremy. It crashed right into his back and Jeremy fell flat on his face and chest on the ground in front of them. The chief and Mr. Peterson simultaneously bent down to help Jeremy get up. By the time they got him to his feet they noticed the other deer standing beside the first one, again about sixty feet away. Before the chief could ask Jeremy if he was okay, it started charging them. Jeremy's mouth opened and no words came out. He was about to be run over again by the same deer, but this time from the front. It was extremely fast. All of Jeremy's muscles tensed up to brace for impact.

A loud gunshot echoed through the woods.

The chief raised his three-fifty-seven magnum in time and got off one round hitting the deer in the chest. It dropped about ten feet away from Jeremy.

"Thank you. Thank you, Rainmaker. Chief, thank you." a very hyper excited Jeremy said. His arms were shaking and he had a look of relief all about his face.

Everyone close to the chief called his cannon, the Rainmaker. A three-fifty-seven magnum that had been passed down from his grandfather, a family relic. Everyone in town was aware that the chief carried it with him on and off duty.

The three men studied the dead deer in front of them. The chief was impressed by the size of it. He looked at Dave and asked, "Is that the biggest doe you've ever seen?"

Dave looked up at the chief and said, "I bet you it's over two hundred pounds. Probably two-forty, two-fifty, maybe."

Jeremy interrupted and said, "Fucker must be rabid!"

Mr. Peterson walked forward and kneeled by the dead deer.

"Hey, where's the other one?" asked Jeremy.

The chief and Mr. Peterson looked up and they both noticed the other deer was gone.

Mr. Peterson looked at his childhood friend and said, "Must have been the report of the gun shot, frightens them away every time."

"I can't imagine it will live long with that knife in its head." replied Jeremy.

The chief and Jeremy walked over to the dead deer and started examining it. Dave opened the mouth and said, "Look at those canines."

The chief noticed that the teeth were sharper and bigger than any dog or wolf he had ever encountered.

Jeremy looked confused and said, "Those are not deer teeth."

Mr. Peterson lifted the front hoof. When he squeezed it, the three of them were shocked at what happened next.

"Holy shit! What the fuck am I looking at?" asked Jeremy.

A puzzled Mr. Peterson responded, "It looks like a talon. Like on an eagle."

"More like a claw from a velociraptor. Like from those movies, you know, those dinosaurs at the amusement park attacking people." explained Jeremy.

Dave Peterson looked up at the chief and said, "This could definitely rip up a backpack."

The chief looked at both men and said, "It could most definitely rip up a jacket."

Mr. Peterson started crying again. Jeremy looked at the chief. The chief motioned him to just stand there quietly. So the two men waited for a little while for Mr. Peterson to gain his composure again. And when that happened the chief said, "We must get this deer to the D.E.C. I'm going to walk back to the car and call this in and get the D.E.C. boys out here to pick this up. You guys stay here."

"Why do we have to stay here?" a nervous sounding Jeremy asked.

The chief pointed at his deputy,

"We need that carcass. I don't want coyotes dragging it off.

Dennis started heading back towards the car. He wasn't quite running; no, it was more of a jog, but he wasn't walking either. He kept turning his head to both sides anticipating an attack from his peripheral. A noise from behind startled him enough to make him freeze in his tracks. He turned around expecting to get run over by one of those things, but to his surprise he saw Jeremy and Dave Peterson close behind.

Before the chief could open his mouth and protest their actions Jeremy said, "I'm not staying behind no way!" Jeremy was moving at a faster pace than the chief and he walked right by him toward the car.

"I agree with the kid, Colt." said Dave.

Suddenly the chief was in last place and all three

men were headed toward the car. By the time the chief got to the car, Jeremy and Mr. Peterson were already inside. The chief didn't throw any shade at either one of them, he got inside the car himself and felt safer. Colt Reuger sat there for a moment and contemplated on telling his deputy to get back out of the car and go stand guard by the dead deer. But the more he thought about it, the more he decided against it. He would never ask a subordinate to do anything he wouldn't do himself. The chief grabbed the handle of the radio and pressed the button and said, "Deputy Rose, pick up. Over."

"This is Deputy Rose. How could I be of service, chief? Over."

"Call the DEC and put me through to Phil. Over."

"Ten-four Chief. Over."

Chief Reuger put the handle back on the radio.

Jeremy was shaking in the back seat and he wasn't sure if it was from the cold damp temperature outside or his nerves. "Chief, can you turn the car on? I'm freezing."

He turned the car on and a few moments later it started to get warmer. There were still a couple hours of daylight left and the temperature hovered around freezing. It was a wet kind of cold that sent a chill down your bones. The chief expected his radio to crackle with a response from ENCON officer Phil any moment. Cell phones had no reception out here in the woods. Jeremy and Mr. Peterson sat quietly soaking up the warm air blasting out of the car heater. There was a quiet uneasiness the three men shared, but it was quickly broken by the radio. "Chief Reuger, this is Phil. Over."

"Hey Phil, I need a favor. I'm out here on Forest Home Road about a mile down toward town from Mc-Master Road. I need you to send somebody out to pick up a deer carcass. Over."

"What's the issue with the carcass? Over?"

"It's mutated. Something is wrong with the teeth and hooves. Over."

There was a pause on the other end of the radio for a few seconds. Chief Reuger waited patiently. A few more seconds went by and finally the chief decided to respond.

"Phil, are you still on the other end? Over."

"Sorry chief. I'm not sure I understood what you were just asking or telling me. Over."

Before the chief could respond, Jeremy started talking from the back seat. "Tell him about the attack. Dinosaur teeth, sharp claws."

"Relax!" said the chief as he gave Jeremy a stern look.

"Look Phil, I don't know what's going on out here. This deer attacked my deputy. I shot and killed it. Over!"

"Aren't you out of your jurisdiction? Over."

"You're not wrong. But there's something wrong with this deer."

The chief looked over his shoulder at Jeremy and Dave and thought about what he was about to say.

"Trust me when I tell you that you need to take a look at this thing. Over."

"Okay chief, it's going to be awhile. Do you have something to mark where the deer is? Over."

"I have an orange flag; the deer carcass is about a quarter mile into the woods from there. There's almost a game trail that leads to it and footprints. Over."

"Thanks chief. Over."

The chief put the handle back on the radio and he put the car in drive. The three men headed back toward Saranac Lake.

CHAPTER THIRTY- NINE

YOU WORK FOR US

A smug looking Major Vierra was in his office with agents Mason and Barrett from the FBI. They had just finished a press conference with a room full of anxious reporters. He felt like he had surprised the agents by unexpectedly throwing them into the press room. If anything, the major felt like they were less arrogant, the thought made him grin. His door opened unexpectantly and there stood Dr. Yogerra smiling at him. She seemed a bit surprised at the company that was also in the room.

"Excuse me major, I'm sorry to interrupt your meeting."

The three men looked in her direction and the major responded, "Gentlemen, this is Dr. Yogerra from the Biogen Farm here in Adirondack Park. Dr. Yogerra, this is Agent Mason and Agent Barrett from the FBI."

Dr. Yogerra stood in the doorway and seemed to study the two agents for several seconds, her face remained expressionless. She looked at the two agents and said, "A pleasure to make your acquaintance."

Without an invitation, she walked into the room and chose an empty chair past the FBI agents by the window of the room. She took a few moments to get settled. The major was used to her theatrics, but he noticed the two FBI agents watching her every move. She seemed to be fumbling with something in her pocketbook and a few seconds later she produced a cigarette and a lighter. All three men watched as she slowly lit the end of her smoke and then took a long deep drag. She seemed to hold it in for an eternity. Eventually, she exhaled, and the smoke came out of her mouth perfectly. Dr. Yogerra focused her attention on the two FBI agents and asked, "What is the Federal Bureau of Investigation doing in the Adirondack Park?"

Major Vieira sat a little farther back in his chair. He started to grin just a little. He knew who was going to win this conversation.

"Just what is it that you do over at the Biogen Farm?" asked agent Barrett in an accusatory way.

Dr. Yogerra took another long drag off her cigarette. This time she concentrated on agent Barrett, measuring him up. She exhaled and the smoke floated over toward him and then said, "Agent Christopher Barrett. Enlisted in the United States Marine Corps. Graduate with your bachelor's in psychology from Penn State University. Accepted into the Academy of the Federal Bureau of Investigation. You have five years' experience on the job. Born and raised in Pennsylvania, a younger brother Michael and an older sister Beatrice. Of course, you had to go to Penn State because mom and dad are alumni. Your father Robert is an engineer."

Her accent was thick. European thought Agent

Barret. Small in stature, short cropped black hair, glasses. He started to hypothesize how this woman knew so much about him. Dr. Yogerra took another long drag off her cigarette and turned her head toward the other agent. Agent Mason focused on her cigarette and noticed the long red ash forming at the end.

"Agent Gregory Mason, graduate of Pembroke High School. Bachelor's degree in criminal law justice from Pittsburgh. After the Academy, you applied to be in the Central Intelligence Agency, but you were rejected. You have two older sisters and your mother is widowed. Father died of pancreatic cancer. I'm sorry for your loss."

She wasn't reading from a tablet or document, noticed Agent Mason. All memorized. The room became incredibly silent. The two agents seemed to be frozen. They were afraid to speak or move, they both had their eyes on Dr. Yogerra. All three men watched as she took another drag off her perfect cigarette. She exhaled slowly and flicked the long ash off to her left onto the floor without remorse. She then reached into her pocketbook, this time pulling out her cell phone. They watched as she hit a few buttons, presumably making a call. "Hello Jonathan, it's Dr. Yogerra."

She held out her phone and the three men assumed it was on speaker.

"Hello Dr. Yogerra, what can I do for you today?" said the voice on the other end of the call.

"I am here sitting in Major Viera's office at Troop B

headquarters, and I have just been introduced to two members from the Federal Bureau of investigation. Agents Barrett and Mason."

The voice on the other end of the call delayed for a few seconds and then said, "This is Deputy Director Miller. Agents, Dr. Yogerra and the Biogen Farm are an asset for us to work with in the Adirondack Park. Do I make myself clear!"

"Yes, Sir." responded both agents in unison.

Dr. Yogerra pulled the phone back towards her mouth and said, "Thank you, Jonathan."

Dr. Yogerra hung up the phone and put it back into her purse. She still had half a cigarette left. Agents Barrett and Mason watched as she took another long drag, the end of her cancer stick glowed bright red. She then exhaled a perfect smoke ring. Again, she flicked the ash off to her left on the floor disregarding the consequences of the burning hot amber.

Dr. Yogerra fixed her sight on the two agents and said, "So, let's start this conversation over again. Just exactly what are you two agents doing in the Adirondack Park?"

"We're investigating the missing snowmobilers and their proximity to the Hogansburg Indian Reservation." replied agent Barrett.

"Where do you suppose those missing snowmobilers are?" asked Dr. Yogerra.

"We think it's a drug deal gone bad." responded agent Mason.

Agent Barrett turned his head and looked at his partner in disgust. He then turned his head back towards Dr. Yogerra and said, "That is a working theory. No disrespect, Dr. Yogerra, but my partner and I are not allowed to discuss any details of the case."

"Well if there's anything I can do, the Biogen Farm has several assets at my disposal. It's not easy traveling around the park, especially this time of year with all the snow. We do have a helicopter and several four-wheel drive vehicles, snowmobiles and ATVs. All have on and off-road capabilities."

Agent Barrett stood up and looked at the major and said, "Thank you major, we will be taking our leave now."

He then turned his head toward his partner who was still sitting down, this caused Agent Mason to stand up. Agent Barrett turned his head and looked at Dr. Yogerra and said, "Nice to meet you, doctor. I will give you a call if we are in need of the Biogen Farm."

Dr. Yogerra crossed her ankles and nodded her head at Agent Barrett and took another long drag off her cigarette. The two agents exited Major Viera's office and closed the door.

The major stared across his desk at Dr. Yogerra. He wasn't sure why she was paying him a visit. He did have several questions for her, so he waited patiently for the good doctor to get herself together and begin their conversation. A few moments later Dr. Yogerra dropped her cigarette on the floor and stepped on it. She then twisted her left boot back and forth a few times and said, "You really do need to get me an ashtray."

"You do realize this is a no smoking zone. As a matter of fact, every state building in New York is a no smoking zone." replied the major.

"I didn't come here to discuss New York State's policy on public smoking."

The major quickly responded, "Then what can I do for you Dr. Yogerra?"

"It seems that the Adirondack Park has been invaded by mountain lions."

"Do you have any proof of these mountain lions?" asked Major Viera.

She looked at him, and then flashed a grin and said, "You're going to help me acquire the proof."

The major had a confused look on his face. He looked at Dr. Yogerra and asked, "And just how am I supposed to do that?"

"The Biogen Farm will contract out an expert hunter. Qualified to hunt big game like mountain lions. He will bring back four to five large cats, and you will explain to everybody during your press conference that the menacing threat to the park is over."

The major leaned forward from his chair toward his desk and asked, "Are you really going to hunt these mountain lions? Are you telling me that there are several mountain lions in the park?"

The major sat back in his chair and ran his hands

through his hair. Suddenly the major's face lit up. He looked across his desk at Dr. Yogerra and said, "Or, are you planting these big cats in the park and then claiming that they are responsible for all these missing hunters and snowmobilers?"

Dr. Yogerra looked at the major for a long time. It made him a little uncomfortable. She lifted her arm and pointed her finger at him and said, "We own you!"

The major leaned back in his chair and his whole body started to sink. That gray feeling started to overcome him again. He was determined not to let that happen, he suddenly got a burst of energy and leaned forward again in his chair. He pointed his finger at Dr. Yogerra and said, "What the hell are you people doing in the park? Why is everybody talking about deer attacks?"

Dr. Yogerra stood and pointed her finger at him again and said, "We own you!"

She then walked to the door and let herself out of his office. The major noticed she didn't close the door. He then looked over to where the doctor had been sitting and also noticed that she didn't pick up her cigarette butt off the floor. He leaned back in his chair again. His head started to hurt, and that gray feeling was starting to overcome him.

CHAPTER FORTY

COVER UP

Chief Reuger was sitting in his office drinking a black cup of coffee. He couldn't stop thinking about the deer they encountered in the woods off Forest Home Road the day before. He had been an advent hunter his whole life. Deer with carnivorous teeth and claws: he was having a hard time wrapping his brain around the idea. It was like he was stuck in a science fiction movie. A bad one.

"Chief, you better come out here and take a look at this." shouted Jeremy.

The chief stood up from his desk and walked out of his office to where his junior patrolman was watching the morning news.

Jeremy was pointing up at the television, he then said, "Some reporter out of Watertown. They got video of the perpetrator going crazy in his cell up at the wacky hospital. You know, the Fuller guy from Santa Clara, the one who survived."

The chief looked up at the TV. There was a video of some guy holding two men, one in each hand, off the ground.

An excited Jeremy asked, "Chief! Are you watching this!"

Chief Reuger continued to watch the video. The man seemed to toss the other two against the wall. He then screamed for them to get out, and they did.

"What's wrong with his face?" asked Jeremy.

The chief ignored him and continued to watch the TV. The man seemed to look out toward the doorway of his cell and then started screaming. The video stopped and then the reporter returned.

"For several weeks now there has been a cover up in the Adirondacks. Missing hunters, five missing snow-mobilers, a missing woman. Troop B in Ray Brook issued a statement a couple weeks ago that mountain lions are on the loose in the Adirondack Park. I also had an opportunity to interview one of the orderlies that work in this psychiatric hospital where John Fuller is being held. Mr. Fuller is the lone survivor of the hunting party that went missing in the Adirondacks several weeks ago. There is speculation that he went rogue and killed the missing members of his party. The District Attorney's office in Franklin County, led by Mr. Allen Rodstein, would not return our calls. But word on the street is that he is assembling a grand jury with the hope of leveling charges against John Fuller."

The reporter on the TV screen disappeared and then a separate video started. It was another man but his face was blotted out, and they had obviously dubbed his voice.

"Sir, can you tell me again what you heard John Fuller say about his hunting party out at Santa Clara in the Adirondack Park?"

"Yeah, he said they were attacked by man eating deer. That his brother and all his buddies were killed by these things, torn to pieces. He said they have sharp teeth like a wolf or something. Oh yeah, something about a claw on their feet. Yeah, they use this claw to rip a man open. At first I kind of laughed when I heard him tell this story. I mean this is a crazy hospital, I figured the guy is nuts. But you've seen this video, this guy's not right, he's got superhuman strength. He's like Superman, and his skin has some type of rash, it's all over his body. That guy's not right. Part of me believes him, about the monster deer. But the other part of me thinks this guy is a serial killer."

The video stopped and then the reporter came back and started talking again.

"For several weeks a local reporter in the Saranac Lake area has been asking a simple question. Are the deer responsible for attacking these hunters and snow-mobilers? I had a chance to ask why he thinks there are deer in the park attacking people."

Jeremy looked at the chief and said, "We know what the fuck is going on don't we chief! Guy should be interviewing us."

Chief Reuger continued to ignore his deputy and focused his attention on the TV monitor.

"Pete Wilson has been a resident of the Adirondack Park for over thirty years and has worked as a reporter for the local newspaper for over twenty. Mr. Wilson, why do you think there are deer attacking people in the Adirondacks?"

"Deductive reasoning. I've been investigating this phenomenon for the last couple years. We had a local hunter a couple years ago go missing, and his companion said that they were attacked by deer. Nobody believed him, they never found the body. When I went out and talked to the people from the Department of Environmental Conservation, they told me that deer harvesting in the Adirondack Park is way down. If you talk to the local hunters, they will tell you there are no deer left in the woods. The regular, normal deer are gone. Also, the local wildlife like rabbits and foxes seem to be vanishing from the park. And then almost six weeks ago, we had that hunter from Altona go missing, and his hunting party says they were attacked by deer. Now we have hunters and snowmobilers missing. I'm simply asking a question, and nobody from Troop B or the DEC will answer me."

The interview stopped and then the reporter returned to the TV screen.

"So what exactly is going on up in the Adirondacks? Is John Fuller responsible for the deaths of his hunting party, including his own brother? Or are there mutated deer attacking hunters and snowmobilers in the park? One thing is certain: we have yet to see evidence, physical evidence, of mountain lions, killer deer, or bodies. When I was a little boy my father told me monsters weren't real. I'm not sure anymore. My family and I are canceling our skiing vacation at Whiteface Mountain that we take every year. This is Joe Hunt reporting from the scary Adirondack Mountains."

The chief walked back to his office and sat behind his desk and shouted, "Jeremy, call the DEC and get Phil on the phone."

"Yes sir chief."

The chief's cell phone buzzed. He looked down and noticed a text message from his brother. He started thinking of his nephew. The chief had taken him on a few fishing trips way back when he was eight or nine. He was a quiet kid, and didn't talk much. Didn't have a lot of friends, mostly kept to himself. But he was a good kid, and he was family. He didn't have the heart to tell his brother that his son was never coming back home again.

"Did you hear back from Phil?" asked Mr. Peterson.

The chief looked up from his cell phone and noticed Dave standing in the doorway.

"Chief. Phil on line two." shouted Jeremy.

The chief looked up at Dave and said, "That's him right now. I'll put it on speaker."

"Chief Reuger, it's Phil. What can I do for you?"

"What do you think of our specimen deer?" asked the chief.

"I sent two guys out where you said it was, but they never found anything." responded Phil.

Chief Reuger looked at Dave and started shaking his head in disapproval.

"Phil. Are you sure your boys went to the right spot?" asked the chief.

"Yes, they found your flag. They said they walked in about half a mile. Followed the gaming trail but came back empty handed." responded Phil.

"Motherfucker!" Dave said out loud.

Chief Reuger gave Mr. Peterson a dirty look.

"What was that chief?" asked Phil.

"No, that wasn't me. It's Dave Peterson, he was with me yesterday." said the chief.

"Hey Dave." responded Phil.

Dave leaned closer to the phone and said, "Thanks for your help the other day out there at Troop B."

"Did they get you out any quicker?" asked Phil.

"Ya, after they processed me. Probably took an hour."

The conversation became quiet for a few seconds and then Phil asked, "What's so special about this deer?"

"Phil, have you ever come across a deer that has sharp teeth and claws that can rip a man open?" asked the chief.

"No, I can't say that I have. Look, Colt, we've known each other a long time. Hell, I've known both of you a long time. I've been fishing and hunting with you and Dave since we were kids. I have no clue what you fellas found in the woods yesterday. I'm sure you found something. I've come across rabbits with five legs and frogs with two heads."

"Phil, this wasn't a rabbit or a frog. These fuckers killed my little girl! They're real!" shouted Dave.

"Dave I'm really sorry about your little girl. I pray every day you find Cheryl. Chief, I don't know what to tell you. Maybe you can find me another one. Gentlemen, I've got to go." Phil hung up the phone.

CHAPTER FORTY-ONE

MRS FULLER

Rachel Fuller had been a widow for almost two years. Her husband Butch had been a great husband and a good father. The two of them were married almost forty years and raised two boys they loved very much.

The last several weeks could only be described as horrendous. What was supposed to be a routine trip up to the family hunting camp for the boys in the Adirondacks, had turned into a nightmare. News outlets and newspaper reporters were calling her son a mass murderer. Lifelong friends were giving her the cold shoulder and not returning calls. And Beth Davies, mother of one of her son's friends, kept knocking on the door asking where her son Karl was.

Heck, she wasn't sure where her son Darrel was, and she refused to accept that he was dead. It was hard to listen to everybody say they were gone, murdered. Now they were pointing the finger at her son John, calling him a monster. The community where she and her husband raised their family had suddenly turned on her.

She wasn't even able to see John. They had locked him up and sent him to a psychiatric hospital.

"Aunt Rachel, we're here." said her nephew Scott.

The car pulled into the hospital parking lot. Rachel

started thinking about the video of John she had seen on the news. How he had lifted those two men off the floor, screaming at them. His face had been awful, all red and swollen. She started to cry.

"Aunt Rachel are you all right?" asked Scott.

"No, I'm not!" she screamed at her nephew.

He lowered his head and tried not to make eye contact with her.

She looked over at him and said, "I'm sorry Scott."

"All good. You've been through too much. Let's go see Johnnie." he replied.

They both exited the vehicle and started walking toward the entrance. It was an unusually warm late December day. The temperature had to be in the mid-thirties and there wasn't a cloud in the sky. The psychiatric hospital was located two hours north of the Adirondacks. It was about a six-to-seven-hour drive from Bronxville, New York. Rachel had asked her nephew to drive her up so that she might have a chance to see Johnny. They had left at midnight and other than a couple stops, they made good time.

The hospital was a large two-story rectangular building and it was painted white. It had a brick facade and every window had steel bars on them. It was around ten in the morning when they walked up the steps and Scott opened the door for his Aunt Rachel. When they got inside there was a desk in front of them. Scott noticed that Rachel seemed to be in a hurry, so he let her go first.

"Hello. My name is Rachel Fuller. I'm here to see my son John Fuller."

The woman at the front desk behind plexiglass lifted her head and looked at Rachel for what seemed to be a long time before she said, "I'm sorry, but this hospital does not have visiting hours."

"You don't understand. My nephew and I just drove seven hours all through the night to get here. I really need to see my son John." demanded Rachel.

The woman behind the plexiglass gave Rachel a half smile, half smirk and said, "Did you make an appointment with Dr. Baumer?"

Rachel started crying. The tears started running down her cheeks and the words didn't quite make sense coming out of her mouth.

"We drove all night. I need–I have to. John. Please. My baby boy."

The woman behind the plexiglass didn't show any remorse for Rachel Fuller or her plight.

"Hello, I'm Scott Fuller, I'm her nephew and John is my first cousin. Is there somebody else we can talk to about possibly seeing John?"

"I can take your phone number and your name. I will contact your son's doctor and someone will give you a call later on today." replied the woman behind the plexiglass.

"I need to see my son now! I'm not leaving unless I see my son now!" screamed Rachel Fuller.

The woman behind the plexiglass picked up the

black phone from the desk. She pressed a button and started speaking. Scott couldn't quite hear what the woman was saying because his Aunt Rachel was crying out loud hysterically and she would occasionally scream that she needed to see her son. Suddenly Scott heard a buzzing noise. The door to the left behind the woman at the desk opened and three men came into the room. Scott noticed that two of the men were dressed in all white, shirt and pants. The other gentleman had a white lab doctor's jacket on and a shirt and tie and black pants. The three men walked up to the plexiglass and stared across at Scott and his aunt Rachel. She was still emotionally out of control.

Scott tried consoling her and said, "Aunt Rachel, it's okay, relax. It's okay, we're gonna go see John."

He put his hands on her shoulders and gently twisted her body so that they were face to face. This seemed to calm her down. At least she stopped wailing and screaming.

"Excuse me, let me introduce myself. I am Dr. Baumer, John's doctor here at this facility." said the man with the shirt and tie.

Rachel turned away from her nephew and looked at the man with the shirt and tie and asked, "Can you please take me to my son?"

"Yes, I can." replied Dr. Baumer.

A glow started to come over Rachel's face and her whole posture became more rigid. The other two gentlemen dressed in all white, walked over and opened a door to the left. Rachel and Scott walked through the door and stood face to face with Dr. Baumer.

"If you will please follow me." asked Dr. Baumer.

They walked through the second door and into a long hallway. Scott was holding on to his aunt Rachel's hand. He noticed that the other two gentlemen dressed in white were walking behind them and Dr. Baumer was in front of them. They walked down the hallway and turned a couple times right and then left. A few moments later they arrived at Dr. Baumers office. He invited them in.

Dr. Baumer sat behind his desk. Rachel and Scott selected two chairs that were in front of his desk, and the two gentlemen dressed in white stood at the door.

Dr. Baumer smiled and said, "We normally don't allow visitations, even from family members. But I do believe it would be good for John if he saw some family right now."

Rachel interjected, "The video of John was just terrible."

"I am so sorry that you experienced that. The local news affiliate that's responsible for that video will be held accountable." explained Dr. Baumer.

"What's wrong with his face?" asked Rachel.

"John has experienced some kind of allergic reaction. We're not quite sure what it is from, but a rash has spread all over his body over the past several weeks. We've treated him with antibiotics, and this has helped slow the spread of the rash, but it hasn't stopped it." explained Dr. Baumer.

Scott asked, "Why haven't you moved him to a different facility? You know, one that is more capable of treating his symptoms. I mean this is a psychiatric hospital, not a medical hospital?"

"I assure you we are more than capable of treating John's ailments. We have the best medical staff equivalent to any hospital in the area." responded Dr. Baumer.

Rachel excitedly asked, "I just wanna go see my baby."

"And I'm about to take you to him but there is one condition." said Dr. Baumer.

Scott and Rachel both looked at each other in a very confused way, and then they looked back at Dr. Baumer, anticipating his next sentence.

"We don't know how contagious his rash is, so you will not be allowed to go into his cell to see him."

Rachel started to scowl again, Scott put his arm around her and pulled her close to him.

Dr. Baumer then said, "You will be able to talk to him through the door, he will be less than a foot away. It's the best I can do under the circumstances."

"Doc, we drove all night to get here. She hasn't seen her son for almost two months. This woman's an emotional wreck. It would do her soul good to just see her son's face." responded Scott.

"Again, let me reemphasize, this normally doesn't happen. I'm going to get in trouble by my superiors for letting this happen. Not to mention a district attorney from Franklin County who possibly might be pressing charges against her son." explained Dr. Baumer.

"John never hurt anyone!" Rachel said with authority.

Dr. Baumer softened his voice and said, "I'm sorry Mrs. Fuller. I'm just stating the facts."

Scott started rubbing his aunt's shoulder and he brought her closer toward him.

Dr. Baumer could see the disappointment in Rachels face, he then said, "Listen, this will be good medicine for John and great medicine for his mother. It's the best I can do under the circumstances."

"We're ready when you are, Doc." said Scott.

Dr. Baumer stood from his desk and motioned for Scott and Rachel to follow. They walked out of his office again down the hallway. They turned right and left a couple more times and then stopped in front of a set of double doors. They were obviously locked because the two gentlemen dressed in white walked forward and one of them pulled keys out and unlocked the doors. The two gentlemen pulled the doors open and Scott, his aunt Rachel, and Dr. Baumer walked through. They continued to walk down another long hallway and a few moments later they arrived at a cell door.

This one was different from the other cell doors they had just walked by Scott noticed. It had dents in it, like it had been hit with force from the other side several times. The door itself looked to be pretty thick and seemed to be made of metal. It wasn't like a regular jail cell door with bars, it was solid. The other doors that they passed had a small window, but John's window seemed to be covered up with another piece of metal.

"Go get a chair for Mrs. Fuller." Dr. Baumer said to the gentleman wearing white.

Scott watched them disappear.

"John are you awake? It's Dr. Baumer."

"I said go away!" John screamed.

Scott and Rachel were taken back by the voice that came from behind John's door. Rachel had a frightened look on her face and she grabbed Scott's hand. Rachel thought to herself that his voice sounded different. It was deeper, angrier.

"John, I have two visitors for you. Your cousin Scott is here. He brought your mom."

Dr. Baumer looked at Rachel Fuller and nodded his head for her to speak.

"Johnny, it's Mommy."

The three of them made eye contact anticipating what John was going to say next. But instead of words forming a complex sentence, it was crying that filled the void. It started off quietly and then started to build to a crescendo. John Fuller was crying. This started a chain reaction. Rachel started crying almost as loud as her son. Then the tears started falling down her nephew Scott's cheeks.

"Mom, is that really you?"

A mother's instinct took over. Rachel Fuller turned her tears down to a trickle and took control of the conversation.

"Honey, I'm right here."   Rachel looked at her nephew Scott to coax him to join the conversation.

"Hey Johnny boy, it's Scott. You know, the cousin you always liked to beat up."

Scott was overtaken by emotion, and he started to break down. This time it was Rachel putting her arm around her nephew and consoling him.

"Hey Scott, how's my mom?" asked John.

Scott was too emotionally distraught to answer his cousin, so Rachel took over. "Your mother is worried about her baby." responded Rachel.

"I'm sick, Mom. I got this rash and it's all over. I can't stop itching and my muscles hurt. It's like a throbbing pain that comes and goes, all over my body!"

The three of them were startled by a huge bang on the other side of John's door. Rachel and Scott and Dr. Baumer all took a step backwards from the door.

"Open this fucking door now!" John screamed.

Before anyone could respond verbally, more pounding happened on the inside of John's door. It was like he was punching the door with a sledge-hammer. Scott and Rachel could see new dents appear on the door.

Dr. Baumer took a small step forward and said, "Now John, you need to calm down please. Your mother is here. I got your mother here John just like you wanted."

John continued pounding on the door from the inside. Dr. Baumer looked at Rachel and said,

"You have to convince him to stop. I'm afraid he's going to hurt himself."

The tears started flowing down Rachel's cheeks again, but she knew she had to take control of the situation.

"Johnny. Johnny. You must stop hitting the door. Remember Sammy?"

The pounding on the door suddenly stopped.

"Of course, I remember Sammy, Mom." responded John.

"He never left your side, John. He loved you. I remember the time you brought home glazed donuts, and you put them on the kitchen table. You were so excited to eat them. But Sammy jumped up on the table and ran out the door with the whole box." Rachel laughed as she recited the story of John's family dog. A few seconds went by, and nobody said anything.

Scott noticed the two gentlemen dressed in white come down the hallway with a chair. They put it down in front of the door and motioned for Rachel to sit in it. Rachel sat down and asked John, "Where's Darrel?"

Only a few seconds went by after Rachel asked the question but to Scott and Dr. Baumer, it seemed like an eternity. John started to cry again, not as loud as the first time, but he was definitely crying.

He tried to tell his mother that his brother was gone, but it was hard to understand what John said back to his mother. The words were mixed in with tears and emotion.

"Johnny, honey, where's your brother?" Rachel asked with more clarity.

"The monsters killed him!" John responded a little louder.

"No, no, no!" Rachel Fuller started shouting. She started crying and a wave of emotion overtook her. She bent over in the chair and started shaking her head. Dr. Baumer made a move to put his hand on her shoulder for support but before he could, Rachel stood up and asked, "Honey, I need to know where Darrel is."

A loud bang hit the door from the inside and then John started screaming again. "Nobody will listen to me! They killed Darrel. Karl's gone; they're all gone."

Rachel Fuller sat back down in the chair and put her face into her hands and bent over to her knees and started wailing.

John stopped screaming and then said, "Mom I'm sorry, please don't cry. Mom, it was the deer."

Rachel lifted her face from her hands and responded, "What do you mean, it was the deer?"

"They're not regular deer, Mom. They're bigger, stronger and faster. They've changed somehow. They have teeth like a dinosaur and their claws, I watched them rip everybody up with those claws."

"John, I'm your mother. Please, please son, tell me what happened to Darrel."

"Mom, I'm telling you the truth. They're monsters. Darrel is gone. Sal, Karl, they're all gone!"

Rachel Fuller stood up from the chair and looked at

Dr. Baumer and said, "I have to go."

Mrs. Fuller looked at the door that was all banged up from the inside, the door that was separating a mother from her son and said, "Johnny, honey, I love you."

Dr. Baumer and Mrs. Fuller started to walk back to his office. Scott started to follow but stopped and said, "Hey, Johnny, it's Scott. Listen, your mom and I are spending the night. I'm going to get her back to her hotel room. We'll be back tomorrow. Hang in there buddy."

"I didn't do it! it wasn't me! It was the monsters. Tell her Scott, it was the monsters!" John continued to scream from his cell.

He got stuck on one word and kept screaming, "Monsters, monsters, monsters!"

His voice started to lose volume the closer they got to Dr. Baumer's office. A few moments later they walked into his office and sat down. Dr. Baumer sat at his desk and looked across at Scott and Rachel Fuller. He noticed she wasn't crying anymore. She had a stone cold look on her face and her eyes were fixed somewhere on the floor. Her mascara was noticeably out of place. There were black blurry streaks running down her cheeks from her eyes.

"I recently lost my husband. And now my youngest son is telling me I've lost my oldest boy to monsters that I know don't exist."

Rachel Fuller lifted her head up and looked Dr. Baumer in the eye and asked, "Do you think my son Johnny is crazy."

Dr. Baumer looked at Mrs. Fuller and nodded his head yes.

She continued to stare into his eyes for some time, not blinking. She then asked, "Do you think he killed his friends?"

Dr. Baumer looked down at the floor, trying to avoid eye contact with Mrs. Fuller.

Rachel raised her voice at him and asked, "Do you think he would murder his own brother?"

Dr. Baumer lifted his head and looked John Fuller's mother in the eyes and shook his head yes.

Rachel stood up from her chair and turned to look at her nephew Scott and said, "Thank you Scott for bringing me here."

Dr. Baumer and Scott then watched Rachel Fuller collapse to the floor. The staff and Dr. Baumer did CPR for some time but finally gave up. She was pronounced dead a short time later and taken away by the county coroner. Scott Peterson drove back to Bronxville that night and told his family that Aunt Rachel had died of a broken heart.

CHAPTER FORTY-TWO

THE WELLER GROUP

Doctor Yogerra was expecting a call from her boss, The Brain. She half chuckled thinking about the name of her boss. She had been with him for several years and he was definitely not a man she wanted to cross. He was the smartest human being she had ever encountered. He could solve the most difficult problems, and his solutions were way out of the box from conventional scientific thinking. She admired his genius, but she also was afraid to interact with him. He wasn't the type of boss that patted you on the back and told you what a great job you were doing. She always felt like she was on thin ice around him, and she was afraid to disappoint him or be wrong. Her job security was about results. If she didn't produce for The Brain, she wouldn't exist.

Dr. Yogerra understood her position very well. There was no firing process with this job. Human resources didn't exist at The Weller Group. When The Weller Group was finished with you, they terminated you. She had experienced colleagues get terminated. She had a friend that just went missing. The local police were called in, but they never found her. Then there were always accidents like car crashes, drownings, and disappearances. Most scientists at The Weller Group didn't last three years. She had been around for over eight. During that time, she had helped plan and execute some of the disappearances.

A few years ago, they gave her a new research facility built brand new in the Adirondacks. That's when she knew she was finally somewhat safe. She started reporting directly to The Brain. Even though he showed no emotion, he confided in her. He told her about how things worked in the company at the upper management levels. That the company was ruled by six people who comprised the chairs. Strategically located throughout the world so that they had influence with the major superpowers: America, England, Germany, Russia, China, and India had all been infiltrated. Australia, Africa and South America were next, according to The Brain.

Over the past ten years, The Weller Group had risen from nothing to become one of the most powerful companies in the world. Funding was never a question, all she had to do was ask The Brain, and he always came through. As long as she could justify what the funding was going to be used for. The Brain did say no occasionally, he had to be convinced. In other words, The Brain needed to be swayed that the funding for Dr. Yogerra's research would benefit him in the long run. She didn't do much business with The Weller Group. She was called in occasionally by The Brain to assist in certain high-tech operations. But she never spent much time in the main facility of The Weller Group. When her business was conducted, she retreated back to the Biogen Farm.

The red phone started blinking. She picked it up and the voice on the other and said, "Hello Dr. Yogerra, I have found them."

Dr. Yogerra was confused. She wasn't quite sure what The Brain was talking about.

"I'm sorry boss, what have you found?" asked Dr. Yogerra.

"I have found the man-eating deer that are wreaking havoc in the Adirondack Park."

A minor buzzing sensation reminded her to activate her HCI. Dr. Yogerra used her eyes and looked up to her left, she became immersed in a video of a drone high above a landscape that included trees and mountains. The drone had several high-tech features.

"We have found where they live." said The Brain.

The drone hovered above a mountainous region and there seemed to be a cave opening in the rock face.

"This is where they live. I'm going to deploy a team to extract one sample."

Dr. Yogerra watched as three men with assault rifles repelled down from a helicopter, they were about sixty feet away from the opening of the cave. A few moments later, she watched as a deer came out of the cave and then the men open fire upon it. The deer falls, and then three men walk up to the deer and they start to strap a harness around it. Suddenly several other deer attack the three men from behind. There is screaming and gunshots, but within a few seconds, the three men are down on the ground and seem to be immobilized by six deer. The three men struggle and try to get up but are quickly subdued by the deer. Dr. Yogerra notices a few seconds later that the men are not moving; they're just laying on their backs. The three men are then dragged into the cave by the deer. Dr. Yogerra is amazed at how the deer simply bite down on the shoulders of the men and drag them into the cave effortlessly. Within a minute of the assault, the men and the deer are gone. Presumably in the cave, and Dr. Yogerra and The Brain are left with questions.

"Well that didn't go the way I wanted it to." said The Brain.

Dr. Yogerra was still in a state of bewilderment.

"I am going to go to Plan B, and it will consist of two phases. My next team will be responsible for phase one. Their job will consist of getting a sample of this carnivorous deer running amok in the Adirondacks."

Dr. Yogerra started to wonder where she was going to fit into the next chapter of his plans. And then he said, "Look at this video that the news media has been sharing the last couple days."

The video started to play on Dr. Yogerra's HCI. It showed a man around one hundred and eighty to two hundred pounds lifting two other men up off the floor. He had each man in his arms. Their feet were dangling in the air.

"That is John Fuller, survivor of the Santa Clara hunting party disaster." explained The Brain.

Dr. Yogerra continued to watch the video. She noticed how John Fuller's face was swollen and red.

"So, I ask you Dr. Yogerra, how can a human being that weighs less than two hundred pounds and no more than six feet tall, hold up two men, one in each arm and both weighing well over two hundred pounds, off the floor?"

Dr. Yogerra continued to watch as John Fuller tossed these two men against the wall like they weighed nothing.

"I need a theory." said The Brain.

Dr. Yogerra was not going to throw out a hypothesis that didn't have a chance in the Brain's world. She simply said back to The Brain, "I need more input, more information."

"That is a fear request Dr. Yogerra. But before I totally call you out, I'm going to share previous information with you. John Fuller was scratched on his back several times by these mutated deer. He was also bitten on both ankles and dragged a couple hundred feet back into the woods. Over the past several weeks he has developed a rash that has spread throughout his body. They have tried ointments and antibiotics, but he has not responded to the treatment."

Dr. Yogerra didn't have to elaborate long to come up with a rebuttal. "He's infected by Mother."

"This is why you're still alive, Dr. Yogerra. You tell me

what I already know. You confirm or believe, and this is why I love to confide in you."

Dr. Yogerra wasn't sure whether to take The Brain's words as a compliment or a death threat.

The Brain continued, "I need you to extract John Fuller from the psychiatric hospital. You will oversee phase two."

CHAPTER FORTY-THREE

LET ME OUT!

"Hey, how's it going Gordie?" asked Todd.

"Yo, Gordie, I bet you can moonwalk like Michael Jackson." chimed in Warren.

The whole room broke out in laughter. Gordie had to walk into the coffee room before his shift. He was hoping that the boys, his coworkers wouldn't be there, but they were. Almost like they were anticipating his arrival.

"Who the fuck is watching the freaks?" asked Gordie.

Freaks was a term that the staff used to describe the current population or residents of the psychiatric center.

"The lobster." replied Scott.

Again, the whole room started laughing. Gordie knew who Scott was referring to. The freak with the bad rash that had lifted him off the floor with one hand, feet dangling.

"Gordie, can you tell us again how you and Rason became an instant YouTube sensation?" asked Jim.

"Fuck you!" replied Gordie.

The whole room started laughing again in unison. Gordie walked out of the coffee room and started to head to the front desk. The last forty-eight hours were a blur. It all started with the incident, where the rash man went crazy in his cell. Rason ordered them to go in there and restrain the guy. But there was something obviously wrong with the guy to begin with. He was punching dents in his cell door. No human could possibly do that. The outside of the cell door, which was eight-inch steel, had fist impressions protruding outward.

"Hey Gordie, have you been floating off the floor lately?" asked Karen at the front desk.

Gordie shook his head no. He started thinking of how many likes the upload to the video got. It had over three million views. Everyone in his family, all his close friends were harassing him about it. Instead of being concerned about his safety, everyone thought it was a big joke. The freak could have killed him, but no one cared, they all just laughed about it.

"Hey, did you hear about lobster man's mother?" asked Karen.

Gordie broke away from his thoughts and concentrated on the overweight white woman with brown hair and caked on mascara.

"Well I guess Dr. Baumer brought the freak's mother into the facility, to his cell. Let her have a conversation with him. Apparently, afterwards, they all went back to his office, Baumer's office, and she dropped dead on his floor."

"What did you say?" asked Gordie.

"That's right, lobster man's mother dropped dead on the floor in Dr. Baumer's office."

Gordie started walking down the hall, Karen was still talking but he ignored her. It was so embarrassing, the YouTube video. Him and Mr. Rason being lifted off the ground by this freak. Everyone got a big laugh. And of course, Pete Thill suddenly whipped out his cell phone and recorded it. Instead of helping subdue the freak, no, Pete decided to turn into a YouTube camera man. What an asshole, thought Gordie. He was getting mad. The whole town was laughing at him. He was downright angry, and he needed to vent at someone. The wheels in his head started turning and he cracked a smile.

Gordie hung a right and headed toward the lobster man's cell. He might not get even, but Gordie had some ammunition, and he was going to use it. He hung another right and then turned left and stopped at the double doors. The double doors that separated the freaks from the outside world. He found his keys in his pocket and unlocked the door, he then let himself into the hallway on the other side.

Gordie walked up to this cell that had protruding fist dents in it. He could hear groaning emanating from the other side of the door. It sounded like someone was in pain. Gordie didn't want that pain. The groaning was inconsistent and every few seconds it would spike a little louder. To Gordie, it was very unsettling. He didn't feel comfortable standing this close to that freak on the other side of the door. Gordie started to concentrate on why he was there, he started to grin.

"Hey Johnny, I got some news for you."

"Get the fuck outta here now!" screamed Johnnie.

Gordie became instantly startled and took a couple steps backwards. He was frightened by the thing on the other side of the door. His brain refocused and he concentrated on why he was there; he started to grin again.

"No, hear me out. I got important information about–"

A loud bang surprised Gordie and made him step back some more. "I said get the fuck outta here now!" screamed Johnny.

There was a foul odor emanating from the other side of the door, the door with all the fist protrusions in it. He took pause and stepped back a bit, evaluating the damage done to the cell door. For all Gordie knew, this guy could have pissed and shit himself, but he didn't care. This freak was going to pay.

"Don't you want to hear about your mother?"

"What about my mother?" replied Johnny.

"She's dead!"

There was a silence that seemed to last a long time. Gordie's grin expanded on his face from ear to ear. All this shit that he took from his family, close friends and the community over the past couple days seemed to drift away. The grin started to turn into a smile. He was gonna make this freak pay.

"Hey loser, I said your mother's dead!"

"No, that can't be. She was here last night. I talked to her." Johnny's voice seemed normal, not aggravated but instead it was full of bewilderment.

Gordie didn't wait for Johnny to become aggravated. Instead, he needed to throw more gasoline on the fire. In his mind he needed to make this freak feel lower than whale shit, especially after all the embarrassment and ridicule over the YouTube video.

"Well after she was done talking to your sorry ass, she fell flat on her face dead. That's right, fell flat on her face dead in the doc's office. Probably because of you. She must have realized what a big fucking mistake you are, and that she couldn't handle life anymore. So she just dropped dead right on the floor, and couldn't take it anymore!"

Gordie was smiling and he relaxed his shoulders like he had just exhaled a deep long breath. He said out loud, "Boy, do I feel better."

Bang! Bang! Bang!

Gordie was startled and stepped all the way back to the wall of the hallway opposite of the freak's steel door. He kept banging on the door from the other side. And again, Gordie could see new protruding dents appear in the steel. Each time Johnny hit the door, part of Gordie's soul jolted in his body.

"You lie! Get my mother now!" screamed Johnny.

Bang! Bang! Bang!

Johnny continued to abuse the door with each hit.

"I said get my mother now!"

Gordie tried to back up more but he was already flush to the wall.

Bang! Bang! Bang!

Johnny continued his assault on the door.

"Let me out!" Johnny screamed.

Bang! Bang! Bang!

With each hit, the noise reverberated down the hallway a little louder.

"What is all this ruckus?" asked Mr. Rason.

Gordie turned his head to the right and noticed his boss walking toward him. "Fucking guy is freaking out."

"Let me out!" Johnny shouted.

Mr. Rason gave Gordie a glance and then turned his gaze to the door that was being abused.

"Johnny settle down. You must settle down; you're going to hurt yourself."

Another loud salvo of bangs. Both men noticed the door move.

"LET ME OUT!" Johnny screamed again.

The banging started to get louder, faster. Mr. Rason started to have doubts about the integrity of the door. Gordie noticed more dents appear and that the whole door seemed to be shifting off its hinges. Mr. Rason looked at Gordie and asked, "What are you doing on the ward at this time? Your shift doesn't start for another twenty-five minutes!"

More intense banging interrupted them.

"What did you say to him?" asked Mr. Rason.

Before Gordie could respond the door was hit with the loudest *bang* of the night. It flew across the hallway and pancaked Gordie into the wall. Mr. Rason was lucky enough to be standing to the right, the door just missed him. He was not sure if Gordie survived the impact and it was clear that Gordie was somewhere between the wall and the door. Mr. Rason turned his head back to where the door was or used to be. There stood Johnny.

He looked different. Johnny had changed since the last time Mr. Rason had seen him. And that was less than twelve hours earlier. Johnny was thicker. His skin was completely red, like a bad sunburn. Worse than a bad sunburn. The two men stared at each other separated by about eight feet. Mr. Rason had never been threatened to the extent that he thought he might lose his life. But doubt was starting to creep in and he wasn't sure what was going to happen next. This thing separated by only a few feet could end his life.

Mr. Rason stood perfectly still. The freak, Johnny, turned right and started running down the hallway away from the double doors. He was extremely fast; Mr. Rason never saw any human being run that fast before. Mr. Rason grabbed his radio.

"Karen, we have a breach in the detention block, wing five. Send reinforcements. Over."

He then looked over to where Gordie was behind the door. It was leaning against the wall at an angle. He managed to tilt it back off the wall upright. He looked down and saw Gordie laying on the floor in the fetal position. He looked dead. Rason then pushed the door farther down the hall. The door was extremely heavy and hard to move. It made a scraping noise and ripped several tiles on the floor.

Mr. Rason immediately walked back over and crouched down to evaluate Gordie's condition. He found a pulse and then did a quick head-to-toe check. Didn't notice anything severe except for a significant bruise and swelling where the door hit him on the forehead.

Suddenly three more orderlies appeared. Mr. Rason looked at them and pointed in the direction that Johnny had gone and said, "He went that way."

He grabbed his radio and said into it, "Karen, Gordie's down, he's unconscious. Send medical staff down to the detention block, wing five. Over."

"They are on the way. Over." crackled Mr. Rason's radio back at him.

Mr. Rason started walking down the hallway toward where Johnny was going. He started to think about what he would do if he cornered Johnny. Mr. Rason started to walk slower. Mr. Rason watched as the three younger orderlies pursued Johnny down the hallway. With each passing second the most comforting thought Mr. Rason had was that more distance was happening between him and Johnny. Mr. Rason noticed up ahead that the three orderlies had stopped, they were just standing looking at the wall. A few moments later he caught up to them and realized what they were looking at. The wall was gone. Johnny seemed to have run right through it. Mr. Rason started to smile. If an eight-inch steel door couldn't contain him, then how did they expect a wall made of plaster and wood to do any better.

Mr. Rason looked at the three other orderlies and said, "Looks like lobster man has escaped."

The four men walked through the opening that Johnnie had made and their faces were suddenly immersed in morning sunshine. Mr. Rason squinted and looked in all directions but there was no sign of Johnny.

"What do we do?" asked one of the orderlies.

"Our job stops here. The lobster man is no longer our problem." responded Mr. Rason.

All four men turned their gaze toward the front of the building as the familiar sound of a helicopter approached in that direction.

"I think it's going to land in the front." said one of the orderlies.

Mr. Rason started walking toward the front of the building and the three other orderlies followed. The four men started to quicken their pace. The helicopter lowered and disappeared from the horizon behind the front of the building.

"It just landed on the front lawn." said another orderly.

They rounded the corner of the building and were still about one hundred yards away from the front door. Mr. Rason had worked at the psychiatric hospital for over ten years, and he had never seen a helicopter land in front of the building before. He recently was promoted to department head of the night watch. The hours sucked, but the pay raise was worth it. They were getting closer and noticed one person in the helicopter, probably the pilot. There were two people outside, dressed in black suits. Mr. Rason started jogging and the orderlies followed close behind. He noticed that the helicopter was all black, no markings, no serial numbers. Sleek stealthy black. It wasn't small; bigger than the news helicopter that fit four. He narrowed his sight at the two outside the helicopter. Men, really big dudes and the closer he got, the bigger they became. Well over six foot, maybe six-four. They were thick guys, two hundred fifty to three hundred pounds and not fat.

Mr. Rason slowed down to a walk. He was about fifteen feet away from the helicopter, panting for more oxygen. Before he could say anything, one of the colossal figures guarding the helicopter raised his arm and stuck his hand out in a stop gesture. Mr. Rason and his orderlies stopped moving and stared at the giant, black-suited man.

"You can't land this thing on the lawn!" said Mr. Rason.

"Dr. Yogerra is inside." replied the giant.

Mr. Rason wasn't surprised by the voice that came out of this big guy. It was deep and measured, every word.

"I don't give a damn who's inside or who you people are! I oversee buildings and grounds at this facility. Nobody ever lands a helicopter on my front lawn!"

said an irate Mr. Rason.

"Sir, I understand your confusion. My superior is inside the hospital explaining everything. Her name is–"

"Yeah, Yeah, I know. Dr. Yogi or something."

The orderlies followed Mr. Rason to the front door of the facility which was a little more than a few hundred feet away. Upon entering, Mr. Rason was expecting to confront this so-called doctor but to his surprise, there was nobody. This building was supposed to be secure, hard to gain access to. In the span of a few minutes an inmate had escaped, a breach in one of the walls, a helicopter on the front lawn and now there was no one at the front desk manning the front door. Again Mr. Rason used his keys to gain access, he let his orderlies in and they pursued the strange intruder. They heard voices and traveled down the hallway toward that direction. They stopped at Dr. Baumer's office. Outside stood two more big men. They looked identical to the two that stood outside the helicopter. Mr. Rason tried to walk into Dr. Baumer's office but was denied access by the giants.

"Excuse me." said Mr. Rason.

He looked into the open doorway and could see a man sitting at Dr. Baumer's desk. Another woman was standing behind looking over his shoulder.

"I tried to stop them."

Mr. Rason turned to the voice behind him and noticed Karen Gordon, the nurse who was supposed to be manning the front door.

"They have higher-up authority. Do you recognize the man at Dr. Baumer's desk?" whispered Karen.

Mr. Rason looked closer at the man typing away on the computer keyboard. He didn't recognize him.

"Mrs. Gordon. How long before Dr. Baumer arrives?" asked the gentleman at the desk.

Karen stepped forward near the doorway but stopped and looked at the massive men standing there and responded, "He's a few minutes away."

The man kept typing.

"Excuse me." said Mr. Rason again.

Without looking up, the man at the desk responded, "Who are you?"

"Mr. Rason. In charge of buildings and grounds."

The man stopped typing. He lifted his head and looked at Rason. He had gray hair and a gray beard. Sixty something. Blue sport jacket, white button-up shirt and paisley blue tie.

"I am Robert Muldowner. President of the board of directors that run this facility."

"Can I help you?" asked a very confused Mr. Rason.

"No."

The man looked back down at the computer and then started typing. Somebody could be heard walking fast toward them. Mr. Rason turned his head and noticed Dr. Baumer.

The doctor tried to enter his office but was denied. A very confused Dr. Baumer said, "Excuse me. This is my office."

"No, Dr. Baumer. This office and all its contents belong to the board of directors." responded Robert Muldowner.

A surprised Dr. Baumer said, "Mr. Muldowner, what do I owe this surprise visit to?"

"Please come in." responded the president of the board of directors.

Dr. Baumer walked in and was ushered to his desk. Mr. Muldowner stood up and motioned for his subordinate to sit down.

"This is Dr. Yoggera from the Bio Gen facility. She will need all records of patient two-hundred-SD2." said Mr. Muldowner.

A confused-looking Dr. Baumer was trying to calculate who, what and where patient two-hundred-SD2 was.

"Mr. Fuller will also be released to Dr. Yoggera. Here is all the correct paperwork." said Mr. Muldowner.

"Well good luck to that!" said Mr. Rason from the hallway.

An embarrassed Dr. Baumer looked up at Mr. Muldowner and said, "I'm sorry about that."

"Is this how your staff talks to you, Dr. Baumer?" responded Mr. Muldowner.

An angry looking Dr. Baumer looked at Mr. Rason and said, "I need you to go and bring patient two-hundred-SD2 to the front desk. Prepare him for transportation."

"You better put your track shoes on." said Mr. Rason.

"Excuse me!" responded Dr. Baumer.

"John Fuller just blew the door off his cell and ran down the hallway and busted through the wall. That cat is gone!" explained Mr. Rason.

CHAPTER FORTY-FOUR

BIG CATS

Pete Wilson was waiting patiently for the press conference to start. The room was packed with other reporters and to Pete, there were a few new faces. He looked over to Joe Hunt and asked, "Where are you staying?"

"I'm not. Traveling back to Watertown tonight." responded Joe.

Pete had been interviewed by Joe recently, the TV news station out of Watertown. The aftermath had started a firestorm in the surrounding communities. Pete's hypothesis proclaiming man-eating deer running amok in the Adirondacks had ruffled quite a few feathers with local authorities. Pete's editor at the Adirondack Daily Enterprise had reprimanded him over several calls: the mayors of Lake Placid and Saranac Lake, the chief of police from Lake Placid, and Major Vierra from Troop B were just the tip of the iceberg.

It was difficult to hear Joe, the room was abuzz with several other conversations among the reporters. The room became quiet when Major Vierra walked up to the podium, everyone was fixated on the major, hanging on his next word.

"Good afternoon. I would like to report that with utmost certainty that we have captured and euthanized several large predators in the park."

Pete and Joe looked at each other in a confused manner. Like a match igniting gasoline, the room erupted into chaos. Reporters from all directions started firing questions toward the major, but before he picked a reporter to answer, Major Vierra raised his airhorn up. Like Pavlov's Dog, the room became silent.

"Please, there will be time for questions after." explained the major.

Movement from the left captured Pete's attention. A trooper was wheeling into the room a rectangular stainless-steel table, the kind of table a human cadaver would be resting on. There was something on top of the table, but Pete couldn't make out exactly what because it was covered by a white sheet. Within a few seconds, three more tables were wheeled into the room. The tables were placed to the left of the podium next to each other.

"What we have here are some big cats!" said the major.

The major looked over at his troopers standing next to the tables and they uncovered the specimens under the sheets. The room started to fill with the noises of cameras and small talk. Pete noticed the extremely big cats laid out on the tables. His mind started racing, without a doubt he could see these predators taking down a man. Pete noticed another man walk into the room. The major made eye contact with the man and motioned him to come up to the podium. The major said, "I would like to introduce everyone to our expert big game hunter, Berenger Legrande."

The man was around six foot four and weighed well over two hundred and twenty pounds. He had brown straight hair and sported a matching goatee. Probably mid-thirties. He was dressed in brown Carhart pants and a wool plaid red and black button-down shirt. To Pete, this guy was a mountain of a man.

With a slight French accent he said, "Thank you, major."

The new man at the podium looked out over the room and took a few seconds to acclimate before he started talking. He pointed over to the door at another man. Pete recognized him, it was Phil Stewart, a long-time department of environmental conservation officer.

"With help from the DEC we have tracked four mountain lions and managed to kill them." proclaimed Berenger Legrande.

Pete immediately did a Google search for the name Berenger Legrande and a hyperlink navigated to a web page. It showed this man standing behind a huge tiger that he'd obviously killed. Pete did a quick glance of the website while the room erupted with questions for the big game hunter. According to the site, Berenger had hunted all over the Americas, Africa, Europe, Asia and Australia. Everything from moose to caribou, wolves, grizzly bears and he specialized in big cats. Pete looked up from his phone and honed in on a question from another reporter.

"Mr. Berenger, do you believe that these cats are man eaters?"

"Without a doubt. Upon dissection, two of the animals were found to have human remains inside them." stated Berenger Legrande.

The noise in the room increased to a rock concert decibel level, Pete was thinking about covering his ears. The major walked up to the podium and started to raise his bull horn. The room quieted down and several hands went up simultaneously. Berenger Legrande pointed at a reporter.

"Kyle Thompson, Channel Five News, were you able to identify the human remains?"

Berenger looked over to the major, and the commander of Troop B answered Kyle Thompson's question without hesitation.

"No. We hope to be able to answer that question soon."

The major stepped away from the podium and more questions started up at Mr. Berenger again.

"Hello, Christine Blue, Press Republican. Whereabouts in the park did you shoot these mountain lions? Also, are you concerned that there might be more of them in the mountains?"

"We shot two of them out near Meacham Lake. The other two were found on the backside of Whiteface

Mountain. It seems they travel in pairs. I'm not sure if there are more mountain lions in the Adirondacks, but these four came from outside the park." said Berenger Legrande.

"Joe Hunt, Watertown Daily Times. Do you have any idea of where they came from?"

The major started to walk towards the podium. Pete noticed the major whisper something into Mr. Berenger's ear. The major then pointed over to Phil, the Encon officer, to come up to the podium. A moment later Phil was at the podium and started answering the question.

"One of the mountain lions had a tag. We were able to pinpoint its origin to the Sierra Nevada Mountain range."

"What is that, like two thousand miles away?" asked another reporter, one that Pete didn't recognize.

"Pretty far away." responded Phil.

"Were you able to track its journey from Nevada to the Adirondacks?" asked Joe Hunt.

"Apparently the tag has stopped working. The last known location of this mountain lion was around two months ago out in the Sierra Nevada's."

The major walked up to the podium and responded, "Mr. Hunt, your false narrative has had severe consequences on our local communities. Several residents have called our phones in states of panic. Our major industries here in the Adirondack Park, everything from skiing to snowmobiling are reporting low attendance numbers because of your irresponsible reporting!"

Pete looked over at Joe and then turned his gaze back to the major and responded, "If these animals were behind the recent disappearances, then surely Mr. Hunt's reporting has helped save lives."

"And you Pete. You call yourself a serious news man? Telling everyone that there are man-eating deer in the Adirondacks." Major Vierra shot a skulking smile back at Pete.

The whole room broke into laughter.

"Excuse me, I just have one more question." asked Pete.

"I think you've asked enough questions." responded the major.

The room started to echo more laughter, and it was directed toward Pete and Joe. This didn't bother Pete.

"I have one more question for Mr. Berenger."

The Major was about to shut Pete down, but Berenger Legrande stepped right into the question. He pointed at Pete.

"Go ahead and ask."

"Are Mountain lions known to travel across the continent in that short of a time?"

"These big cats have been known to travel great distances. I'm not surprised how far they've come in such a short period of time." responded Berenger Legrande.

Pete looked over at Phil and asked, "What does the Department of Environmental Conservation have to say on the matter?"

Phil seemed caught off guard. He looked over at Pete and responded, "No comment."

Pete noticed Phil's doubtful expression in a brief period of eye contact before Phil looked away.

The major leaned over and whispered something into the great hunter's ear. Berenger Legrande then walked over to the door where Phil was standing. The Major said into the microphone, "I would like to thank Mr. Legrande and the DEC for tracking and removing these deadly predators from the park."

The major turned toward the door where the two men were standing, and he started clapping his hands. Suddenly the whole room broke out into a chorus of clapping directed at Phil and Berenger. A few moments later the room quieted down and the major began to speak again. "For the first time in a couple months, I'm going to get a good night's sleep. I suggest you all go home and do the same."

The Major walked out the door, ignoring the questions that followed him out the hallway.

CHAPTER FORTY-FIVE

THE POLITICS OF DEER

There are no political parties among deer. The politics of deer, however, do consist of three major concerns.

One: forage for food. A deer will constantly move to find suitable grazing areas.

Second: they must bed down in a safe place at night where predators can't find them.

Third: they must find a suitable mate.

The alpha always gets the female. Or, rather, females. The bucks in this species battle for dominance over the doe. Male deer must win their battles to mate with a doe and there is no second place, the winner gets them all! For well over ten-million years, deer have been programmed to operate in this way. The whitetail deer have been so successful, they have migrated all over the Western Hemisphere, Europe, and have even been spotted in New Zealand. Even so, there is a fine balance between predator and deer that keeps deer populations under control. Even the human world has strict control over deer harvesting during hunting season. Humans have learned over time that, if left unchecked, deer can drastically increase their numbers in only a handful of years. Agencies like the Department of Environmental Conservation help control deer populations by outlining hunting seasons.

Doe usually give birth in the springtime and can have from one to three fawns at a time. Happy's off-spring were happening faster.

It took him two years to establish a decent harem that consisted of twenty-five doe and over forty fawns. It was an all-girls club overseen by one alpha buck. No other boys were allowed.

His doe were giving birth twice a year and some-times three. They also were delivering between three to six fawns. The first generation of fawns that Happy had mated with were mostly gone. Several didn't survive the pregnancy, or they succumbed to death shortly after delivery.

The offspring grew quickly. Within six months, they were fully-grown adults. Happy started mating with his daughters and they proved to be better at birthing fawns than their mothers. They did it faster and their offspring were healthier. Happy had strict control over the male population within his herd. Whenever a male was born, Happy would kill it immediately.

The herd was growing at a very fast rate. The first generation of Happy's prodigy were born to be meat eaters. Within a few weeks, they were already skilled hunters, catching squirrels and rabbits. After a few months they were going after coy dogs. At six months they were attacking moose and other big game. Then, Happy taught them how to bring down black bears, their strength in numbers. He also taught his daughters to kill all other indigenous deer they came upon. Happy would have one bloodline and he was at the top.

Their appetites were voracious, they were always hungry. They ate anything, including their sisters, or the ones that were injured or died unexpectedly. He also taught his daughters to waste nothing. All kills would be brought back to the herd and consumed.

Happy liked to wander off from time to time, away from the herd. He never went too far but he did appreciate his alone time. He came upon a small river and stopped to get a drink. The water was cold and thirst-quenching. He lifted his head up and focused on a small four-legged dasher up high in the trees. He quickly turned his head to the left and focused his attention on a creature hiding in the brush. He couldn't see it but he could hear it. Happy was curious about what it was. He focused in on its breathing and figured it to be a small to medium four-legged dasher. It was breathing fast and this meant it was going to spring out and try to run away. Happy started to grin, he loved hunting.

Suddenly a noise off in the distance caused Happy to freeze. It was a perfect distraction for the fox that was hiding. The fox leaped out of the brush and sprinted across Happy's path and just kept going. Happy just stood there, he didn't give chase. Staring off into the direction where the noise came from, Happy started to trot. A few moments later, he entered the thicket on the other side of the small river. He could smell animals, and he could hear them. There were several of them. He poked his head out of the thicket and was surprised to see so many dashers. They were all different sizes, just walking around, not paying attention. Happy started to grin. There were small two-legged dashers that couldn't fly. They looked like they should fly but they never did, they just made a lot of noise. There were also medium dashers and some of them had small spikes on their heads. Happy's grin widened when he saw how big the four-legged dashers were. They made a different sound.

"Mooooooooooo."

Happy remembered seeing these creatures before when he was little. With his mom and sister, they happened upon a field where these big dashers were. He remembered how they ate grass. That's all they seemed to do, these things, just eat grass and make strange noises. Happy noticed that the dashers were surrounded by strange trees. No branches or leaves and the trees were laying down instead of standing up. But they were all connected to some shorter trees that did stand up.

Happy started to wonder what these mooers tasted like.

CHAPTER FORTY-SIX

THE G MEN

The two agents were questioning a Native American who seemed to be in possession of critical knowledge. They had spent the last three days interviewing everyone involved. They started with family members, and then interviewed staff at Charlie's Inn, the Airport Café, Deer Valley, and Owls Head. Agent Barret and Agent Mason hadn't learned anything new. Same information that Troop B came up with during their investigation. Five guys out snowmobiling, enjoying the newly fallen snow.

They ate breakfast at the Airport Café in Lake Clear. Had lunch at Deer Valley near Meacham Lake. Then finished off at Owls Head up towards Malone. Several alcoholic beverages were consumed. The snowmobilers never showed up back home. Snow machines found between Owls Head and Charlie's Inn off Route Thirty. When they tried to interview suspects on the Hogansburg Reservation, they got shut down by the tribal police. Forms had to be filled out, hoops jumped through. It was a bureaucracy of red tape. They had to play the political game, and it would take weeks before they could interview any suspects from the Indian reservation. Both agents thought there was a high probability that drugs were involved. The trail went cold at the reservation. This didn't stop them. The casino was a great place to ask questions, and it was always open to nonresidents of the reservation.

"So just how many times a week would you see Mr. DeFalco?" asked Agent Mason.

"In the summer, he was here four nights a week." responded the blackjack dealer.

She was around five foot four, one hundred fifty pounds, shoulder length black hair. Agent Barret had a nine in the whole with a ten showing. There were two people playing on his right and Agent Mason to his left. He was betting ten dollars and Agent Mason was letting it ride. Mason had won the previous hand and had a seven showing, with a ten in the whole. The two agents were not dressed like G men, they were donning civilian clothes. Agent Mason was wearing jeans and a blue navy t-shirt with a blue down filled winter jacket. Agent Barret wore a black similar winter jacket, button up gray shirt and black khaki style pants. The dealer flipped her second card up, a queen of hearts.

"Dam! Every time!" exclaimed the gentleman to Agent Mason's left. He was clearly agitated by the dealer's card. Agent Barret noticed the aggravated man had a sizable bet in front of him. He glanced over at the rules of the table. They said, minimum bet ten dollars, maximum bet three hundred dollars. Agent Barret noticed that the man had the maximum bet in front of him. The man was a large Caucasian, severely overweight, balding, in his fifties. He was sporting a Hawaiian shirt and big tan pants.

An uncomfortable silence hung around the table. Everyone was anticipating what the dealer had buried in her second card. She went around the table right to left and asked if anyone wanted a hit. The two people to Agent Barret's right passed, as did Agent Barret. Agent Mason took a hit and the dealer flipped him a seven of clubs.

"Too much." replied Agent Mason.

She then flipped his card over and said, "Twenty-four. Sorry." the dealer took his money.

"That was my card!" proclaimed the overweight man.

He gave Agent Mason a scowling look and said, "Hey buddy, we play by the book at this table."

Agent Mason looked at the large man with confusion and asked, "The book. What's the book?"

"Why you taking a hit when you have seventeen? You screwed me. If the dealer is showing a ten or face card, hit on sixteen or below. But seventeen or higher, stay!" replied the profusely sweating angry man back at Agent Mason.

Everyone with money bet on the table gave Agent Mason a despondent look and then turned their sight toward the agitated man. He looked at the dealer and said, "I need a seven."

The dealer flipped over a king of diamonds.

"Thanks a lot, pal." said the large man to agent Mason.

He turned over his cards and revealed a ten of spades and a four of clubs. The dealer took his three hundred dollars in chips. The big man stood up from the table and turned to walk away. Before he did, he looked at Agent Mason and said, "You're welcome for the three-hundred-dollar lesson, asshole."

Agent Barret looked at Agent Mason and smiled.

The dealer turned over her card and showed a king of hearts.

"Pay twenty-one."

The two people to Agent Barret's right got up and left the table with a look of disgust. The dealer then flipped over Agent Barret's card and said, "Nineteen, sorry." she took his ten dollars in chips.

"Do you know Talon Cree?" asked Agent Mason.

"Yes." replied the dealer.

"Did you ever see Talon hanging with Tony DeFalco?" asked agent Barret.

She took her time answering the question. Studying both agents from head to toe.

"Are you guys playing?" asked the dealer.

The agents both put out a ten-dollar chip. The dealer started shuffling the cards.

"Talon doesn't work in the casino." said the dealer.

"You have never seen those two hang out together?" asked agent Mason.

The dealer raised her head and looked at both agents and then asked, "Has Talon done something wrong? Who are you guys? Are you friends with Talon?"

Before the agents could answer, a Native American man dressed in a black suit with the casino insignia on the breast pocket interrupted, "Angel, is everything okay?"

Agent Barret did a quick look over the man. Ponytail, mid-thirties, six foot one, close to three-hundred, overweight. One of many pit bosses on the floor.

"These two guys are asking questions about Talon."

With a stern voice, and an eye piercing gaze the pit boss said, "Gentleman, I hope you're here to gamble and enjoy our hospitality. If there is anything I can do for you, please don't be afraid to ask. My dealer is here to shuffle and deal the cards, she won't be answering any more of your questions. Have I made myself clear!"

"Yes, sir." responded Agent Barret.

The dealer dealt the cards, but before they could even play, she flipped over a blackjack. King of diamonds and ace of spades.

"She is unbeatable." proclaimed Agent Mason.

"Apparently." said Agent Barret.

The two men made eye contact and decided to try their luck at another table. They walked by the next three tables, stopping for a brief moment to see if there were any open seats.

"Looks like we have a shadow." said Agent Barret.

Agent Mason turned his head and noticed the pit boss that had just reprimanded them, was following at a distance.

Agent Barret looked at his partner and said, "Time to go."

The two G men found the exit and started walking back to their car.

"Excuse me!"

They stopped and turned to see the pit boss quickly approaching them.

Agent Mason looked at his partner and said, "Could be trouble."

"I'm not afraid of him, besides there are two of us."

The pit boss stopped a few feet in front of them and asked, "What do you think happened to those boys?"

"What exactly are you talking about?" inquired Agent Mason.

"You guys are the feds, right. You're definitely not here to gamble; I mean you suck at it."

Agent Barret smirked at his partner and then produced his badge and said, "Agent Barret and this is my partner, Agent Mason."

The pit boss looked at Agent Barret and asked, "So what do you think happened to those snowmobilers?"

Agent Mason had a pen and small note pad out and asked, "And your name is?"

"Geronimo, to you."

Agent Barret chuckled but his partner wasn't amused. Barret knew what was going to happen next. His partner was about to throw the FBI academy book at this man, and it just wasn't going to work. He gave Agent Mason a look, the kind that told his partner to back off. Agent Barret then looked at the pit boss and asked, "What do you think happened to those men, in the woods?"

The man who referred to himself as Geronimo looked at both agents and said, "Stay out of those woods. Bad things have been happening to my people, real bad things."

"What kind of bad things?" a confused Agent Mason asked.

With a grave look, Geronimo said, "It's the deer, they are not right. They're not normal. They're demons. It's their woods now, it belongs to them."

CHAPTER FORTY-SEVEN

WINTER CARNIVAL

The village of Saranac Lake has one of the oldest winter carnivals in the United States. In the late 1800s, the small logging community had quickly become a popular location for Tuberculosis patients, the fresh winter air improving the health of those with the disease. Around this time, the village decided to break up the long cold winter with a carnival. They included events and activities such as sledding, snowshoe racing, and skiing. They built an ice castle where blocks of ice would be sawed out of Lake Flower. These blocks can weigh up to almost a thousand pounds. The century-old tradition of carving out the blocks and erecting the castle slowly takes shape over the span of a few weeks in mid-January. When they're finished with construction, a majestic castle becomes the focal point of the community for two weeks.

Over the decades, more and more events have been included in the Saranac Lake Winter Carnival. Local sports teams play games in the snow. There's music and dancing. The locals elect a king and queen from the community to oversee all the events. A parade filled with floats, marching bands, and colorful characters rounds out the last Saturday of carnival. The last event of the whole week, on the hungover Sunday after the parade, is a slide show at the ice palace with fireworks. Pictures are taken professionally throughout the carnival and pieced together for everyone's entertainment.

The entire community comes out and supports the winter carnival annually. Of course, alcohol is consumed in large quantities. Locals celebrating birthdays in late October through early December can often tie their conception to the annual celebration of Winter Carnival.

The only residents in town who didn't look forward to the carnival were the chief of police and his staff. Chief Reuger oversaw security, and that responsibility encompassed every event throughout the two-week span. His departments were short staffed, and this meant overtime for everyone. This also put a huge dent in his annual budget for the department. There were other pressing needs like new vehicles and training. He also had to deal with more domestic disputes and the rowdy downtown district that fueled alcohol-infused shenanigans.

The chief understood the fiscal importance of the carnival to the community. It did drive tourism for the local businesses at a slow time of year. But it also created more problems, and most of these problems were alcohol related.

"Chief, the king is here!" shouted Deputy Knowles.

He was lost in thought and didn't respond right

away, so Jeremy shouted again, "Chief!"

Colt popped out of his dream-like state and asked, "What?"

"The king of Winter Carnival is here." Jeremy responded in a quieter voice.

The chief got up and walked out of his office to greet the local royalty.

"King Thomas, what do I owe you for this unexpected visit." asked the chief.

Thomas Mullburgh was the recently crowned king of the year's winter carnival. He ran an insurance agency and had an office on main street. He sponsored youth athletic teams and volunteered his time throughout the community. On the surface, he was a popular man. However, behind the scenes Thomas was a conniving backstabber who would kiss the right asses to get ahead. A prominent member of the village board who liked to try and tell the chief of police how to run the department. He was in his mid-fifties, around five foot eleven, brown hair with a large midsection. Colt thought of him as a narcissistic blowhard. The kind of man that had to stop and look at himself in every mirror and window along the way.

"Chief, if you could keep the area in front of the ice palace blocked off tonight for the fireworks, it would be much appreciated. The queen and I along with other members of the court are going to have pictures taken in front of the castle an hour before the fireworks go off." Thomas stated confidently.

"My department is short-handed this weekend. I don't have enough men to help out with your request." responded back the chief.

King Thomas looked perplexed by what the chief had just said. He waited a few more seconds and then said, "Well, where are they? Surely you didn't give them the weekend off, come on man, this is winter carnival!"

"Those budget cuts you helped pass with the village board last spring caused me to let go of two of my men." the chief explained.

King Thomas's cheeks turned a shade of red.

"Well, I suppose we can manage. I am on my way down to the castle now to meet up with a few family members. Thank you, chief, for your time. If you could spare a man or two I would be forever in your debt."

The king winked at the chief and walked back out of the station.

"Enjoy and congratulations again, Thomas, well deserved." said the chief.

The chief snickered and thought about how cheesie the king's wink was. As if it would help get more officers down to the ice castle to help out with the pictures. Colt started thinking about how close Thomas lived in proximity to the ice palace, about a mile. He walked back into his office. He couldn't stop thinking about the deer he had shot out on Forest Home Road. The teeth would rip a man apart. And when Dave had squeezed the leg and that sharp talon protruded out like a claw, it didn't make sense. Deer were not predators. He had been hunting deer his whole life.

But when he connected the dots–all the disappearances from dogs, small animals, and people–the picture created a disturbing trend. Nobody would believe him. He needed evidence that the monster deer were attacking people. He had to go out and kill another one, and this time they wouldn't leave it in the woods.

"Chief, we have another fight going on!" shouted Deputy Knowles.

The chief hated the Winter Carnival. His deputies had broken up too many fights to be counted and arrested several drunks over the past week.

"Send Sergeant Davis and Williams to deal with it." responded the Chief.

His radio started talking, *"Chief. Chief pick up, over."*

He grabbed his radio on his belt and said, *"This is Chief Reuger."*

"Sorry Chief, we're down here at Rockies and there is a big bastard that just sent a guy to the hospital. He punched the guy's front teeth out, blood all over. Over."

"So, arrest him and book him. Over."

"The guy is over three hundred pounds. He won't let us touch him. Over."

"Aren't there two of you? Over."

"We can't handle him. Do you want me to pull my side arm on him? Over."

"Negative, Sergeant. Be right there. Over," responded Chief Reuger.

The Chief stood up and grabbed his coat and hat off the wall. He walked out of his office and looked at Deputy Knowles and said, "Let's go."

Deputy Knowles smiled and grabbed his jacket.

"Aren't you forgetting something?" asked the chief.

The deputy turned around and grabbed his police hat. The two men exited the station and walked about a quarter mile up the road along Main Street to where the perpetrator was.

Rockies was established about five years ago; it was one of the local beer and shot bars located on Main Street. The owner was a hustler, thought the chief. A bit full of himself. Rockie Joe Butzker.

The place was packed, like all the other bars in town during Winter Carnival. Everyone was getting a buzz on before the fireworks and slide show. There was a line of people dressed warmly in their winter clothes waiting outside to get in. The chief knew the guy at the door. The bouncer made eye contact and said, "Hey, chief."

"Hey Richard."

He was a local kid. Twenty-something, brown hair, six foot and overweight. Kid had been partying since he was twelve, thought the chief. Really bad teeth, kid had to get them fixed.

They walked inside and it took a while for them to make it to the bar. People were bumper to bumper. The chief spotted the owner, or maybe the owner spotted him first.

"Chief, you have to get that asshole out of here. I tried; my guys tried. He sent Shawn to the hospital, knocked out his teeth, probably a concussion." said Joe Butzker.

"Hey Joe, it looks a little too full. What's your total occupancy again?" asked the chief.

Joe's face went from one of confidence to despair, the wind had just got knocked out of his sails, he started pleading, "C'mon, chief. It's Winter Carnival. I won't make another dime until summer, cut me some slack."

The chief looked at the owner of the establishment and asked, "Where is this guy?"

Joe pointed and said, "He's in the back by the rest rooms. Good luck, he's a monster."

The chief gave Joe a not-so-impressed look and walked back toward the bathrooms. He recognized the song playing on the jukebox, it was from the sixties. It was hard to hear because there were so many people talking over it.

The two men continued to walk toward the back of the establishment. The room was like a long rectangle with a bar shaped like a small rectangle in the middle. There was usually a pool table up front, but it had been removed for Winter Carnival. Dart boards were still on the wall but the tables and chairs and bar stools had all been removed for the weekend. Just a big rectangle with a bar, nowhere to sit, just stand and drink massive amounts of alcohol. Good for business, bad for peacekeepers.

Deputy Williams spotted the chief and said, "Chief, glad you're here."

Sergeant Davis looked at his boss and then turned his attention back to the behemoth monster of a human standing against the back wall.

"That's him?" asked the chief.

Sergeant Davis and Deputy Williams shook their heads yes.

"That's a big guy, chief!" proclaimed Deputy Knowles.

"I've seen bigger."

The chief looked at the perpetrator standing against the wall. He started to step toward him when a girl interrupted him and asked, "Excuse me, I need to use the lady's room."

The chief looked to where the door to the girl's room was just ahead. It was next to where the big guy was standing.

"You'll have to hold it."

"Hey, I have to go bad. You can't stop me." said the girl.

She was approximately five foot four, one hundred thirty to one hundred fifty pounds. Blonde hair, shoulder length, green eyes, definitely a college student. The chief was sure his deputies were checking her out. She was a looker, thought the chief.

"Let me see your ID." asked the chief.

The girl turned bright red.

"It's in my jacket pocket, I'll be right back."

The college girl escaped into the river of humans

behind them. The chief looked back at the monster and stepped towards him, and said, "Hey buddy, what's up."

"They disrespected me!" shouted the big guy.

"Who?"

"I was minding my own business. They tried to cut me off. I only had a couple beers."

The chief took a closer look at the man. Guy was big–no he was colossal. Over six foot four and well over three hundred pounds. The size of an offensive lineman that played in the National Football League. He was wearing a shirt with a big middle finger on it.

"My sergeant tells me you physically assaulted another man. Sent him to the Hospital. You're going to have to come down to the station."

"No fucking way! That pussy deserved to get punched. Nobody grabs my beer!" shouted the big man.

"Chief, this guy is on more than just beer." whispered Sergeant Davis.

The chief nodded in agreement. He looked at the big guy and said, "I am going to ask nicely, just one time. Turn around and put your hands behind you."

The big fellow was about ten feet away. He looked at the chief for a long time. The two men didn't blink. The jukebox was still playing the same song, but the chief was almost too far away to hear it. The big man then turned around and faced the wall.

"Put your hands behind your back," demanded the chief.

The man did as instructed.

The chief looked at his deputy and said, "Cuff him, Williams."

Deputy Williams walked hesitantly forward and pulled his handcuffs off his belt, the big man spun around and shoved Deputy Williams into the wall. The chief watched his deputy bounce off the wall and crumble to the floor.

Everything seemed to slow down. The chief watched the big man step toward him. The chief was going to wait until the right moment. He said to himself, a little closer. The big, colossal giant was almost upon him when suddenly the chief stepped forward and raised his right knee. He then extended his right leg and drove his foot directly into the stomach of the big man. Everyone could hear the wind escape from the big man's lungs as they watched him collapse to the floor.

"That's a perfectly executed front kick." said Deputy Knowles.

The big fellow got to his knees, turned his head to the side and threw up violently.

Sergeant Davis smiled and then said, "There go the drugs."

A moment later, the big man looked up at the chief and said, "I'm going to kill you!"

The chief stood his ground as the giant got to his feet and stepped towards him. He noticed the big guy pull his right arm back. The chief knew what was coming next. He waited one more second and then tilted his head down, exposing his hard forehead. The big fellow threw an overhand right punch that connected with the chief's head. His wrist broke instantly, along with several fingers and knuckles. The chief took one step backwards, lifted his head and regained his balance. His hat flew off his head and hit the floor behind him. He watched the big fellow grimace in pain and clutch at his damaged hand.

"My turn." said the chief.

Chief Reuger stepped forward with his left foot and swung his overhand right across the man's face, instantly breaking his nose. The big fellow fell back down into a pile of vomit that belonged to him. He was out cold. The chief looked at Sergeant Davis and said, "Clean this mess up."

CHAPTER FORTY-EIGHT

HEY BUDDY

King Thomas was all smiles. Since his coronation, he had become the most popular man in town. He was a celebrity, stopping to take pictures and giving inter-views to local journalists and reporters. The last two weeks were an incredible rush. He was exhausted, the itinerary every day was demanding. There were a lot of events scheduled, and it was almost impossible to make them all. But King Thomas did his best to keep up appearances. Just one last event to go tonight. The slide show and fireworks at the ice castle. He'd promised his wife to meet at the ice castle, to take a few pictures with the family. Secretly he dreaded spending any time with his family. He wanted to dump his wife but his ac-countant told him it would ruin him financially, so he played the game. He couldn't stand being around his daughter, she was a total bitch. His wife told him it was just a phase, the teenage years, that she would grow out of it. But she was always nasty to him, even as a little girl, he never connected with her. The thought of spending any time with them was a big disappointment. He told himself that he would push through, take a few pictures and pretend, put up a good front for the com-munity. This could also help propel his future mayoral campaign. Then after he was going to go home and take a much-needed siesta.

He had just left the police station, and it was a short walk along Lake Flower to the castle. That arrogant gorilla, the chief of police, had better come through and help out with the pictures before the fireworks. Thomas cracked a smile, thinking of how he would fire that asshole once he became mayor.

It turned out to be a warm sunny day with temperatures in the mid-thirties. Not too warm though. In years past if the temperature was too hot, the village would rope off the Ice castle and not let anyone near it. People didn't take too kindly to the idea of getting crushed by thousand-pound blocks of ice.

"King Thomas!" came some shouts from a small group of people across the road.

"Hello!" responded a smiling Thomas.

The town was full of people anticipating the fireworks later. Good for business, and always good for the insurance business, thought the king. As he walked along the lake, Thomas marveled at how a thick blanket of snow covered it. Up to this point, it had been a good winter with colder temperatures and lots of snow. Thomas had remembered years past where it wasn't like this. Hardly any snow, and temperatures not cold enough to build a good ice castle.

"Hey look, it's the king!" proclaimed a passerby.

"Hey buddy."

It was hard not to stand out. Thomas was wearing

the crown and a long elegant royal robe. Another small group of people walked toward him and asked,

"King! Can we get a selfie?"

"Of course."

They all gathered around the king. The girl that had asked, had a selfie stick connected to her phone. Thomas had seen this advertised on TV. It worked brilliantly. She extended her phone in front of them and said, "Smile! Everyone say, "Winter Carnival!"

Everyone said it in unison. The phone clicked. She took a couple more and then said, "You da man!"

They regrouped and started walking in the opposite direction.

Thomas could see small pockets of people getting their pictures in front of the castle. He couldn't help smiling, his grin went ear to ear. He just loved all the attention, and everyone seemed to like him, as the king.

"What a dork!"

Thomas looked across the street and saw a small number of college kids pointing at him and they seemed to be laughing. His mood changed from gratification to instant embarrassment.

"Mom, it's the king!" proclaimed a little boy.

Thomas looked down and said, "Hey buddy."

The embarrassment started to go away. Surely those college kids must have been pointing at someone else, thought Thomas. He took a few more steps and then spotted his wife, Doris. They made eye contact. She instantly smiled and started pointing in his direction.

The gratification started to slip away again. As he got closer, he could see his teenage daughter Michelle. She wasn't smiling, her usual teenage self. She also brought her best friend Susan.

"Hello, my amazing family!" said Thomas.

He walked over and hugged his wife, and she recoiled at first, and then reciprocated. Thomas looked at his daughter and said, "Hi, honey."

Michelle rolled her eyes, looked at him and said, "Can we just get this over with already!"

He had a sudden thought where a two-thousand-pound block of ice ends up sliding off the ice castle and crushes his wife and daughter. What he could do with the insurance money, He started to smile. Thomas looked at her friend and said, "Hi, Susan."

"Hi, Mr. Mullburgh."

Susan and Michelle had been best friends since kindergarten. Some people thought they looked like sisters. Black hair, blue eyes, long straight hair, a little overweight.

"Susan, you may address me as King!"

Michelle rolled her eyes again and said, "Please, Dad, stop."

Thomas looked at his wife and said, "Shall we?"

Doris positioned her posse in front and around the castle over the next ten minutes and took several pictures. Occasionally getting interrupted by other people to have their picture taken with the king. Every time this happened, the king smiled, Doris was patient and

Michelle rolled her eyes. After a while Michelle asked, "Mom, can we go already!"

"One more picture, just the king. Yes, Thomas, go stand to the left of the castle. I want to see the lake in the background."

Thomas did as he was told. Doris lined up the shot. The sun was hiding behind a cloud, so it wasn't too bright. Ice castle to the left, lake behind.

"Perfect." said Doris.

"Hey king, stay there, let me take one more. It's for the slide show." said a tall man with a red ski jacket and solid blue winter hat.

Thomas knew him. The guy was a local photographer, but he couldn't remember his name. The king nodded and posed for the picture.

"Thanks!" said the photographer.

Thomas walked up to Doris and said, "I'm going to stick around for a few more pictures and then walk home."

"Remember, you need to take a nap before tonight." She then looked at her daughter and told her to say goodbye. She gave her mother a look that could kill, then looked at her father in a disgusting way and said goodbye. Thomas started thinking of falling ice. He gave his wife a glance and she reciprocated with a more loving one.

"Goodbye, Mr. Mullburgh."

The king said goodbye to Susan. He then watched them disappear into the crowd, presumably walking back to the car. He was a lucky man, but he just wasn't in love with his wife anymore. Doris he met in college and they had been together for almost twenty years. Michelle was fifteen going on I-know-everything. The last two years he had been flirting with his secretary in his office. At first it was one sided but a year ago she started flirting back. She was in her late twenties, divorced with a kid. Brunette with a great figure, and she knew how to turn him on. The king smiled at the thought. They had turned things up a notch, snuck out on a couple dates. She didn't want to go any further and said she wasn't going to be a homewrecker. Just last week he told her that he was going to get a divorce and then they could start a new life together. That gratifying feeling started to return again. The insurance business had been a good year, and the future was looking bright.

"It's the king!" declared a strange man.

"Hey, buddy."

He stayed there for another twenty minutes and took pictures with everyone interested. Thomas really liked the attention. He looked at his watch, then noticed that the sun was starting to set. He had a mile walk so Thomas started in the direction home. He was going to take a shortcut and use the snowmobile trail that ran along Pine Ridge Cemetery.

The train tracks that cut through Saranac Lake and led to Lake Placid had been ripped up and a combination bike-and-snowmobile trail had been constructed between the towns. Within a few minutes he had reached the trail. Thomas noticed it was well groomed for the snow machines. The road was to his right and the cemetery to his left. It was the oldest cemetery in town. He started thinking of his mom and dad. They had been gone for some time now. Thomas looked over to where their graves were. He couldn't see the headstone, it was far across on the other side, but he knew the general direction they were located.

Thomas noticed movement to his right. He looked over and up on the road he saw a deer. Thomas smiled. It didn't have antlers. Thomas could never tell the difference between the males and the females. Other than the antlers, they fell off every year. He wasn't a hunter.

The deer was walking parallel, seeming to keep step with him. It was approximately one hundred feet away. Thomas stopped to get a better look and noticed that it stopped also. He started to walk and the deer did too. Thomas started walking backwards and the deer mirrored his movements. Thomas stopped and said, "Hey, buddy."

The deer obviously didn't respond. Thomas looked at his watch and remembered he needed a nap. He started walking again.

"Heyyyy buddyyyyyyyy."

Thomas stopped and glanced to his right at the deer. It just stood there looking at him.

"Heyyyyyy."

This noise came from behind. Like the first, it was

nearly a whisper. Thomas looked behind and there was another deer, back a hundred or so feet.

"Must be the wind." Thomas said aloud.

He started walking again and noticed movement down to his left. Another deer. He had one on the road to his right, one behind and one walking down in the cemetery.

"*Windddddddd.*"

Thomas quickened his pace and said aloud, "This is creepy."

"*Creeppyyyyyyyy.*" Thomas looked to his right.

"*Creepyyyyy.*" He then looked behind.

"*Creepyyyyy.*" This time to his left. It was like an echo all around him. His feet started walking even faster. He smiled at the thought of creepy deer. He had never been afraid of deer. There was nothing to be afraid of. His friends hunted them, he himself liked eating venison. He thought about anything that wasn't what was happening around him.

His thoughts were interrupted by movement up ahead. Thomas focused and could see the outline of another deer. It had stopped in front of him. When Thomas got about fifty feet away, he stood still. It was a deer, but it was different. It was big with no antlers. He still wasn't sure the sex of it. Thomas couldn't help but look at the knife that was sticking out of its head. There was a knife protruding out between its eyes.

"How are you even walking?" asked Thomas.

"*Walkinggg.*" A whisper from his right.

"Walkinggg." A whisper from his left.

Walkinggg." A whisper from behind.

The deer with the knife sticking out of its skull tilted its head in a strange grin, exposing a mouth full of razor teeth. Thomas said, "I, am fucked."

"Fuckkkk."

"Fuckkkk."

"Fuckkk."

*   *   *

A huge crowd gathered around the ice castle and witnessed a spectacular fireworks display, it lasted for almost twenty minutes. Small talk resonated throughout the people comparing the fourth of July fireworks to winter carnivals. After the final barrage of pyrotechnics, the slideshow started just to the left of the ice castle. A culmination of pictures taken throughout the community over the past two weeks that started with the coronation of the king and queen.

"Where the hell is Thomas?" asked Queen Lillian.

She continued to scan the extremely large crowd, in the thousands. The royal court had showed up to take pictures an hour before, all set up in advance by King Thomas, but he never showed.

"King Thomas!" several people in the crowd shouted in unison.

Queen Lillian smiled expecting to see her king, and then noticed several people pointing at the huge projector screen. There he was, larger than life. The crowd started chanting his name.

"Thomas, Thomas, Thomas!"

Queen Lillian also noticed a deer several feet in the background of the picture. It seemed to be grinning, almost smiling and it was looking straight at the king.

CHAPTER FORTY-NINE

THE MEN OF AUTHORITY

Major Vierra was in his office having a meeting with the two men from the FBI when an unexpected visitor arrived.

"Well, come on in," said a not so surprised Major Vierra to Dr. Yoggera.

The three men watched as the small woman settled into a chair next to the major's desk. There was a moment of silence before Dr. Yogerra said, "Please don't mind my intrusion, proceed with your conversation."

The three men stayed silent.

"Gentleman, I can only assume you're discussing the missing snowmobilers."

The door to the major's office flew open again but this time it was Chief Reuger. Major Vierra noticed how surprised the chief was to see a full room. He also recognized how distraught the chief looked.

"Yes chief, come on in. I'll remember to return the favor next time I come see you."

"Next time?" questioned a confused chief.

"Yeah, I'm going to rush past your deputy at the front desk and bust down your door. Hopefully you won't be in a meeting."

"I'm sorry major. He just went past me and wouldn't listen when I told him you were in a meeting." said a familiar voice from behind the chief. Janet was standing behind Chief Reuger in the doorway.

"It's okay." responded the major.

Janet disappeared and closed the door. The chief walked up to the major's desk and dropped an eight by ten picture on it.

The major picked it up and asked, "What am I looking at?"

"Recognize the man in the picture?" asked the chief.

"The King, Thomas. So what?"

"That's right, Thomas Mullburgh, he's the latest missing person in the park!" responded the chief.

An uncomfortable silence blanketed the room. Then the chief said, "He never showed up for the fireworks."

"Is this the reason why you have come, barging down my door and interrupting my meeting?"

"He also never made it home. Last time he was seen was around 4:00pm with his family taking pictures at the ice castle."

"It's only been twenty-four hours, not even. Do some police work. Guy is probably on a bender or at his girlfriend's house." said a smirking major.

"Look at that picture closer." said the chief.

The major picked it up and studied it up close. He then said, "I see the king, ice castle, the lake, and–"

"What else?" interrupted the chief.

The major threw the picture back down on his desk

and stared at the chief. "I think you've been talking to Pete from the Adirondack Daily Enterprise too much!"

"Those cats aren't from the Adirondack Park, and you know it! Someone planted them!", shouted the chief.

"Can I look at the picture?" asked Agent Barret.

The major leaned forward in his chair and slid the picture to the end of his desk. Agent Barret stood up and looked at it. He then looked at the chief and said, "A deer."

The chief looked at the major and said, "That's right. There's a deer behind the king."

"Where did you get this picture?" asked Dr. Yogerra.

"It was in the slide show last night, at the fireworks. The whole town noticed it." The chief looked across the room and asked, "I'm Chief Reuger of the Saranac Lake Police Department. Who are you people?"

"I'm Agent Barret and this is my partner, Agent Mason. We're from–"

"I know. The FBI."

Another long pause as all four men looked over at the only woman in the room, who was preoccupied lighting a cigarette. Agent Barret remembered his first time meeting her, he started to grin. She took a deep drag off her cigarette and created a very bright ember on the end. Her exhale produced a long puffy white cloud that seemed to momentarily extinguish the ember.

"I am Dr. Yogerra from the Bio Gen facility in Ray

Brook. You, Colt Reuger, I know much about."

Chief Reuger was looking at a short middle-aged woman with a thick European accent. Cropped black hair shoulder length. She was wearing a black pantsuit and wore a pair of black glasses. In the Adirondack Mountains, this woman stood out, thought the chief.

"We don't smoke anymore in public buildings, lady."

She took a long drag off her cigarette and pulled a cell phone out of her bag. She dialed in a number and then started to talk into the phone.

"Mayor, I have one of your village employees on speaker."

"Who am I speaking to?" asked the voice on the speaker phone.

The chief looked over at Dr. Yogerra and noticed she was wearing a small smile. He leaned closer to her phone and said, "Chief Reuger."

"Now you listen here Chief. Dr. Yogerra is an asset to the village. You assist her with anything she needs."

The chief didn't wait long to say, "Yeah, and how much money has she assisted you with your campaign?"

The chief grabbed the phone out of Dr. Yogerra's hand and hung it up. He then put it on the major's desk and looked back at the major and said, "Listen, I bagged one of these sons of bitches out on Forest Home Road last week. It wasn't a regular deer."

"What do you mean, not regular?" asked the major.

"It had teeth, sharp ones like a predator. When Dave Peterson squeezed its leg, a sharp talon came out.

Sharp enough to rip a man up real bad."

"Dave Peterson?" asked the major.

"You know him. About six-foot, a buck eighty, always wears a red and black plaid hunter's jacket. Worked at Dannemora, retired from corrections about a year ago." responded the chief.

The major still looked confused and then asked, "The guy that I arrested for punching out his daughter's boyfriend?"

The chief looked across at the major with a confirming head nod.

"Come on, chief. You want me to validate your horror story from a perp I just arrested?"

"I'm telling you it all makes sense. The hunters, snowmobilers, missing dogs."

"Missing dogs!" screeched the major in disbelief.

"Where is your evidence?" asked Dr. Yogerra.

The chief glanced over at Dr. Yogerra and asked, "Just what is it that you people do up there anyway?"

He glanced back at the major and said, "I called Phil. He said he would send his DEC boys out to get it. But they never found it."

The major grinned at Chief Reuger and said, "Sounds like a big fish story if you ask me, I have bigger problems to deal with. Oh, and that reminds me, I have something to ask you."

The chief seemed to lose track of his thoughts and looked at the major somewhat surprised.

"Did you arrest a man by the name of Billy Joe

Tallabear?"

"Yes I did." the chief responded.

The major pointed his finger at the chief and said, "Well you're going to need a good lawyer. He is in the process of suing the village, the Saranac Lake Police Department, and you. You beat up the wrong guy Colt. Kid is connected."

"That fat bastard put two guys in the hospital and took a swing at me." explained the chief.

The major gave the chief a threatening look and said, "I'll be in charge of this investigation. You might want to take some time off and get your house in order."

"You got a real problem on your hands. I will get your proof. I just hope more people don't go missing before then." shouted the chief.

Chief Reuger turned and opened the door and walked out of the room. A few moments went by and then Agent Mason said, "Guy reminds me of Clint Eastwood."

"Is there anything else I can do for the FBI?" asked Major Vierra.

"No major, thank you for your time." replied Agent Barret.

The two G men exited the room. Major Vierra stood up from his desk and walked over and locked the door. He then picked up the phone and hit a button. Janet picked up on the other end and the major said, "No more visitors and hold all my calls."

The major hung up the phone, sat down and

picked up the picture on his desk, he looked at it and started shaking his head no. He then handed it to Dr. Yogerra and asked, "Have we got a deer problem in the Adirondacks?"

Dr. Yogerra looked at the picture and took another long drag off her cigarette. She exhaled and said, "I think we have a chief of police problem in the Adirondacks."

CHAPTER FIFTY

THE FIXER

Dr. Yogerra then said, "I cleaned out all the information regarding patient John Fuller. All medical files and administrative notes have been expunged from that facility."

"Excellent work. Do we know where our fugitive is, approximately?" asked the Brain.

"Thirty minutes after the escape, home video captured Mr. Fuller breaking into a private residence in Canton, New York."

"How far away are we talking?"

"Almost twenty miles."

There was a pause for a few seconds, and she waited patiently for her boss to start talking again. And then he said, "It is conceivable to assume that John Fuller's anatomy is mutating exactly like the deer. He has superhuman strength and speed. This is astonishing. Have you thought about his intended trajectory."

"I believe he's going back to the Adirondacks, where everything started for him." replied Dr. Yogerra.

There was silence on the other end and this made Dr. Yogerra nervous. He could be calculating an impossible question that she didn't have the answer to or planning an inhuman task where people lost their lives. His voice reengaged on the other side asking, "What is his ETA?"

Dr. Yogerra was confused at first with the acronym and then it came to her, estimated time of arrival. She responded, "It's another seventy miles. If he uses an automobile, one hour. He could already be there. But if he travels on foot, three to four days. His problem is that the roads are blocked off with security checkpoints. The state police and border patrol are manning the checkpoints. I believe Mr. Fuller is on foot. He will not risk getting stopped in a vehicle. He must navigate around them and this will slow him down through the wooded terrain of the Adirondacks."

The voice on the other end of the red phone was silent. Dr. Yogerra again waited patiently for a response, and it didn't take too long. "Whenever I have a broken situation, or a problem that needs fixing, I send in the fixer. He can kill two birds with one stone. He will obtain a sample by capturing one of the carnivorous deer. And while he is there, I will have him capture Mr. Fuller. He will be in contact with you shortly. I expect you, Dr. Yogerra, to stay out of his way."

The red phone went dead. Dr. Yogerra became slightly queasy thinking of the fixer, of spending any amount of time in his presence. The Brain called him the fixer, but he had other names. Shadow, death, inhuman, barbaric, horrifying, formidable and nerve racking, these names were just the tip of the ice burgh. She knew his true name but dared not speak it. Why poke the bear while it's sleeping? Every time he showed up, people died, disappeared, accidents happened. If the boogieman did exist, he was afraid of the fixer. The worst thought Dr. Yogerra had was this thing coming for her. It always dressed in an elegant shimmery black suit. Black tie, black button up shirt, black shoes and a matching black fedora hat. She assumed he had black skin, but Dr. Yogerra was wise not to get too close.

She never made eye contact with it. It moved more like an animal, a sleek predator with such grace and agility. She did admire its athleticism and the way it spoke. Perfect pronunciation of the English language. The words rolled off his tongue like he invented them. It was the meaning of those words, what they represented in the end that frightened her. At the end of his long soliloquies, violent actions followed. She would dread waiting for the fixer to call her over the next few hours. She tried to not think of his real name, but it was hard to forget.

CHAPTER FIFTY-ONE

RUN FAST

It had been a couple days since he broke through the wall. John remembered running, running fast. The more distance he put between him and that awful place, the better he felt. He couldn't believe how strong he had become. At first it felt good to punch the door. It made the itching and burning sensations go away for even a second. After a while, he noticed that his punches were putting dents in the door. The itching and burning became unbearable. The burning turned into an excruciating pain. Then his mother showed up. It was good for his soul to talk to her but everything got worse. The itching and pain were throbbing. It was all over his body. Then that bastard had told him that his mom died. John had hit it harder than ever. He was stunned when the steel door flew across the hall. He remembered Mr. Rason just staring at him, like he was afraid for his life. He had been running ever since. John remembered coming upon a farm, with a house, and nobody seemed to be home. One of the first things he did was ditch his hospital uniform and find a change of clothes.

A car honked and sped by, his thoughts were interrupted and he refocused on where he was. John was hiding in a culvert on the side of the road. Back at that farm he grabbed a black Harley Davidson T-shirt, and it was a little tight. He found a pair of blue jeans that were baggy, he didn't have time to check the sizes, he just grabbed them and flew. He remembered his hospital slippers and socks falling off after the first mile. He just kept going, his feet didn't seem to mind. The snow was falling but he wasn't cold. John looked down at his feet, they were red. He could see his breath when he exhaled. A noise off in the distance caused every muscle to freeze in his body. He heard dogs barking. He lifted his head to check the road and saw no cars. John took two strides and easily glided across the two-lane road. He headed for the tree line.

The sun was setting. It would be dark soon. John had to get back, back to where this whole nightmare had started. Something was drawing him back. He couldn't explain it to himself, he was going to go back to the cabin. The hunting camp.

John was easily traversing the obstacles on the forest floor. There were stumps, fallen trees, and branches. When he came upon a wet area, he simply went through it. The cold and wet environment didn't bother him. The pain and itching were gone. It was gone after he'd blown through the wall. He destroyed that wall, and it didn't even slow him down. He was different, he'd left the old John and all that pain back at that place. His mom, she was gone too, like Daryl.

Part of him tried to hold on, to the thought that his

mom was still alive. Maybe that guy had been lying. But in his soul he knew she was gone. For some reason he knew, he couldn't feel her anymore. At the hospital he'd felt her presence on the other side of the wall. John didn't understand how, he couldn't explain it. He even knew she was down the hall in Dr. Baumer's office. For some strange reason, he could feel her down in that direction of the building. Having gone to Dr. Baumer's office several times before, John simply extrapolated that she was there. And then she wasn't there. It was like she instantly disappeared or that feeling wasn't there. He didn't sense her anymore after that. He wasn't sure who the new John was, but that didn't matter. His life was over and he had one mission left. That red demon was going to die.

He kept running, and he was running fast. The smell of pine filled his nostrils, and his hearing was enhanced. Strange sounds, he wasn't exactly sure what they were. Small critters rustling up in the branches, up in the trees. Wood cracking, what you hear sometimes when the temperature drops close to freezing. There were smaller animals moving on the ground off to his peripheral. John stopped and noticed a rabbit, brownish gray leaping to his left. He instantly darted in that direction. As soon as its feet hit the earth, the rabbit sprang back up to the right. John anticipated its movement and caught it in midair with his hands. For a moment he just stood there in amazement. John wondered to himself, questioning what had just happened.

The rabbit squirmed violently in his hands. He tightened his grip and the rabbit stopped moving. John tilted his head and smiled slightly. He noticed how fluffy and soft the fir was.

"Holy shit!" John said out loud.

He couldn't believe that he had just caught a rabbit with his bare hands. He was afraid that he might hurt it so he lowered his hands and released his grip on the rabbit and then watched it hop away. He then noticed a light not far away. John ran in that direction and stopped when he came upon a house.

John stayed in the brush and tree line that separated him from the building. It was a two-story structure with a detached garage. There was about an inch of snow that had freshly fallen and John did not see any tracks. He assumed that nobody was home. John carefully walked to the garage, there was a side door. He checked to see if it was locked, it wasn't. He quietly opened the door and walked in; it was dark. The sun was gone from the horizon and it was dark everywhere. But John still could see. He didn't understand how, but he could see a car and a toolbox, a big one. The kind of toolbox you would see at a car repair shop. The garage was big enough for one car and he could see the outline of shelves on the wall. John walked around the car to the driver's side door. He checked the handle, and it was unlocked, so he opened it up. Instinctively, John looked in the back seat and noticed there was a long-sleeved blue and black flannel shirt.

"Bonus." he said out loud.

John reached in the back and grabbed the shirt. While he was doing this, he noticed boots on the car floor. John thought to himself, just imagine if they fit me. He smiled and grabbed the boots. Sitting on the driver side with the door open he swung his legs outside the car. They were work boots, a tannish leather, that had been weathered. John tried them on and they fit. Normally he wouldn't have put them on without socks, but his feet didn't seem to mind. John swung his legs back into the car and thought about the keys. He looked in the ignition and then the tray, and then checked the glove box but found no luck, just an old road map. His eyes shifted upward, and he reached for the visor pulling it slightly down. The keys dropped out of the sky and landed on his lap.

"Double fucking bonus!" a smiling John Fuller said.

He also noticed a garage door remote pinned to the car visor above him. He reached up and pushed the button and the garage door behind him opened up slowly. He shut the door of the car and put it in reverse. He slowly backed out of the garage and turned the car around in the driveway.

John grabbed the map from the glovebox and opened it up. It took him a few minutes to get his bearings. He then found Santa Clara and figured to be about sixty miles from the hunting camp. John nosed the car out into the road and headed in that direction. He figured it would take him about an hour to get there.

His teeth were hurting. The last few days they started to ache, all of them. His stomach started to growl; he was hungry. John had not eaten since his escape. He turned on the radio and found a station at 106.3 FM. It seemed to be the only station he could get without static. John remembered how hard it was in the Adirondack Mountains to get a radio signal. A song was playing, it was a seventies tune. He didn't know the name but he remembered hearing it when he was little. The song was suddenly interrupted:

"Breaking news. Authorities are still on the lookout for fugitive John Fuller who escaped from the Ogdensburg Psychiatric Facility on Wednesday morning. He was last seen in the Canton area on a home video security camera. He is considered dangerous. Authorities are asking citizens to lock their doors and report all suspicious behavior. A hotline has been set up at 888-717-4444. Again, the authorities are asking anyone who comes into contact with John Fuller, to not engage. Call the hotline at 888-717-4444."

The radio went back to playing the forgotten seventies song. John stayed around the speed limit cruising at fifty-eight mph. He entered into the town of Potsdam and followed local traffic through to the other end of town. These were small villages with a couple of red lights. It didn't take long to drive through. The speed limit changed to fifty-five and John accelerated back up. John glanced over at the map; it was laid open on the front passenger seat. 11B for fifteen miles and then catch 458. There was another car a few hundred feet ahead. John stayed at a comfortable distance and matched its speed.

Those fucking deer. They were demons. He had to kill them all. The only thing that mattered now was revenge. The big one, the red one. John was going to kill it last. Look it in the eye as it took its last breath. It was the king, the nucleus of mayhem and disaster. True definition of a monster. It was going to pay for what it did to his brother. Nothing else mattered. Darrel was gone, Karl, Sal, Dan, Billy and now Mom.

His mouth was throbbing with pain. John reached inside and pinched his back molar with his forefinger and thumb. He wiggled it slightly and pulled it straight out of his mouth.

"What the fuck!"

He examined the tooth with extremely long roots.

The lights of an oncoming car made him focus back on the road. When the car sped by in the opposite direction, John looked back at his molar.

He wasn't a dentist by any means, but he didn't see any abnormalities. John put the tooth in the tray of the car's center console and focused on the car ahead. His tongue found the hole in his mouth along the gum line where his molar recently vacated. It was deep and John could taste his own blood. He liked it. He had tasted his blood before but this time it seemed different. His tongue explored the cavity in his mouth with more robust vigor. He really liked the rich salty taste. John noticed the car ahead slow down and put on its right turn signal. A sign indicated NY-458. John followed the car, again staying a few hundred feet behind. Matching the other car's speed, John accelerated back up to fifty-six miles per hour. He noticed that the tree line on both sides of the road seemed to get closer.

He was inside the blue line of the Adirondack Park. The designation on a map that was created over one hundred years ago, to protect this vast wild forest preserve. There would be few buildings and houses along the rest of the way and a couple small hamlets. Suddenly the car up ahead started to slow down and John followed suit. He could see lights up in the distance. John's blood pressure rose when he realized what it was, a roadblock. John slowed the car down to almost a stop. He watched as the car ahead pulled away closer to the state police vehicles waiting with their lights flashing brightly in the dark canopy of surrounding trees. There were other vehicles present. One said, *"border patrol"*, and there were dogs. Two state troopers had German Shepherd dogs. John watched as troopers and border patrol agents walked around and looked inside the car in front. He was about one hundred and fifty feet away. John brought the car to a stop. The agents lifted the trunk and peered inside the other car. John didn't hesitate, he put the car in park and opened up the driver side door. As he exited the vehicle, he heard someone shouting, "Sir get back into your car!"

John started running for the tree line.

"Stop or I will shoot!" screamed the voice.

John kept running. Suddenly loud reports of gunfire opened up. John could hear the bullets getting closer. When they were about to hit him, he simply moved out of the way. The bullets whizzed by and he kept on running. He made the tree line and the bullets stopped chasing him. He slowed down and stopped by a big sugar maple tree. It was barren of leaves, all discarded in the fall. He was protected from the surrounding conifer trees. Pine trees that kept their needles during the wintertime. He said out loud, "How did I do that".

But he didn't have time to reflect. The sound of barking dogs brought John back to reality, and the sound was getting closer.

John instinctively started running again. It was dark out and there was no starlight. John assumed that it was much darker inside the forest. But he could see better than he could ever remember. It was like he was wearing night vision goggles, except he wasn't. John noticed that with every leap, the sound of the barking dogs became further away.

He slowed down and stood beside a tall birch tree. He looked up, it had several branches, but they were forty feet off the ground. John smiled slightly and reached out a hand to grab the tree. Suddenly intense pain traveled down his hand to his fingertips. John screamed in agony and watched as blood and one-inch claw-like nails protruded out the end of his fingers. He withdrew his hand and noticed the nails disappeared back inside his fingers. John grabbed the tree again and they appeared again, but this time less blood and no pain. John turned his head to his left hand and repeated the same process. Again, agonizing pain and blood and sharp one-inch nails. The barking dogs were getting closer. John made an up-down motion alternating both hands and scraped the tree like a grizzly bear. He tore about an inch into the tree. It was easy and it didn't hurt. John looked back up the tree and started climbing. His boots were slipping on the bark of the birch, but his claws had no problem digging in. The agonizing pain returned, but this time in his toes.

His feet were no longer slipping on the birch bark. John easily traversed to a branch and stood motionless looking down on the ground. The branch was thick and easily supported his weight. His boots didn't have the best traction, but he had no problem keeping his balance. John noticed blood on his boots, where his toenails punctured through. The dogs were getting closer. John looked in the direction that the barking was coming from and spotted them. There were two of them and there were three troopers following about one hundred feet behind. John stayed perfectly silent and watched as the dogs trotted up to the tree and sniffed around it. The two dogs looked up and started barking as soon as they spotted John.

John tilted his head to the side and grinned.

From forty feet above, John pounced on one of the German Shepards. It happened so fast that the poor animal never had a chance. John drove his nail-like claws into the sides of the dog. He easily broke through the rib cage and crushed the soft organs inside. The animal let out a yelp and went limp. John made eye contact with the second dog. It was about ten feet away. It backed up another ten feet and ran back towards the oncoming troopers yelping loudly. John looked down at the dead dog and felt no remorse. He retracted his hand with the heart in his grip. John put it up to his mouth, smelled it long and then ran his tongue over it. It was warm and salty. John ripped it into bite size pieces and gobbled it down in a matter of seconds. It was the first meal he had had in almost three days.

His dinner was interrupted by someone shouting, "Stop!"

John looked over and saw the three state troopers. They had flashlights and behind them was a whimpering German Shepard. The flashlights were almost too bright for John. He looked away and refocused. His eyes adjusted and the light was more tolerant.

John studied the troopers and then said, "I didn't do it."

"You killed my dog."

They were all pointing their guns at John, two had pistols and one had an AR-15.

John looked down at the dog and said, "Yup, I did

kill this dog." John looked back up at the troopers and said, "But I didn't kill my friends or my brother."

"Get down on the ground. Put your hands behind your back!" shouted the trooper in the middle.

"You're going to pay for what you did to my dog, asshole!"

John tilted his head, grinned, and said, "Your dog was a pussy."

The trooper who belonged to the dead dog pulled the trigger on his pistol. John turned slightly and watched closely as the bullet breezed by his right ear. Then John leaned out of the way in time as the second bullet was targeting his face.

The three troopers lowered their weapons and looked at John in disbelief. They stood there for a long time just staring at him. The trooper to the left said, "What are you? How did you move like that?"

Before the troopers could get off another shot, John Fuller quickly escaped into the darkness of the Adirondack Forest Preserve.

CHAPTER FIFTY-TWO

TOO MANY PRESS CONFERENCES

The room was full of reporters. This time around, the major had help. To his left stood the two FBI agents and to his right stood the District Attorney from Franklin County. Phil was farther down to the right, representing the Department of Environmental Conservation. There was one person missing, noticed the major, and he was not happy about it.

"Okay, let's get this started. Before I take any questions, I would like to give Mr. Allen Rodstein, District Attorney from Franklin County, a chance to give us an update on the escaped fugitive, John Fuller." The major stepped back from the podium and Mr. Rodstein stepped up to the microphone.

The major took a good long look at the voice that had hounded him from the other side of the phone the last few months. He was a short man, barely five foot five, the major guessed. A stump of a man, large in the mid-section, well over two hundred pounds. Black hair, bald on the top with a thick mustache. The guy spent more time arguing with people and not enough time working out, thought the major.

The DA adjusted the microphone to his mouth and then said, "Franklin County is charging John Fuller with five counts of second-degree murder."

The room roared to life with questions. The major stepped forward and raised his hand, this time without the blowhorn. The reporters lowered their volume and a few seconds later the noise level dropped off to just the camera clicking. The question shouting was gone but the hands remained raised. The DA, Mr. Rodstein, pointed at a reporter.

"Hello, Kyle Thompson Channel Five News, how can your office bring charges against John Fuller if there aren't any bodies?"

"My office and I believe we have sufficient evidence to win in court, if need be." The DA pointed his finger at another reporter.

"Christine Blue Press Republican, why did your office wait so long to charge Mr. Fuller? I mean, it seems like you're doing this now because of his recent escape from authorities."

"You could say it was the straw that broke the camel's back. But my office was getting ready to file these charges anyway. The escape and timing of the charges are just a coincidence. Although, I must say that in my view an innocent man wouldn't escape. This doesn't look good for Mr. Fuller's defense." The DA then pointed his finger at another reporter.

"Vic Gordon, Lake George gazette. Can you provide the details of how Mr. Fuller was able to break out of the mental facility?"

"This is an ongoing investigation, I am not at

liberty to say."

The room started to raise their voices in disapproval. The DA pointed at another reporter.

"Joe Hunt, Watertown Times. My sources are saying Mr. Fuller physically broke his cell door down and ran through the wall. Can you confirm this?"

The room exploded with questions, the major stepped forward and grabbed the air horn under the podium. A second later a loud blow horn filled the room and drowned out everyone's voice. It lasted a few seconds and then stopped. The major looked at Joe Hunt and said, "Joe, I'm ready to arrest you for disturbing the peace!"

"Major, we have all seen the video of John Fuller lifting up two men with their feet dangling off the floor. It seems there is supporting evidence that Mr. Fuller does possess superhuman strength." said Pete Wilson from the Adirondack Daily Enterprise.

The major lifted his hands up and said, "Here we go again, these two so-called reporters are a couple of conspiracy nuts."

A wave of laughter swept across the room.

The major waited for the laughter to subside and then said, "Video gets doctored all the time on YouTube. The employee who downloaded that video was later fired and arrested. So, I am here to tell you that the validity of that video is in question."

"Phil Silverman from the Albany Times. Do the authorities know where Mr. Fuller is?"

The major looked at the district attorney and motioned him back.

The DA then said, "We have roadblocks set up at several different places leading into the Adirondack Park. These roadblocks are manned by the New York State Police and Border Patrol. Last night, at one of these checkpoints, John Fuller was stopped on NY-458 outside of Nicholeville. He exited his vehicle and ran into the surrounding woods. Mr. Fuller killed a member of the New York State Police canine unit before he disappeared into the tree line."

"Major, can you release the name of the fallen trooper?" asked a reporter in the back.

The major leaned into the microphone and said, "Ralph, a five-year veteran of the force."

"Does the trooper have a last name?" asked the same reporter.

The major tried to place a face with the voice but there were too many reporters in the room.

"We don't give our dogs last names."

The room vibrated with small voices filled with confusion and laughter. The major became irate and shouted, "What is so funny! That animal was a valuable member of our canine unit."

The room became silent, and the silence lasted for several seconds until the major said, "Agent Barret is here to discuss the missing snowmobilers."

Agent Barret walked up to the podium and said, "We have had all the snow machines sent to forensics and have also recovered blood samples that are being tested. We are in the process of following up on several leads and we have recently set up a hotline and several great tips have started to come in. Any questions?"

"How do five snowmobilers just go missing?" asked Pete Wilson. "These were local boys who knew the backwoods. You're the FBI, surely you have some idea. Can you give us anything more?"

The major walked up to the podium and leaned in and said, "Whadda ya know Pete, maybe your deer got them."

The whole room erupted with more laughter. Even Agent Barret cracked a smile. The major signaled with his arms to quiet down and the room did.

"At this time, I would like to have Phil from the Department of Environmental Conservation come up."

Phil walked up to the podium, everyone could tell he was uncomfortable, definitely out of his element. He looked over the crowded room and said, "The DEC is recommending that the residents inside the park stay out of the woods. We believe that there may be another predator on the loose."

The room started to fill with low level chatter. Suddenly several hands went up.

"Vic Gordon, Lake George Gazette. Is there any correlation with the missing man from Saranac Lake, the king of the Winter Carnival?"

Phil looked at the major. The major motioned him to step away from the podium and then took his place.

"As for the whereabouts of Mr. Mullburgh, the Saranac Lake Police Department has an open investigation ongoing. I was hoping to have Chief Duprey here today to give us an update, but I can only assume that his duties have prevented him from joining us here today. As far as staying out of the woods, it's a precautionary measure. The DEC is sending out a hunting party and setting up gaming cameras throughout the park. We're asking residents to stay away from the woods for a couple weeks just to be safe."

"How do you know they won't end up missing too?" asked Joe Hunt.

The major looked long and hard at the reporter from Watertown and said, "These are trained men from the Department of Environmental Conservation. They work in the woods. They know every tree, stream, mountain and stump in the park."

"Yeah, but are they trained to take down a mountain lion?" asked the unseen reporter from behind everyone else.

"Excuse me, sir, who are you?" asked the major.

Reporters in front of the unseen voice stepped to the side and there stood a twenty-something Caucasian man, about six foot, two hundred pounds. He had long straight blonde hair about shoulder length. The major noticed he was wearing a blue ski parker and donning blue jeans.

"George Rivers, Syracuse Daily."

The major just stared at the reporter. He looked over the room and noticed several new faces, reporters he didn't know. The major asked, "So, is there anyone from Buffalo?"

Everyone started looking around at each other. The room stayed silent.

"Phil, can your men at the DEC take care of a rogue mountain lion?" asked the major.

Phil nodded and gave two thumbs up.

"Major! Alice Merrit from the Rochester Chronicle."

"That is getting close to Buffalo." said the major.

"Yes, I suppose. How are you going to prevent the residents or tourists from staying out of the woods?" asked Alice.

"That is virtually impossible. The Park is too big, and the state doesn't have the manpower. If we catch anyone in the woods, we will give them a warning to leave. If they won't leave, they will be ticketed and must appear in front of a judge where a hefty fine will be levied."

"Major, Christine Blue Press Republican."

"Chris, I know you. You don't have to keep introducing yourself." said the major.

"Thank you, major. What about the residents who live in isolated areas within the park?"

"We are in the process of communicating with those people. They have to be very vigilant on their property. There's a possibility that they're being watched by this type of predator. We are suggesting that they leave for a week or two, if possible. But we understand that some of them can't afford to do that. So they will have to be extremely careful."

"Major how did John Fuller kill the police dog?" asked Peter Wilson.

The major looked at Pete with a disgusting scowl on his face. He started to leave the room when Pete hit him with another question. "Is it true that the dog was missing its heart?"

The major stopped and walked back to the podium and said, "Okay, this concludes our press briefing. If you have any questions please see my secretary, Janet. Thank you."

Major Vierra walked out of the room and down the hallway towards his office. The reporters were shouting his name. With every step he took toward his office, the noise dissipated. He was followed by Agents Barret and Mason. The District Attorney from Franklin County and Phil were behind the FBI agents. He couldn't help but wonder how Pete Wilson knew about the missing heart. Someone in Troop B had loose lips. A minute later they were all sitting inside Major Vierra's office. The major looked at the G-men and said, "Can the FBI throw Pete Wilson and Joe Hunt in jail somewhere, far away from Troop B headquarters."

The agents said nothing.

Mr. Rodstein cracked a smile at the major and then asked, "Do your boys know where he's heading?

The major grinned and said, "If he's on NY-458, he

is only about forty miles away from his hunting camp in Santa Clara. We think he is headed there."

Mr. Rodstein stood up and looked at everyone in the room and said, "Gentlemen. Well I have to get back to Malone."

He then walked out the door. The major stood up and said, "Thank you, I will keep you updated."

"When were you going to tell me that my department was going to go hunt mountain lions?" asked Phil.

The major seemed to be blindsided by the question. He sat back down in his chair and took a long-measured look at Phil.

"Don't worry about that. I have a special team coming in to take care of that."

Without blinking Phil looked at the major and said, "It sounds like you're going above my pay grade, major."

"It is above you Phil."

"Well then don't ask me to speak anymore at your press briefings."

"Come on Phil, I needed an expert who knows the park."

Phil stood and stepped toward the door. He opened it and looked back at the major and said, "You should have gotten that great hunter who planted, I mean, killed those other four mountain lions in the park."

"They weren't from the Adirondacks, we know that. They migrated from out west." said the major.

Phil walked out the door.

"Phil, come on. That's not fair. Phil!" the major

shouted at him.

The major looked at the agents and said, "He's just mad that he didn't get to shoot those cats."

The F.B.I. agents quietly stared at the major.

The major stared back at both men and said, "I have to go pay a visit to a certain chief of police in Saranac Lake."

The two G-men glanced at each other and then back at the major. Agent Barret asked, "Mind if we tag along?"

A familiar face walked in the door before the major could respond.

"Agent Barret, Agent Mason, good to see you again," said Dr. Yogerra.

The major froze when he saw his uninvited guest. The two of them locked eyes for a brief moment.

"Dr. Yogerra, what can I do for you?"

The two G-men stood near the door. They were watching the interaction with great interest. Dr. Yogerra walked over and sat down in her usual chair next to the major's desk. The major looked up at the FBI agents and asked, "What was it that you wanted?"

"Can we go with you to see Chief Reuger?" asked Agent Barret.

The major had a confused look on his face and then said, "I can meet you there, say in about twenty minutes."

Agent Barret looked over at Dr. Yogerra and then back at the major and said, "See you there in twenty."

The two agents walked out the door.

Major Vierra walked over and closed the door, locking it behind him. He returned to his desk and noticed a thick smoke ring gracefully rising up to the ceiling.

"Don't you think those agents are wondering why you're always coming into my office?" he asked

Dr. Yogerra took a long drag off her cigarette. The end of it was as bright as the sun. A few seconds later she exhaled a steady stream of white smoke in the direction of Major Vierra. He stood up from his desk and walked away from the poisonous secondhand smoke in disgust.

"You can't just walk in here anytime you want! The FBI is going to start asking me questions."

"Don't worry about the FBI, The Weller Group owns them too. Just like they own the Bio Gen Facility and just like they own you!"

Dr. Yogerra took another long drag off her cigarette and then reached over and extinguished it out on the major's desk. After she exhaled, she said, "Tell me about the roadblock last night."

The major walked over and sat back down at his desk.

"What have you people done to this John Fuller guy?"

"Just tell me what happened." demanded Dr. Yogerra.

The major took a moment to collect his wits, and then said, "I'm not sure I believe my troopers. After reading their report, I called them in and interviewed them myself. I still have doubts, so I sent two officers from the Bureau of Criminal Investigators in to interrogate my men. These guys are the best at what they do. I replayed the recording of the interview over a dozen times–"

"Just get to it, major." said an irritated Dr. Yogerra.

"When my men caught up to John Fuller, he was eating something, and his hands were all bloody. They said his skin looked red, like he had a bad sunburn. He was standing over one of the dogs from our canine team, it was dead. Upon further investigation with the Crime Lab System, it was discovered that the dog was missing its heart."

Dr. Yogerra grinned. "Continue."

"My Troopers got off two shots at this man, kill shots. We're talking forehead. They said John Fuller moved out of the way."

Dr. Yogerra leaned forward and asked, "What do you mean?"

"They believe he has the ability to dodge bullets. And before they could get another shot off, he vanished into the woods faster than they ever saw another human move."

"Anything else?" asked Dr. Yogerra.

"Yes, apparently, he can claw into trees. They found evidence of claw marks on the tree that was next to Ralph."

"Ralph?" a confused Dr. Yogerra asked.

"That's the name of the dog."

Dr. Yogerra held back a chuckle and nodded her head in approval.

"At first my guys thought the marks were made by a bear."

Dr. Yogerra watched as the major opened up a drawer in his desk and flopped a small stack of 8x10 pictures on his desk.

"Upon closer inspection, you can see five finger claw marks over an inch deep embedded into the tree."

Dr. Yogerra took a minute to examine the pictures and then said, "That's four fingers and a thumb, and the claw marks go up the tree. Looks like he can climb also."

Dr. Yogerra dropped the pictures on the desk and reached inside her pocketbook. The major watched perplexed as the Doctor produced a tiny black button no bigger than her fingernail.

"What is it?" asked the major.

The major had to focus hard to see it. Dr. Yogerra threw it toward his metal filing cabinet, he watched as it instantly stuck like a magnet.

"You are going to put this on Chief Reuger car. Somewhere he won't find it."

The major's mind was spinning with unimaginable endings, the kind that ends a man's life. He was stone faced, searching for the right words to defuse this situation.

"Don't do anything to the chief. I can arrest him. He beat up a drunk a couple days ago. He won't be a–"

"This is of no concern to you. Simply do as I command. Oh, and major, we want the chief to go into the woods."

"Why?" asked a very confused major. "You just told me you didn't want anyone in the woods."

"Is of no concern to you." repeated Dr. Yogerra.

She stood up and picked up the pictures on the desk and then started walking to the door.

"Hey wait, that's forensic evidence." said the major.

Dr. Yogerra grinned at the major and said, "It belongs to The Weller Group now. Just like I do, and just like you do."

CHAPTER FIFTY-THREE

JURISDICTION

"Hey chief, the DA from Malone just filed murder charges against John Fuller!" shouted Deputy Knowles.

The chief stood up from his desk and walked out of his office to the front desk, the television was reporting the local news. The reporter on the TV was stating how John Fuller, the escaped fugitive, had been charged with five counts of murder.

"That's bullshit! We know what really happened to those guys, don't we chief?" asked Jeremy Knowles.

Chief Reuger ignored his deputy and focused on the TV. The reporter went on to explain how the DEC had recommended that people stay out of the wooded and forest areas of the park. That there might be additional mountain lions on the loose.

"Mountain Lions, my ass!" shouted Deputy Knowles.

The front door opened and in walked Major Vierra and the two FBI agents.

"Chief Reuger, can we speak to you in your office?" asked Major Vierra.

The chief said nothing. He motioned for the four of them to walk into his office. The chief walked in last and closed the door behind him and then sat behind his desk. The major sat down opposite the chief and said, "You missed my press conference."

"I was too busy finding a lawyer." responded the chief sarcastically.

"Let's cut the crap, Colt. I'm going to need your help. I have several roadblocks set up and my manpower is thin."

"My department is pretty thin too, major."

The major acted like he didn't hear the chief's complaint and said, "We think John Fuller is headed back to his hunting camp in Santa Clara. We can't afford to have a bunch of local vigilantes out in the woods trying to be heroes."

"Just how do you plan on keeping the locals out of the woods?" asked the chief.

"You don't have to worry about that. Not in your jurisdiction. I need you to remind the locals to stay out of the woods, in a couple weeks this will pass. Things will go back to normal." explained the major.

The chief looked at the G-men and asked, "You guys buying this mountain lion crap?"

"What are you referring to?" asked Agent Barrett.

The major smirked at the chief and said, "Oh, can we put this crazy deer attacks to bed all–"

The chief interrupted. "I have hunted and fished these mountains and lakes my whole life. I've seen bobcats, but never any mountain lions."

"What is the difference between a bobcat and a mountain lion?" asked Agent Mason.

The chief stood up from his desk and said, "Size! A

bobcat weighs less than forty pounds. A mountain lion can weigh more than two hundred pounds."

The major rushed in to get his next point across. "That's why we need to keep the locals out of the woods."

The chief sat back down at his desk and looked at the major and said, "I agree, we do need to keep people out of the woods, but it's not because of mountain lions."

Agent Mason looked at his partner and then back at the chief and asked, "Then what is it?"

The major raised his voice and said, "Oh, please Colt, can we cut the crap with your mutated zombie deer story!"

The chief shot a piercing look at the major and said, "I'm going into your forbidden woods, and I am going to bag one of these so-called mountain lions."

The major grinned and sarcastically said, "Please, leave the hunting to the professional."

Agent Mason then asked, "I don't understand. Didn't you say that there aren't any mountain lions in the woods?"

The major interjected, "He thinks there are killer deer in the park attacking humans."

"That's right. Man eating deer with sharp predator teeth and talon claws that can shred a man to pieces." shouted the chief.

Agent Barret looked at the chief and asked, "Where is your proof?"

"I told you already. I shot one out on Forest Home Road –

"But the D.E.C. boys never found the carcass." said an interrupting Major Vierra.

The grin on the major's face ran ear to ear. The FBI agents shot a glance at each other and then looked back to the chief.

"That's right. But this thing had a mouth full of razor-sharp teeth and some type of talon. And these things are cunning. Deputy Knowles got run over by one from behind."

Agent Mason repeated, "Run over?"

The chief then explained, "Ya, we were looking at a deer in front of us about forty feet away. It was just standing there looking at us and there was a knife sticking out of its forehead."

A smirking Major Vierra asked, "How could the deer still be alive if it had a knife sticking out of its head?"

"We couldn't believe it either, but there it was. Then, Jeremy got run over from behind by another one, a different one."

The major started laughing, "Did it also have a knife sticking out of its head too?"

The chief scowled. "No, it did not. But you're missing the point. These things were hunting us."

The agents looked at each other again and then back at the major.

The major responded, "Oh, come on. Do you expect me to believe this fairy tale? Deer hunting humans! Deer walking around with knives in their forehead. Claws and razor-sharp teeth, I'm not buying it! Colt, I'm sure you saw something. Maybe the deer you shot was different, a birth defect or–"

"Think of all the missing people in the park over the last four months. The hunting party out at Santa Clara, the Peterson girl out on Forest Home Road, the snowmobilers out towards Meacham Lake. The king of the Winter Carnival, walking back home from the Ice palace. The small wildlife that are nowhere to be found in the park like rabbits, racoons, and dogs. Hell, my own nephew is missing!"

The three men just stared at the chief, and the major wasn't buying his story.

"A few mountain lions aren't going to do all that. But a large group of deer working together as a pack, they would be capable," said a very convincing chief.

The four men sat and said nothing for several uncomfortable seconds. The major sensed that the G-men were being persuaded by the chief's story. He interrupted the silence and said, "Proof! Go get me proof."

"I would, but I don't want to get arrested by your boys for going into the woods."

"Don't worry, chief. My men will leave you alone. Go get your proof or go waste your time. Two things! Stay away from Santa Clara, and if you come across a mountain lion, good luck."

"I will get your proof and drop it right on your desk."

The major stood up and walked to the door. Walking out of the chief's office he said, "Stay safe, Colt."

The G-men stood and looked at the chief. Agent

Barret said, "You tell a good story chief. Now you need to back it up with proof."

The FBI agents exited his office.

CHAPTER FIFTY-FOUR

METAMORPHOSIS

Had to stay away from the road. Since the bullets went whizzing by his face, John figured it was a good idea to stay away from the road.

For the past day he'd traveled along through the woods avoiding houses and cars. He followed route NY-458 but stayed a good distance away in the woods, where he wouldn't be noticed. He stopped briefly before the sun rose and rested. His mouth had been bothering him and he lost four more teeth. He didn't even have to pull them out, they'd simply fallen out into his mouth.

John knew something was wrong, but he didn't think it was all bad. The new abilities were an unexpected gift. He could see in the dark and his hearing was enhanced. He had retractable claws on his hands and feet that made it easy to both climb trees and apparently rip hearts out of German Shepherds.

Fast, yes he could run faster than any other person, he was sure of it. John chuckled with the thought of him winning the one-hundred-meter dash in the Summer Olympics.

And bullets, he could dodge bullets. It wasn't luck either. John had seen the hammers of the gun strike and then he'd tracked the bullet as it exited the muzzle with a fiery flash. It was like time slowed down for him and he'd simply moved out of the way. The whole bullet thing had surprised him when it happened, but the experience didn't seem alien to him. John was never afraid that the bullets would hit him. He wasn't contorting his body or flexing in impossible positions. He simply understood that the bullet was traveling in a straight path. All he did was turn or slide out of the way. He didn't understand how or why, he simply moved out of the way.

John's attention was brought back to the road. He could hear a car coming up from behind, and it was headed toward where he was going. John crouched down behind a tree. It was a pine tree. As the car went by, John could smell it, a mixture of gas and oil. Oh yeah, his sense of smell seemed to also be enhanced. It was a blue SUV, four-door with a dent in the passenger side. There was a female driver, straight blonde hair wearing a red winter jacket. Not a ski jacket but it definitely was a winter jacket. There was a child in the back seat. Winter hat covered the kid's head, John couldn't tell what color hair. Shoulders had on a black ski jacket. The car zoomed by and John focused on the license plate, 6BC722. John noticed one more detail. The bumper sticker on the tail fender said, *I like animals better than humans.* John laughed. The car was out of his field of vision, but he could still hear it. The most extraordinary thing about the car was how far away he was to the road. John was a good football field away and he was able to not only smell the exhaust but also capture the fine details of the car and its occupants.

His mouth was hurting and the pain was getting worse. But at least he wasn't itching, scratching all over his body, that sensation was gone. John started moving again. He liked to run, it was fun. He liked running before also, but this was different. He easily traversed over fallen logs, stumps and rocks. He could anticipate where his foot would land, how the contour of the ground was. John had no fear of the environment he was in, like slipping, tripping or falling down. The more he moved within it, the better he became.

His skin was also tougher. He scraped it on trees and rocks, and it didn't hurt, bruise or bleed. The bark on the trees would tear off when his arms or legs rubbed against it. John could see the landscape up ahead dip down. He anticipated a small valley and leaped across it with ease, landing on the other side without slowing down. John started to recognize the area of forest he was coming into. He had hunted here before; he was getting closer to the hunting camp. John estimated that he was about two miles away. He had to cross the road. John listened until he was sure it was safe. He then closed the distance between him and the road in a few seconds.

His senses became overwhelmed by the intense light that penetrated the open road. He had been traveling within the canopy of the forest for several hours. He knew that it was early morning, but his new senses were no match for the power and warmth of the sun. It took him a few strides to cross the road. He noticed how strange it felt under his feet compared to the natural landscape of the forest floor. John liked running in the woods better. He was running at full stride with a smile on his face. A few strides later, John picked up the sound of voices talking ahead, he came to a stop and crouched down behind a tree. He rested his hand on the bark and tried to focus on the voices. He could see the hunting camp. His car was gone and so was Danny's truck. There were two state troopers standing near the front door.

"This place looks like a dump." said the trooper to the right.

John grimaced. He contracted his left hand and it dug into the tree. The aroma of almonds filled his nostrils. John looked over to where his claw had just dug into the tree. It was a bitter smell. John studied the bark of the tree and recognized it as a type of cherry, a black cherry tree. Something his father had taught him. He focused on the name tags that were pinned on the upper chest of the troopers' uniforms.

Trooper Morley said, "If this clown shows up, I'm not asking questions."

The other trooper, Watson asked his partner, "What do you mean?"

Trooper Morley responded, "This guy is a mass murderer. I will unload my service pistol into him."

John could feel his temper start to rise. He watched the two troopers walk around the front of the property; they seemed to be shaking their heads with disapproval.

Trooper Morley said, "This place is a dump! Not going to catch any deer out here. That's why our perpetrator had to go and bag his whole hunting party."

The two troopers started laughing. John really wanted to end these two, just extinguish their lives and he knew he could do it. Part of him still cared, cared about the sanctity of human life. But he could feel that slipping away and he didn't care about the consequences anymore. John slowly crept backwards and decided to avoid the possible confrontation. He could only think of one other place to go, where Daryl died. Where that big fucker ended him. John recalled his memory of the monster, the big red deer with the massive rack. His own life didn't matter anymore. He had one last job to do and that was to end that fucking monster. Big Red, that's what he would call him. He would get his revenge. John would look into the eyes of Big Red, penetrate its soul and watch the light go out.

CHAPTER FIFTY-FIVE

EVERYONE IS A SUSPECT

Agent Mason was peeping into Chief Reuger's police vehicle. Agent Barret was parked a safe distance away, able to observe but not be detectable. They were both dressed for the elements and were expecting to follow Chief Reuger into the woods, without his knowledge. Agent Mason made his way back to their car and opened the passenger side door.

"The chief's car is full of hunting gear. Twelve-gauge shotgun, a vintage 30-06 with a scope, and gear for traveling into the woods." said Agent Mason.

"Get inside the vehicle," said an annoyed Agent Barret.

Agent Mason did as he was told and closed the door. After he was safely inside he asked, "What's the big deal?"

"We are trying to stay discreet. This is called surveillance."

Agent Mason hesitated and then responded, "I'm sure if we asked him, the chief would take us with him into the woods."

"What are they teaching you guys at the Academy! I suppose you want to make friends with the chief and stroll into the woods together. Has it occurred to you that the chief is a suspect?"

Agent Mason shrugged his shoulders and then said, "I don't know, I think he's just a small-town guy who thinks he saw something in the woods. The man is harmless."

Agent Barret shook his head in disbelief and said, "Everyone is a suspect. Until we put together a few solid leads, we are following the chief into the woods."

Agent Mason tried redirecting their conversation, he then asked, "What do you think of his story?"

Agent Barret gave his partner a look and said, "I, for one, don't believe man-eating deer are killing people in the woods. I am starting to suspect that maybe your buddy, the chief, has connections up on the Indian Reservation."

"You think he's running drugs?"

Agent Barret again looked at his partner, but this time a little longer and said, "I think some people have gone missing and I do think there is a correlation with the reservation. Definitely drugs involved. What a great place for people to disappear. I mean a vast Federal Park with numerous lakes, mountains, streams and rivers."

"What about mountain lions?"

"Well, the man did provide proof." Agent Barret pointed at Agent Mason and then said, "You saw the dead mountain lions they rolled out. But I can't help but wonder if there is some sort of connection with Major Vierra and Dr. Yoggera."

"Ya and she seems to have friends in higher places." responded Agent Mason.

Agent Barret held up his hand, "Hold that thought."

The two men watched Chief Reuger, Deputy Knowles and another man get into the chief's police car, the same one that had the hunting gear and rifles in it. A moment later they were following the police cruiser out of town.

"I wonder where they're headed?" asked Agent Mason.

Agent Barret said nothing and continued to follow from a distance. Before they reached the village boundary, another car pulled out in front of them, perfectly sandwiched between the chief's car and theirs. It was a good buffer and seemed to be traveling in the same direction as the chief's car.

"Run the plates on that car." demanded Agent Barret.

Agent Mason punched in the data on his keyboard and said, "Bob Lilard. Twelve Response Street, Saranac Lake, New York. Age forty-six. No priors, says he's a teacher, Physical Education."

They passed the hospital and a few miles later were headed towards Paul Smith's College.

Agent Barret asked, "Who's the other man in the car?"

"I think it's Dave Peterson." responded Agent Mason.

Agent Barret looked confused. He then asked, "The guy with the missing daughter?"

Agent Mason nodded yes and said, "You're not wrong. It's the same guy who punched out his daughter's boyfriend, was arrested, and now that same boyfriend is missing."

Agent Barret looked at Agent Mason and said, "Everyone is a suspect."

The three cars continued on for a few more miles until they came to a stop sign in front of Paul Smith's College. All three cars took a right and resumed their journey on Route Thirty North towards Meacham Lake. Agent Barret stayed a good quarter mile behind the other two cars.

"Do you think he's headed toward Santa Clara, to the Fuller hunting camp?" asked Agent Mason.

"Possible."

The cars resumed on for about five miles. The two agents noticed the lead car turn right down a dirt road. The second car continued straight, and Agent Barret followed it.

Agent Barret said to his partner, "I'm not following the chief. We will go up the road a little bit and then bushwhack our way in."

A half mile down the road Agent Barret pulled the car over toward the soft shoulder.

"What do we know about that road?"

Agent Mason tried pulling up maps on his computer and said, "No service."

"It's probably an old logging trail." Agent Barret said, "We'll cut a path into the woods from here."

Agent Mason looked around at the terrain. He noticed that the snow was a good two feet deep.

"Maybe we should wait ten minutes and then drive down the same logging road."

Agent Barret smiled and then said, "They're not far ahead. Won't take us long to catch up to them."

The two men commenced putting on their warm winter jackets that had the FBI letters embroidered on them. Winter hats, gloves and ski pants and boots. It was a warm winter day. The sun was out, and the temperature was in the mid-twenties. Agent Barret opened up the trunk of the car and pulled out a Remington TAC-14 12-gauge shotgun. He smiled at Agent Mason and said, "Just in case we run into mountain lions."

Agent Mason replied, "Or killer deer."

The two men started laughing. Agent Barret closed the trunk and remotely locked the car. He started heading into the woods with Agent Mason following. The first couple steps were awkward and clumsy. The snow was extremely deep. They soon made it to the tree line where the snow was shallower. They were moving faster but it was strenuous. They walked for about twenty minutes until Agent Mason said, "The road."

Agent Barret looked over to his right and he could see the logging road, the two men quickly made their way to it. A few minutes later they came upon the police cruiser. Agent Barret looked inside and noticed all the gear and rifles were gone.

"Over here." shouted Agent Mason.

Agent Mason was pointing at a trail in the snow. Agent Barret walked over and studied it; he noticed several animal tracks.

Agent Mason looked at his partner and said, "Looks to be some type of a gaming trail."

"Do you know what a mountain lion track looks like?" asked Agent Barret.

"Nope, not my wheelhouse."

Agent Barret studied the tracks in the snow and then asked, "What type of boot print is that?"

Agent Mason looked down at what his partner was pointing at. It looked like a mesh or grid pattern on top of the animal tracks.

"Must be some type of boot that is designed for deep snow." guessed Agent Barret.

Agent Mason pointed straight into the woods.

"Well, looks like they're following this game trail."

Agent Barret nodded his head in agreement and said, "It also looks like it goes for quite a distance. At least they made it easier for us to walk in the deep snow."

The two men followed what they believed to be a game trail into the forest. The trail seemed to have new tracks laid down recently, but the strange-looking boot prints were on top. A fresh two inches of snow had fallen in the last twenty-four hours. The leafless trees held onto some of the freshly made snow.

"How far in do you figure they are?" asked Agent Mason.

"Probably fifteen minutes ahead of us."

The sound of an owl off in the distance caught their attention. Agent Mason looked in all directions, his partner could sense his apprehension and said, "Out here it's hard to triangulate where the sound is coming from."

They continued to trudge along the trail for some time. Agent Barret was getting tired, and he knew his partner was also feeling the effects of the hike. Up ahead they could see that the trail opened up. They walked out into a small meadow. It was about one hundred feet wide and about twice as long. Agent Barret could see where the trail continued on into the woods at the other end. He then suggested, "Let's stop for a minute."

His words were received with optimism from his partner. The warm sun felt good on their faces. Agent Barret looked around and started noticing the differences among the trees. There were evergreen trees, they kept their needles throughout the year. There were also bigger taller trees that didn't keep their leaves during the winter. Other than that, he couldn't tell the difference between them. In the far-off distance the sound of an owl hooting could be heard. Agent Mason smiled and said, "The forest is full of owls. I hope they're not man killers too."

Agent Barret flashed him a smile.

"Killlllersssss."

Both men looked behind them but saw nothing.

"What you say?" asked Agent Barret.

"I didn't say anything." replied Agent Mason in confusion.

"Killllersssss."

The sound came from their right. They looked over to their right but didn't see anything.

"Killlllersssss."

This time from their left.

Both men turned in that direction, but again there was nothing there.

"Helpppppp meeeee."

The agents looked behind them and saw only trees. The voices seemed to be coming from the tree line, but all around them. Agent Barret turned and looked forward and saw a deer standing about forty feet away, just staring at them.

"Doesn't look like a man eater." said Agent Mason

The deer tilted its head to the side and started grinning. It opened its mouth and revealed a row of razor-sharp teeth.

Barret and Mason looked at each other with their mouths opened wide.

"That is just wrong." said Agent Mason.

"Agreed." Agent Barret nodded his head. A dark nervous feeling started to engulf his soul. He said back to his partner, "We both owe the chief an apology."

Agent Barret lifted his shotgun with the intention to kill the mutated deer, but something crashed into him from behind. The collision caused him to misfire the weapon. He fell forward on his stomach and the snow engulfed his face. Before he could ascertain what had happened, he heard his partner say, "Barret, what do I do?"

Agent Barret lifted his head out of the snow and at first, he couldn't see Agent Mason. He twisted his body and looked behind him only to see Agent Mason surrounded by three deer. They were circling him, and they were only a few feet away.

"Chris, what do I do?" asked a nervous Agent Mason.

Agent Barret searched for the shotgun, but it was over ten feet away from where he'd apparently thrown it. He looked back at Agent Mason. The three deer were so close to Agent Mason, just out of arm's length.

"Very carefully, slowly, reach for your gun." said Agent Barret.

Agent Mason reached for his holstered sidearm, found it and slowly lifted it up.

"OK, now what? a frightened Agent Mason asked.

Agent Barret screamed, "Pull the trigger!"

The gun fired and the shot hit the deer directly in front of him, in the head. Blood splattered in his face, But before Agent Mason could wipe it away, one of the deer bit him on the back of the neck. Vital fluid shot out to the side of his neck. He didn't even have time to scream. Agent Barret watched in horror as his partner collapsed to his knees. The other two deer pounced on Agent Mason. Agent Mason had a look of complete terror in his eyes. More blood started splattering out of his body. He couldn't even fight back; the deer were too strong. Agent Barret looked over at the other deer, the one in front. It was still grinning at him with those very sharp teeth. He sprang to his feet and dove for the shotgun. When his hands touched it, he did a shoulder roll and landed on his back with the weapon pointed up just in time to get the shot off. The charging deer fell a few feet too close for comfort to his left, it was dead.

"Chris!"

Agent Barret looked back over to see his partner pleading for help. Two of the three deer that were eating Chris started charging him. Agent Barret got two shots in succession off and he dropped them both. The last deer ran into the tree line. Agent Barret started running towards his partner and from forty-five feet away, he didn't look good. Out of the tree line in front of him, six more deer came charging. He aimed and fired and one deer went down, but the other five were still charging. Agent Barret shot again but nothing happened, he needed to reload. He stopped and reached inside his jacket pocket but realized that within seconds he was going to be overrun. He looked to his left and saw a tree about forty feet away and started running for it. Right before he got to the tree, one crashed into his back again and he fell forward on his chest. He instinctively rolled over and drove the stock of the shotgun between the deer's eyes. It staggered backwards giving him time to get to his feet. He turned his head toward his partner and saw the mess that the other four deer were doing to him. The noises that were being produced by them made him nauseous. Crunching, tearing, and ripping, he threw up. He was sure Agent Mason was gone and he didn't want to be next. The deer that just ran him over was a few feet away and he assumed it had a massive headache. Agent Barret made eye contact with it and noticed that its eyes were different, almost reptilian. The deer started charging again. Agent Barret swung his shotgun like a baseball bat and made contact on the right side of the deer's face, it went down. The other four deer started charging him, a moment later he was climbing the tree faster than he had ever climbed a tree in his life. There were several branches of different heights. It was a perfect climbing tree. He needed to get as high in the air as he could.

Eventually he could climb no higher. Agent Barret looked down and noticed a deer on its side on the ground, directly below him. He wasn't sure if it was alive, it was the one he hit on the side of the face. The other four deer just looked up at him, grinning with those sharp teeth stained with human blood, his partner's blood. He turned his head to see his partner, the one he left for dead, just lying there. The other four deer ran back over to Agent Mason and started eating him again. He was being torn to shreds. He looked at Agent Mason's face and then made eye contact with his partner.

"Chris, help me." Agent Mason, pleading for his life, managed to get the words out.

Tears started flowing from Chris Barret's eyes. His partner was being eaten alive. Only one thing left to do. Agent Barret reached for his sidearm, but it wasn't there. He had left it in the car. He thought about getting to the ground and grabbing the shotgun. He could see where it was.

"Chris!" Agent Mason screamed with what energy he had left.

Agent Barret started to climb down but then stopped. Right below him was that deer, the one he had done batting practice on, and it was grinning at him with those teeth. He looked over where his partner lay. The surrounding snow was scattered with blood. Agent Mason was being disemboweled; his intestines were laying on the ground beside him. He suddenly started screaming. One of the deer was tearing at his left arm. Agent Barret watched in horror as the deer ripped Agent Mason's arm off below the elbow. It looked up where he was in the tree and made eye contact with him. The deer had his partner's arm in its mouth, just staring at Agent Barret.

The deer's head exploded in a sea of red. It dropped to the ground, dead before it hit the snow.

Agent Barret watched as the remaining deer scattered into the tree line. A moment later three men appeared out of the forest and walked over to where Agent Mason lay on the ground.

"He's still alive!" shouted Deputy Knowles.

"He's in bad shape." said Chief Reuger.

Agent Barret started screaming,

"Over here! Over here!"

All three men looked at him up in the tree. Agent Barret climbed down and then ran over to his fallen partner. He watched as the chief put his partner's intestines back inside of his body cavity.

"Get me the first aid kit out of my backpack!" screamed the chief.

Deputy Knowles started to retrieve it. The chief then removed his belt and tightened it around Agent Mason's upper arm.

Blood gurgled from Agent Mason's mouth as he tried to speak.

"Chris, snowshoes." Agent Mason barely got the words out.

Agent Barret looked at the snowshoes the other three men were wearing and shook his head in approval. The tears were falling out of his eyes like a river.

"Hang in there buddy." Agent Barret gently patted his partner on the shoulder, the one that didn't have bloody bite marks on it.

"Here ya go chief." said Deputy Knowles.

The chief opened the first aid kit and grabbed a roll of bandages. He looked at Jeremy and Agent Barret and said, "You two lift him up. I have to wind this bandage around his waist and stomach. Oh, and he's not going to like it."

They grabbed Agent Mason and started lifting him. He immediately opened his eyes and started screaming. Then he stopped. The chief started wrapping the bandage around Agent Mason.

Dave Peterson started shaking his head and then

said, "He's gone."

The chief looked up at Dave and then looked at Agent Mason.

"He's gone Colt."

"I don't want him to go!" screamed the chief back at Dave.

The other two men put Agent Mason down. They were right, he was gone. His eyes were open, but the light was gone. Colt had seen it happen before, in Iraq with his unit. He left a few lifelong friends over there in the desert. Staring into their faces and talking to them. One moment they're there and then, they're gone. The chief stood up and looked at Agent Barret and said, "What the fuck were you doing up in the tree?"

"We got jumped. It happened so fast; I got knocked to the ground."

"Did you even try to save your partner?" asked the chief.

"He was gone. They jumped him, but I took out three of them." pleaded Agent Barret.

The chief grabbed the agent by the shoulders and said, "Where are the dead deer you shot? Where are the bodies!"

Agent Barret was confused. "I shot three!" he screamed.

"Bullshit, you left him and climbed up a tree to save your own ass!" the chief shouted.

"Colt, enough!" Dave Peterson shouted.

The chief looked Agent Barret dead in the eyes and shoved him backwards. Agent Barret fell on his ass. Agent Barret looked around but didn't see any deer. Impossible he thought, he was sure he shot them dead.

"We got one." said Dave Peterson.

The chief looked over and saw Dave standing over a dead deer, the one that the chief shot. It still had Agent Mason's arm in its mouth. A moment later all four men were standing around the deer looking down on it. Dave looked at the chief and said, "Help."

The chief and Dave removed the arm from the deer's mouth. Dave looked at Agent Barret and handed him his partners arm and said, "Why don't you return this to your buddy."

Agent Barret gently grabbed the arm with both hands and walked over to his partner's body. He couldn't help but notice the different layers of flesh, tissue and muscle hanging raggedly from where the arm used to be connected to agent Mason's elbow. He gingerly put the severed arm beside his partner's deceased body.

Ropes started falling from above and all around them. Then men started sliding down the ropes. They landed on the ground holding assault rifles. The chief counted eight men in a tight circle, about thirty feet back surrounding them. They were dressed in all black, with boots, gloves, helmets and full-face coverings. Some type of paramilitary group. All four of them looked up and noticed a hovering black helicopter about two hundred feet off the ground. The chief was amazed at how quiet the helicopter was. They couldn't hear the rotors like on a usual helicopter, and there didn't seem to be any engine noise.

"Agent Barret, please tell me these guys are from the FBI." asked the chief.

"No, they're not from the bureau."

The chief looked at the closest ninja dressed black clad soldier and asked, "Who the fuck are you guys?"

Then another man dropped down from the helicopter except he didn't repel down a rope. He jumped from the helicopter that was too high off the ground and landed in a crouched position with one hand touching the ground. The guy should have broken both his legs and his back, the man should have died from the fall, thought the chief. The man slowly rose into a standing position. He was less than twenty feet away from the chief. Definitely a guy, but the chiefs' brain was questioning if it was human.

"Hello, Chief Reuger. I'm Mr. Ebony."

The chief's eyes and ears were trying to make sense of what was standing in front of him. Stood around six foot three, weighed over two hundred. It was also dressed in all black. A black leather jacket with black leather pants.

"I work for The Weller Group, and these are my merry men." explained Mr. Ebony.

"More like a small army." said Dave Peterson.

He wore a tight black winter cap that followed the

outline of his head and covered the ears. The chief wondered what its ears really looked like.

"Mr. Peterson, I am so sorry about the disappearance of your daughter." said a smiling Mr. Ebony.

It spoke perfect English, like the funny talkers from England, thought the chief.

Mr. Ebony then said, "Gentleman, you won't be needing your weapons."

The eight paramilitary soldiers raised their assault rifles and red laser dots started to paint their four bodies. A moment later, one of the soldiers walked over and stopped in front of Dave Peterson and held out his hand.

"No way. I'm not giving up my shotgun."

"Please, don't make my men take it from you by force." said the reassuring and calming voice of Mr. Ebony.

Dave looked at the chief. The chief nodded and then Dave handed his shotgun over to the soldier. The soldier then walked over to Jeremy and without hesitation he handed him his pistol. The soldier then stopped in front of the FBI agent.

"Agent Barret. Have you found the missing snowmobilers or the drugs they were peddling up there on the reservation?" asked Mr. Ebony.

Agent Barret focused on the black clad man, or thing in front of him and then asked, "What department are you from?"

"Oh, I don't work for the United States Government. I don't work for any government." explained Mr. Ebony.

The soldier patted down Agent Barret but found no weapons. Agent Barret then said, "Mister, you have broken more than a half dozen federal laws. Tell your men to lower their rifles."

Mr. Ebony walked over to where Agent Mason lay dead and seemed to examine the body for a few seconds. The chief couldn't discern what it was. It walked effortlessly upon the snow and moved so graceful and athletic.

"It appears your partner has succumbed to his wounds."

The soldier stopped in front of the chief. Colt handed his 30-06 rifle over.

The chief watched as it walked over to the dead deer. It opened the deer's jaw and revealed a mouth full of carnivorous sharp teeth. It flashed a smile at the chief and said, "Now that's interesting."

He then picked up one of the front legs and squeezed the front hoof area. The four men and small group of soldiers were taken aback when they saw a sharp three-inch talon appear. Mr. Ebony looked at Agent Barret and said, "I think I know what happened to your partner."

He then turned his head and looked at Dave Peterson and said, "How long has Cheryl been missing?"

Dave Peterson took two steps towards the thing and screamed, "You fucker, I'm going to kill you!"

Before he took his third step, one of the soldiers hit him in the back of the head with the butt-end of his assault rifle. Dave was knocked out before he hit the ground face first.

"Are you here to rescue us, or not?" asked the chief.

Mr. Ebony walked over to the chief and stood about three feet away, just staring at him. The chief tried to make sense of the outline of the thing's face. Cat-like features, he thought to himself. The chief grinned at it and said, "You're not human"

"Thank God. Although I consider myself an atheist" replied Mr. Ebony.

It held out its hand and said, "Let's have a look at it."

"A look at what?" asked a confused Chief Reuger.

"Oh, come now Colt. Everyone knows in the Adirondacks about your Rainmaker. How you boast about it to all your friends and enemies. What is it you tell them, that if you shoot it at a foe, it will bring a rainy day down on their grave?"

The chief reached inside his jacket and found his family heirloom holstered to the side of his hip. He then produced his three-fifty-seven magnum and handed it over to the thing.

Mr. Ebony graciously accepted the cannon and said, "Thank you. What a fascinating piece."

The chief watched as the thing studied his gun, rolling it over in his wrist. He then tucked it behind himself in his pants.

The chief looked long and hard at the thing and said, "I want it back. That belonged to my grandfather."

Mr. Ebony looked at the chief and grinned, slightly

turning his head to the side and said, "I respect that."

Mr. Ebony turned and walked back over to the dead deer and said to his small army, "Let's get the specimen secured and up to the chopper."

"The Bio Gen Facility and Dr. Yoggera, there must be a connection." asked Chief Reuger.

Two of the soldiers started to put a harness on the deer.

"That facility is a small piece of The Weller Group, and Dr. Yoggera belongs to us." responded Mr. Ebony.

"And Major Vierra?" asked the chief.

Mr. Ebony tilted his head and grinned, exposing a mouth full of razor-sharp teeth, and said, "He belongs to us too."

The chief was taken back a bit when he noticed that this thing had the same type of teeth as the deer. Suddenly a loud howling holler filled everyone's ears. Even Mr. Ebony looked confused. The soldiers were looking in different directions all around them. The chief had never heard such a noise before. It reminded him of a grizzly bear roar and a laughing hyena all at once. The noise caused the hair on the back of the chief's neck to stand up.

A moment later deer started stepping out of the tree line. Everywhere the chief looked, deer were just standing in a circle surrounding them. The chief chuckled with the thought that his group had been surrounded by paramilitary soldiers, and now the soldiers were surrounded by man-eating deer.

Mr. Ebony looked around at his men and said, "Don't move a muscle."

Everyone watched as the deer knelt down on their two front legs and bowed their heads. All of the deer in the circle did it. Then a giant specimen of a buck appeared and stood sideways so that everyone could see its massive rack. The chief counted sixteen points. It had a red tint to its heavy fur, and it was a massive deer. It was thick and had to weigh well over three hundred pounds, thought the chief, probably four or even five hundred.

"You are truly magnificent." said an admiring Mr. Ebony.

The big buck looked at Agent Mason's body and then grunted. Two deer stood and trotted over to where Agent Mason lay. They grabbed his feet in their mouths and disappeared into the tree line, dragging him away. Nobody said anything. Agent Mason's arm lie there in the red snow, a reminder to everyone that a man used to be there.

The king of the man-eating deer then looked over at the dead deer that was already harnessed up and grunted again. Two different deer started to trot over to where it lay on the ground. The two closest soldiers raised their weapons in protest but were quickly subdued by four deer behind them. Within a few seconds the soldiers were disarmed and on the ground. They both had a deer applying pressure with their front legs on the chests of the soldiers, and the look on their faces told everyone that they were helpless. They didn't even manage to get a shot off. The other soldiers saw the fate that potentially awaited them, so they turned around and opened fire on the surrounding deer. The chief dropped to the ground and watched the mayhem unfold around him. Every time a deer got shot and fell, two more deer would take its place. The soldiers managed to kill a few but there were too many of them and they moved so fast. One by one the soldiers were subdued and dragged off into the woods. Screams of agony slowly faded off into the tree line. All that remained were the repelled ropes hanging from the helicopter and the four of them, five counting Mr. Ebony.

"Wait!" shouted Mr. Ebony.

He seemed to be talking to the big buck. He was about fifteen feet away from the king of the maneaters with his arm extended and his hand out in the stop position. Mr. Ebony then bowed down to the massive buck and took a knee. A moment later he stood up and locked eyes with the majestic creature. The two of them tilted their heads and then grinned at each other. Mr. Ebony flashed his teeth, and the big buck returned the gesture. He then walked over to the dead harnessed deer, looked over at Agent Barret and said, "Very carefully walk over to me."

Agent Barret did as ordered. He then stood next to Mr. Ebony. The thing grabbed Agent Barret behind the neck and said to him, "Do you trust me."

"Yes." said a wide-eyed Agent Barret with hopeful faith.

Mr. Ebony looked at the big red buck and said, "Let's make a trade."

Mr. Ebony motioned toward the dead deer and back to Agent Barret and asked the king of the monsters, "One for one."

The surrounding deer started speaking, mimicking like a parrot.

"One forrrrr one. One forrrrr one. One forrrrr one."

It was the creepiest thing the chief had ever experienced. The deer were echoing the words all around.

""One forrrrr one. One forrrrr one. One forrrrr one."

"What are you doing?" asked a terrified Agent Barret.

Mr. Ebony grinned at him and said, "This is totally on you. You shouldn't have trusted me."

Mr. Ebony smiled again at the big red buck and pushed Agent Barret towards the beast. Agent Barret stumbled forward into four deer. They slashed him up and had him on his back in no time at all. A few seconds later he was being dragged back into the woods, screaming help me the whole way.

"Help meeeee. Help meeee. Help meeee." the deer continued to echo a man's dying words.

"You are a fucking monster." shouted Chief Reuger.

Mr. Ebony smiled at the chief and said, "No, there is only one monster here, and he's red."

"He trusted you." shouted Deputy Knowles.

"Never trust anybody, kid." Mr. Ebony reached over

and picked up an assault rifle that used to belong to one of his soldiers. He pointed it at Jeremy Knowles and shot him in the leg.

"Ahhhg, Chief!" Jeremy fell to the ground in excruciating pain.

The chief immediately assisted his deputy. He moved him over to where Dave was still lying on the ground unconscious. Colt turned his head to see Mr. Ebony rising up to the helicopter. He had the harnessed dead deer hooked to one rope and he held onto another.

"You can't leave us like this. At least throw me a weapon?" pleaded the chief.

"I have faith in you, Chief Reuger. But I must confess. You were never going to make it out of this nightmare alive." explained Mr. Ebony.

"How can you do this to your fellow-" Chief Reuger stopped himself from finishing the sentence.

"That's right chief, like you said, I'm not human. And don't worry about this, I will take good care of it for you." Mr. Ebony waved his new three-fifty-seven magnum at him.

The chief watched Mr. Ebony and the dead deer lift up into the helicopter. A moment later the chopper was gone, silently departing as it had arrived.

The chief looked around and surveyed the situation. Dave was on the ground unconscious; Jeremy had a bullet wound to the leg and they had no weapons. Oh, and they were surrounded by man eating deer that were starting to walk closer to them, grinning with razor-sharp teeth. He just hoped it would go quickly. He wasn't afraid of dying, but for the kid's sake, he hoped the end would come fast.

"Is that the one we saw on Forest Home Road?" asked Jeremy.

Colt looked up and saw Mary, the deer with the knife sticking out of its head.

The chief started shaking his head and said, "I'm beginning to dislike that fucking deer."

He looked over at the big red one, the king, it *was* truly amazing. Colt thought about how great that head and rack would look over his fireplace.

"Chief, what do we do?" asked a terrified Deputy Knowles.

The chief watched as the deer creeped closer and closer. They only had seconds to live.

"Close your eyes Jeremy, it will be over soon."

The chief closed his eyes, anticipating the final attack. He wrapped his arms around Deputy Knowles and pulled him tight to his chest.

"I hate you fuckers!" a scream echoed off the trees.

The chief opened his eyes to a voice he didn't recognize. He saw what looked like a man stabbing a deer about fifty feet away. The deer dropped dead at the man's feet. Another deer charged the stranger, but the man was ready, he slid to the side with incredible athleticism and drove his knife under the belly of the beast. Its entrails fell to the ground in a bath of liquid and a few steps later it lay dead.

"I want you, you red bastard! It's my turn now!" screamed the strange man as he pointed at the king of the man eaters.

The chief watched as the big red monster grunted two times and then two more deer charged the stranger. The man sliced the neck open of the first deer and then moved to the side and leaped upward, somehow landing on the back of the second deer like he was riding a horse. The chief watched the strange man drive two knives into the neck of the deer. The man then rode it to the ground where it stopped moving. The stranger was covered in blood, but the chief also couldn't figure out what color the stranger's skin was.

The monster grunted three more times and again three more deer attacked the strange man. Again, the stranger leaped on the back of the first deer and seemed to twist its neck. The chief heard a loud snap and then watched the deer fall to the ground. The second deer drove its head into the man's abdomen, but the man held onto the head and rolled backwards, throwing the deer behind him. The chief was amazed at how far the deer flew in the air before hitting a tree. The stranger stood up and charged the third deer, driving his hand deep inside the deer's rib cage. Blood started spilling onto the ground and then the stranger pulled his hand out clutching the heart of the animal. The deer fell to the ground. The stranger turned and faced the king of the monsters, lifting up his trophy, looking straight in its eyes. He then took a massive bite out of the heart and swallowed it in one gulp, throwing the rest at the beast.

"Your next!" the stranger screamed at the king.

The chief noticed that the stranger had claws, not knives but actual claws protruding from his fingers and they looked extremely lethal.

"*Johnieeeeee.*" the king of the monsters spoke.

"*Johnieeeeee. Johnieeeeee. Johnieeeeee.*" whispered the deer all around them.

The big red deer rose up on two legs and hollered at the top of its lungs, producing that blood curling sound that caused the chief's hair to stand up on the back of his neck. The chief watched as the surrounding deer disappeared into the tree line. All of them within seconds were gone, even the dead ones. The last one left was Big Red. The stranger and Big Red were separated by around fifty feet, just staring at each other. At the same time they both grinned showing off their razor sharp blood stained teeth. Big Red turned and escaped into the tree line so fast and so gracefully, it was an incredible exit, thought the chief.

"I will find you! I hate you!" screamed the strange man.

"*Johnieeeeee. Johnieeeeee. Johnieeeeee.*" whispers from the trees all around them.

The stranger just stood there for a long time, just staring off in the direction where Big Red went.

The chief looked at his deputy and noticed a look of bewilderment on his face. He then smiled and looked at Dave, he was the luckiest one of them all, he was still unconscious, missed the whole show. But the three of them were alive; he shook his head in disbelief. The chief looked over at the strange man and asked, "Are you John Fuller?"

RILEY ROSE

Riley Rose, what an incredible journey you have before you. Your great uncle has a few words of wisdom to share. First of all, try and be a good listener when others talk. Secondly, be more patient with people, especially with your little brother. Also, use that brilliant smile, it's a gift. Lastly, pick up a good book every now and then and become a veracious reader. I hope you experience many genres that make you smile, laugh, cry and ponder.

ACKNOWLEDEMENTS

Gin Matters would like to thank several people, my incredible family and friends in the Adirondack Mountains, extended family in Buffalo and Long Island, my children and my dedicated partner Jodi who happens to be happily married to me.

I would also like to thank my dedicated readers. You have given me the drive and confidence to keep on writing. I can't wait for your feedback; it truly helps me with my finished product.

I must recognize all the fictional characters that I have created. My cousin Brendan is quick to point out that a few people in the Village of Saranac Lake draw close resemblance. I will have to think of how I can plug Brendan into this next book. Let me also set the record straight, Dr. Yogerra and Dr. Monroe are not the same person! Besides, everyone knows that Patricia is way smarter and better looking than Dr. Yogerra.

My editing team did a great job helping me streamline my ideas into the written word on paper. A special thanks goes out to Jennifer Cavage for helping me finish up. I also want to thank Haleigh, for not only being an amazing daughter, but also for your guidance and mastery of the English language. I still don't quite understand sentence structure, pronouns, verbs and how to properly use a semicolon. Thanks to your tutelage, I feel like I can,

"Oh, forget that! Let's face it. Gin Matters is going to concentrate on fictional characters and how to incorporate Brendan. I will never have a grasp of the written part of the English Language. For that I must rely upon the pros!"

ABOUT THE AUTHOR

Normally I have no problem bragging about myself and my exploits. It's the people around me who keep me humbled, grounded. I could write a book about me, I could also write a book about my alter ego, Gin Matters. My family and friends in the Adirondack Mountains already know so much about me, I feel like it would be redundant talking about who I am.

So, let's talk about what I like to write about. Genres like science fiction, horror, bullying, falling down and getting back up, ying and yang, winning and losing, cycle of life, and of course the inevitable apocalyptic events that will destroy mother earth and the human race.

There are so many great things to hang my hat on. It truly is an amazing time to be a fiction writer! I do believe everyone has a few best sellers locked away in their head, the trick is knowing how to get them down on paper.

All you really need to know about this author is that I am having fun, and I hope you continue to read my fiction.

Check out my web site:
ginmatters.com

Always remember,
Gin Matters.